IN THE LABYRINTH OF DRAKES

BY MARIE BRENNAN

A Natural History of Dragons
The Tropic of Serpents
Voyage of the Basilisk
In the Labyrinth of Drakes

Midnight Never Come
In Ashes Lie
A Star Shall Fall
With Fate Conspire

Warrior
Witch

IN THE LABYRINTH OF DRAKES

A MEMOIR BY LADY TRENT

Marie Brennan

A TOM DOHERTY ASSOCIATES BOOK
NEW YORK

This is a work of fiction. All of the characters, organizations, and events portrayed in this novel are either products of the author's imagination or are used fictitiously.

IN THE LABYRINTH OF DRAKES

Interior illustrations by Todd Lockwood

Map by Rhys Davies

Designed by Greg Collins

A Tor Book
Published by Tom Doherty Associates, LLC
175 Fifth Avenue
New York, NY 10010

www.tor-forge.com

The Library of Congress Cataloging-in-Publication Data is available upon request.

ISBN 978-0-7653-7763-0 (hardcover)
ISBN 978-1-4668-5698-1 (e-book)

Our books may be purchased in bulk for promotional, educational, or business use. Please contact your local bookseller or the Macmillan Corporate and Premium Sales Department at 1-800-221-7945, extension 5442, or by e-mail at MacmillanSpecialMarkets@macmillan.com.

First Edition: April 2016

Printed in the United States of America

0 9 8 7 6 5 4 3 2 1

SEGHAYE
Rumaish
Jaydir
Sarmizi
Zathrit
AKHIA
Qurrat
Jefi
HAGGAD
Labyrinth of Drakes
Qedem Mountains
Farayma Mountains
RHYS DAVIES

IN THE LABYRINTH OF DRAKES

PREFACE

I suspect a percentage of my readership will see the title of this volume and expect the entirety of what is contained herein to be devoted to a certain discovery that took place in the Labyrinth of Drakes. I will indeed discuss it in due course—have no fear on that count—but if that discovery is your sole concern, then you should close these covers forthwith and obtain for yourself a copy of Naomi Songfield's excellent study *Under the Watchers' Eyes*. That book will give you what you desire, in all the meticulous detail you could possibly hope for (and a good deal more besides).

The remainder of you, I presume, are here for the rest of it, the incidents and issues that surrounded me during the lead-up to and the aftermath of that discovery. This was an extraordinarily complex period in my life, and the tale is not a simple one to tell. In the space of a single year I grappled with dilemmas ethical, intellectual, and political; risked my life both voluntarily and otherwise; faced some of the worst condescension of my career and attained some of my greatest achievements; and made a decision that changed my course profoundly.

It is, in the end, an exceedingly personal tale. (An odd statement to make of a period that eventually drew such tremendous public scrutiny, I know.) Even I, shameless as I am, have hesitated on numerous occasions in the writing of it, for I cannot discuss many of these elements without sharing in detail the inner workings of my heart and mind. This is of course the purpose of a memoir, and I knew that when I embarked upon my task; but now that the time has come to speak of such matters, I confess my qualms. Whatever acclaim my professional deeds have garnered, I harbour no illusions that my personal thoughts and actions will do the same.

Be that as it may: this is my story, and I will tell it as I see fit. I will therefore follow the winding path that led me to the Labyrinth of Drakes—a path filled with every sort of obstacle, from scientific conundrums to assassination attempts—and invite you, gentle reader, to follow it with me.

Isabella, Lady Trent
Falchester
26 Ventis, 5661

PART ONE

In which the memoirist acquires a job despite the opposition of multiple parties

ONE

An offer of employment—Breeding dragons—Lord Rossmere's requirement—Looking for an old friend—My study—Preparations for departure—Reflections on the past

There is very little pleasure in being snubbed over a task for which one is well qualified. There is, however, quite a bit of pleasure in watching the ones who did the snubbing later eat their own words.

Credit for this pleasure must go to Thomas Wilker, who had for many years been my colleague in matters scientific. He was a Fellow of the Philosophers' Colloquium, as I was not—that august body having condescended to admit into their ranks the occasional man of less than gentle birth, but no ladies regardless of their ancestry. Strictly speaking, it was Tom and not I who received the snubbing.

The post refused to him was the focus of stiff competition. Natural history as a scholarly field was not so terribly old; the more specialized topic of dragon naturalism had only recently begun to emerge as an area of study in its own right. Tom's publications and my own played a part in that trend, but we were not the only ones: there were easily half a dozen people in Anthiope with similar interests, the esteemed Herr Doktor Stanislau von Lösberg not least among them.

Those half-dozen lived abroad, though, in places such as Eiverheim and Thiessin. In Scirland there was no one whose qualifications truly challenged Tom's, now that he was a Colloquium Fellow. When a position opened up that called specifically for a dragon naturalist, he should have been the first choice—as indeed he was.

Any rumour which says he refused the position is false. Tom did not refuse. On the contrary, he told his prospective employers that he and I would be delighted to accept. When they said the offer was for him alone, he assured them I would not need a salary, as my recent speaking tours and publications had left me with quite a comfortable income. (As it happens I would have appreciated the salary, for my income did not go so far as it might—but I would have foregone that for such an opportunity.) They made it clear that regardless of finances, I was not welcome in this endeavour. Tom maintained that to hire him was to hire us both; they hired Arthur Halstaff, Baron Tavenor in our stead; and that was the end of that.

For a time.

A year and a half later, the employers in question came crawling back. Lord Tavenor had resigned his position; he had met with no success thus far, and had difficulty with the locals besides. The offer to Tom was renewed. So in turn was his condition—only this time he said that, upon reflection, a salary for me might be just the thing after all. He made it quite clear that if they did not see fit to meet his conditions, then they could go hang.

This is, in brief, how I came to be employed by the Royal Scirling Army in the deserts of Akhia, to raise for them their very own flight of dragons.

* * *

The problem of dragon-breeding was not a new one. Ever since prehistoric times, mankind has dreamt of harnessing dragons for his own ends. This has taken every form imaginable, from leaping atop the back of a fully grown dragon in the hope of breaking it to saddle—an attempt which almost invariably ends with a broken rider instead—to stealing hatchlings or eggs on the theory that a young creature is easier to tame, to caging dragons and optimistically encouraging them to breed.

That last is difficult to do even with less hazardous wild animals. Cheetahs, for example, are notoriously selective about their mating habits, and will go very rapidly from disinterest to ardour to mauling their erstwhile paramours. Others refuse the task entirely: whether it is for reasons of embarrassment or some other cause, the giant pandas of Yelang have never been known to reproduce within the confines of an imperial menagerie.

(I suppose I should offer fair warning. Because this volume of my memoirs concerns itself with my research in Akhia, it will of necessity say more than a little about the mating habits of dragons and other creatures. Those whose sensibilities are too delicate to endure such frankness might well be advised to have a more stout-hearted friend read them a carefully expurgated version. Though I fear that edition might be rather short.)

Dragons are even less tractable in this regard. The Yelangese in particular have a long history of trying to breed their dragons, but despite some rather grandiose historical claims, there is no reliable evidence of success with anything other than the smallest kinds. Large dragons, the sort that come to mind when one hears the word, simply will not cooperate.

And yet it was the cooperation of large dragons that we needed most, in the third decade of this century.

The reason, of course, was their bones. Astonishingly light and phenomenally strong, dragonbone is a wondrous substance . . . when one can get it. The bones decay rapidly after death, once their peculiar chemical composition is no longer protected by flesh and blood. A Chiavoran named Gaetano Rossi had developed a method for preserving them; Tom Wilker and I had stolen that method; it was stolen from us in turn, and sold to a company in Va Hing. Three years before I went to Akhia, it became public knowledge that the Yelangese were using dragonbone to build effective caeligers: airships that could be used for more than mere novelty.

"If you had shared what you knew with the Crown when you learned it," Lord Rossmere said to Tom and myself during our first meeting, "we wouldn't be in this situation now."

I did not say to him that I had kept the information secret precisely to avoid our current situation. First, because it was only true in part; and second, because Tom was stepping firmly on my foot. He had worked quite hard to get us this opportunity, and did not want to see me squander it by speaking impertinently to a brigadier in the Royal Army. I offered instead a more temperate rendition of my thoughts. "I know it may not seem like it, but we do have an edge over the Yelangese. I believe our research into dragonbone synthesis is quite a bit further along than theirs, owing to the good efforts of Frederick Kemble. He had several years to work on the problem while the world knew nothing of it."

Lord Rossmere ignored my comment, addressing his next words to Tom. "I shed no tears for the deaths of dragons, if they can be useful to us. I'm also a pragmatist, though. Scirland has already exhausted most of its productive iron mines, and thanks to your companion, we've also lost our foothold in Bayembe. If we kill half the dragons now for raw material, then in a generation we'll be fighting over the few that remain. We need a renewable supply, and that means breeding them."

None of this was news to either Tom or myself. Lord Rossmere was not speaking to inform us, though; all that was prelude to his next statement. He said, "Your work must be carried out under conditions of strict security. The formula for bone preservation may be out in the world, but nobody has yet had much luck with breeding. The nation that harnesses dragons for that purpose will have a lasting advantage over its rivals, and we do not intend to lose that chance."

There would be at least two nations with this particular secret. Scirland had no true dragons left, only draconic cousins such as the sparklings with which I had begun my research so many years before. Politics make for peculiar bedfellows; in this instance, we were in bed with Akhia, whose desert drakes would be ideally suited for the purpose—if we could induce the beasts to cooperate.

Tom said, "We will of course do what we can. It will take a good deal more than two people to manage the necessary work, though . . . I believe Lord Tavenor had a staff to assist?"

"Yes, of course. Some Akhian labourers, and the site doubles as a barracks for our military contingent in Qurrat. There is a gentleman you will liaise with—" Lord Rossmere twitched aside a few papers, searching. "Husam ibn Ramiz ibn Khalis al-Aritati. A sheikh of one of their tribes. We've been assured of his trustworthiness."

"I presume we will also have access to Lord Tavenor's notes?" I said. "He has published nothing of his work. Obviously he met with no success, or else you would not be looking for his replacement; but we must know what he has done, so that we do not waste time repeating his errors." Depending on what we found in his notes, I anticipated spending quite a bit of time repeating his errors, to see whether it was his theories or his methodology that had failed him. But Tom and I had discussed this beforehand, and my dutiful question was merely to set the stage for Tom's own response.

His brow artfully furrowed, my companion said, "Yes, the lack of publications is rather troubling, for a scientific endeavour of this sort. It seems rather a waste. I realize that matters related to the breeding of dragons must be kept under wraps—but we would like an understanding that Dame Isabella and I may publish our other discoveries as we see fit."

It was peculiar to hear Tom refer to me as "Dame Isabella." We had not been so formal with one another since Mouleen; indeed, we had an unspoken agreement never to let differences in rank stand between us. Formality was necessary, however, when dealing with men like Lord Rossmere. The brigadier swelled with indignation. "Other discoveries? We are sending you there to breed dragons, not to run about studying whatever you like."

"We will of course devote our full attention to that task," I said, my tone as conciliatory as I could contrive. "But in the process of so doing, we will undoubtedly observe a thousand details of anatomy and behaviour that need not be state secrets. Mathieu Sémery has won a fair bit of acclaim in Thiessin with his study of wyverns in Bulskevo. I should not like to see Scirland lag behind in the eyes of the scientific community, simply because we kept mum about everything we might discover."

This was not a situation where I could form a private vow

to do as I wished, and the consequences be damned. That might suffice for the wearing of trousers in the field, or my friendships with various men come what rumours might result . . . but violating our arrangement with the Royal Army could land Tom and myself in prison. I was determined not to squander this opportunity, but first we needed Lord Rossmere's consent.

Not bothering to hide his suspicion, he said, "What sort of things do you imagine you would publish?"

I racked my brains for the most tediously scientific topic imaginable. "Oh, perhaps . . . the grooming behaviour of the desert drake after feeding. Do they lick themselves clean, as cats do? Or do they perhaps roll in sand—and if so, what effect does this abrasion have on their scales—"

"Thank you, Dame Isabella, that will do." I had succeeded in sufficiently boring Lord Rossmere. "You will submit any materials you write to Colonel Pensyth in Qurrat, along with a list of the publications and individuals to whom you wish to send them. He will consult with General Lord Ferdigan as necessary—but if they approve, then yes, you may publish. But those men will have final authority in the matter."

I did not much relish the notion of military oversight, but this was likely the best Tom and I could hope for. "Thank you," I said, and tried to sound sincere.

"How soon shall we begin?" Tom asked.

Lord Rossmere snorted. "If I could put you on a boat tomorrow, I would. Unless you find a way to make dragons grow to full size more rapidly, it will be years before we have an adequate supply—and that is if you succeed right away. The Yelangese have undoubtedly been pursuing the same goal; we have no time to waste."

"Since you cannot put us on a boat tomorrow . . ." I prompted.

"How soon can you depart?"

His manner of asking made it clear that "the day after tomorrow" would be an ideal answer, and his mood would deteriorate with every subsequent day he was forced to wait. Tom and I exchanged glances. "This Selemer week?" Tom ventured.

I had traveled enough in my life to be able to do so efficiently. "That should be feasible," I agreed.

"Splendid." Lord Rossmere made a note of it and said, "I'll write directly once we have your passage booked. Mr. Wilker, you'll be lodged in the Men's House in the Segulist Quarter of Qurrat. Dame Isabella, you'll be living with a local family, one Shimon ben Nadav. Also Segulist, of course, though as you might expect, a Temple-worshipper. There are few Magisterials in Akhia, I fear. Furnishings and the like will be provided; there's no need to pack your entire household."

Rumour had it that Lord Tavenor had done just that, and been made to ship his belongings home at his own expense after he resigned his position. Fortunately for Lord Rossmere, I was accustomed to making do with quite little. Compared with my cabin aboard the *Basilisk*, even the most parsimonious of lodgings would seem downright palatial—if only because I could roam more freely outside of them.

There were of course a hundred other details to arrange, but trivial matters were not for the likes of Lord Rossmere. He called in his adjutant and made the necessary introductions; that officer would handle the remainder on his behalf. Then we were dismissed to our own business.

Tom and I descended the stairs and went out into the bustling streets of Drawbury, which in those days still held the headquarters of the Royal Army in Falchester. We stood for a moment in silence, watching people go by; then, as if by a silent accord, we turned to regard one another.

"Akhia," Tom said, a grin touching his expression.

"Indeed." I knew why his grin had not fully come to rest. My own excitement was tempered with apprehension. Our research aboard the *Basilisk* had been carried out partially under the auspices of other groups—the Scirling Geographical Association, the Ornithological Society—but that was quite different from the kind of oversight that now loomed over us.

I would never say it to Tom, who had fought so hard for my inclusion in this enterprise, but I was not entirely sanguine about the prospect of working for the Royal Army. My adventures abroad had tangled me in such affairs on several occasions, but I had never sought them out deliberately before now. And I knew very well that if we succeeded in breeding dragons as the Crown desired, we would in effect be reducing them to the status of livestock: creatures fed and raised to adulthood in captivity, only so they could be slaughtered for human benefit.

The alternative, however, was worse. If dragons could not be bred, then they would only be hunted; the wild populations would be depleted in short order. I had grown up in the countryside, where the slaughter of sheep and fowl was entirely commonplace. I must persuade myself to think of the dragons in those terms—however difficult such thoughts might be.

Tom and I walked to the corner of Rafter Street, where a hansom cab might be hailed. By that point in my life I had enough money to maintain a carriage of my own if I wished, but I had gotten out of the habit. (My friends later had to persuade me that while Mrs. Camherst or Dame Isabella might do as she wished, it was not fitting for Lady Trent to go about in hired vehicles.) Once settled in and on our way, Tom caught my gaze and asked, "Will you look for him?"

There was no point in pretending I did not know who Tom was talking about. There was little more in pretending carelessness, but I did my best—more for the sake of my own dignity than out of any hope of deceiving Tom. "I doubt I could find him if I tried," I said, gazing out the window at the city rattling past. "There must be a great many men in Akhia named Suhail."

Our erstwhile companion from the *Basilisk*, the man who had gone with me to the cursed isle of Rahuahane, who had stolen a Yelangese caeliger and tried to rescue a princess. I had given him my direction in Falchester before we parted company in Phetayong, but had not received a single letter in the nearly three years since. Possibly he had lost the notebook page upon which I scrawled the information. But it was not so difficult to find me; there were few lady dragon naturalists in the world, and only one named Isabella Camherst.

My words were a mask for that sorrow, but also a nod to the truth. As well as I thought I knew Suhail, I knew very little *about* him: not his father's name, not his family name, not even the city in which he lived.

As if he could hear those thoughts, Tom said, "I imagine the population of archaeologists named Suhail is rather smaller."

"Presuming he still engages in such work," I said with a sigh. "I had the distinct impression that his father's death meant he was being called home to his duties. He may have been forced to lay aside his own interests."

Although I meant my comment to be temperate, the word "forced" betrayed my own feelings. I had once forsworn all my customary interests for the sake of my family; the "grey years," as I called them, had been one of the dreariest periods of my life—surpassed only by the time spent mourning my husband Jacob. I knew Suhail's passion for his work; I could not imagine him giving it up without a qualm.

"You could ask around," Tom said gently. "What harm could there be?"

Embarrassment for Suhail's family, perhaps—but having never met them, knowing nothing of them, I found it hard to muster much concern for their feelings. And yet, I did not want to get my own hopes up, only to see them dashed. "Perhaps," I said. Tom was kind enough to let me leave it at that.

I did not have much leisure for melancholy after I returned to my Hart Square townhouse. If we were to leave in a week and a half, there was no time to lose. I sent the maid to begin an inventory of my travel wardrobe, and went into my study to consider which books I would bring along.

My study had, over the years, become a source of deep and quiet pleasure to me. It was not elegant, as some gentlemen's studies are; one might rather call it "cluttered." Apart from the books, I had notes, maps, sketches and finished paintings, field specimens, and assorted knick-knacks collected in my travels. Shells acquired by my son Jake weighed down stacks of paper; the replica of the egg I had taken from Rahuahane propped up a shelf of books. (The firestone carved out of the albumen of the real egg was still mostly hidden atop my wardrobe, although I had shaped a few of the pieces and sold them for funds along the way.) High on the wall, above the shelves, a series of plaster cast footprints marched in an unsteady line: the fossilized tracks of a prehistoric dragon, discovered the year before by Konrad Vigfusson in southern Otholé.

A large claw sat on my desk, where I had left it that morning. The claw was a complete mystery, sent to me by a fossil-hunter in Isnats; he guessed its age to be tens of thousands of years old, if not more. It was a fascinating glimpse into the distant past of dragons . . . presuming, of course, that the claw did indeed come from a dragon. The fossil-hunter had found no associated bones, which would ordinarily aid in classifying a specimen. In this instance, the *lack* of bones might be the identifier: if the owner of the claw had been a "true" dragon, then of course its bones would have decayed too rapidly for fossilization. (Although preservation can occur in nature, the chemical conditions for it are sufficiently rare as to make fossil dragon bones nearly unknown—although a great many hucksters and confidence men would have you believe otherwise.)

So: grant that it may have been a dragon. If so, then it was one of prodigious size, dwarfing even the largest breeds known today, as the claw measured nearly thirty centimeters around the curve from base to tip. Tom theorized that the claw might have been out of proportion to the rest of the dragon, which certainly made biological sense; what the purpose of such an overgrown talon might have been, however, is still a puzzle today. Hunting, defense, the attraction of mates . . . we have many guesses, but no facts.

My study also contained a box, high up on one shelf, whose battered exterior suggested that nothing of particular interest was contained therein. Unknown to any but Tom and myself, it held my greatest treasure.

This I lifted down, after first ensuring my door was locked. Shorn of its lid, it disclosed various plaster lumps held together with bits of wire. This, as readers of the previous volume may recall, was the cast I had taken of the gaps inside the Rahuahane egg—the emptiness where once an embryo had been.

The cast, unfortunately, was far too delicate to risk on a sea journey to Akhia, and as near to irreplaceable as made no difference. I had studied it a hundred times and drawn its appearance from every angle; the sketches I could take with me. Nothing replaced the experience of looking at it directly, though, and so I examined it one last time, fixing its shape in my mind.

I believed—but could not yet prove—that it constituted evidence of a lost breed of dragon, one which the ancient Draconeans had indeed tamed, as the legends said. Those legends had always been doubtful, owing to the intractability of most dragon types, but a breed now lost to us might have been more cooperative. Indeed, I sometimes wondered if that cooperative nature was *why* the breed was lost: we have so thoroughly domesticated certain kinds of dogs that they can no longer survive in the wild. If the Draconeans had developed such a creature, it might well have died out after the collapse of their civilization.

Such thoughts were mere speculation, though. Even the shape of the embryo was uncertain, owing to the petrification of the albumen and the flaws of the cast; who could guess what the adult form might have looked like? We knew too little of dragon embryology to say.

But with enough time in Akhia—and enough failed hatchings, which were inevitable—I might find a better answer.

A knock came at my study door. "One moment," I called out, replacing the cast in its box, and standing atop a chair to put it once more on its disregarded shelf. A pang of guilt went through me as I did so: who was I to grumble about the Royal Army keeping its naturalists mum, when I myself was sitting on this kind of scientific secret? Nor was it the only one: I had *two* valuable pieces of information not yet shared with the world, and the other one was stuffed into a desk drawer a meter behind me.

The trouble with the cast was that I did not want to say where I had gotten it. My own landing on Rahuahane had been inadvertent; others would go on purpose, if they knew about the ruin there. And those others would become a flood if they knew that the cache of eggs there also constituted a massive cache of unshaped firestone. I had struggled since the day I made that cast to think of a plausible story for its origins that would not either distort true information with false or give away too much. I had yet to succeed.

As for the paper in my desk . . . there, my motivations were not a tenth so noble.

"Come in," I called, once I was down and away from the relevant shelf.

The door opened to admit Natalie Oscott. Once my live-in companion, she had moved to her own lodgings shortly after Jake went away to school. "He does not need a tutor any longer," she said at the time, "and you need more space for books." This latter was something of a polite dodge. I had once promised to qualify her for a life of independent and eccentric spinsterhood; that had since been achieved, though

I could hardly take the credit for it. Natalie had found her calling in engineering, and a circle of like-minded friends to go with it, who kept her tolerably employed. Her finances were somewhat strait—certainly far less than she could have expected in life had she remained a proper member of Society—but she could pay her own bills now, and chose to do so. I could hardly stand in her way; although with Jake gone, I sometimes missed having company in the house.

She gave me a curious look as she came in. "Living alone has done odd things to you. What were you up to, that I had to wait in the hall?"

"Oh, you know me," I said with an airy smile. "Dancing about with my knickers on my head. I couldn't let you see. Please, have a seat—did Tom tell you the news?"

"That you're leaving next week? Yes, he did." They did not live in the same neighbourhood, but it would not have been much out of Tom's way home for him to stop by the workshop where Natalie and her friends tinkered with their devices. "What will you do with the house?"

I sat down behind my desk and slid a fresh sheet of paper onto my blotter. "Close it up, I think. I can afford to do that now, and this is dreadfully short notice to be looking for a temporary tenant. Though you're welcome to the place if you like; you still have a key, after all."

"No, closing it makes sense. I'll come in for books, though, if you don't mind me playing librarian on your behalf."

That was an excellent thought, and I thanked her for it. The so-called "Flying University" that had begun in my sitting room was now a whole flock of gatherings, taking place in many houses around Falchester, but my library still occupied a vital position in that web. Though of course my shelves did not cover every topic—which gave me another thought. "I also have a few books that should be returned to their owners. One from Peter Landenbury, I think, and two or three from Georgina Hunt."

"I'll take them," Natalie said. "You have enough to concern yourself with. Is that a letter to Jake that you are writing?"

It was, though I had not gotten any farther than the date and salutation. How does one tell one's thirteen-year-old son that one is leaving for a foreign country in a week—not to return for who knew how long—and he is not permitted to come?

Natalie knew Jake as well as I did. Laughing, she said, "Be sure to examine the contents of your traveling chests before the ship casts off. Otherwise you may arrive in Akhia and find your son folded in with your hats."

"Akhia is a desert, and therefore much less interesting to him." But Jake would want to come along regardless. When he was very young, I had left him behind so I might go to Eriga; when he was older, I atoned for that abandonment by bringing him on my voyage around the world. The act had given him Notions. It was true that Jake's greatest love was the sea, but more generally, he had it fixed in his head that traveling to foreign parts was something every boy should do on a regular schedule. I had enrolled him at the best school my rank and finances could arrange—Suntley College, which in those days was not *quite* in the upper tier—but for a boy who had gone swimming with dragon turtles, it was unavoidably tedious.

Thoughts of my son should not have led me to animals, but they did. After all, Jake was no longer dependent on me for care and feeding, but other creatures were. "Do you want the honeyseekers? Or shall I ask Miriam?"

Natalie made a face. "I should be a good friend and tell you that I will take them, but the truth is that I fall asleep at the workshop too often to be responsible for anything living. I should hate for you to come home and find your pets are dead."

"Miriam it is, then." They were not birds, which were Miriam Farnswood's specialty, but she liked them well enough despite that. I set my pen aside, knowing that I would need my full attention for the letter to Jake, and steepled my fingers. "What am I missing?"

"Respectable clothing for when you are in town; trousers for when you are not. Hats. No, you'll want a scarf, won't you, to cover your hair? Your anatomical compendium. They will have scalpels and magnifying glasses and so forth waiting for you there, I presume, and Mr. Wilker has the set you gave him—but better safe than sorry. I'm told Akhians have a kind of oil or paste they use to protect their skin from the sun; you might want to acquire some." Natalie rolled her eyes heavenward, studying my ceiling as if a list might be found there. "Do they have malaria in Akhia?"

"I believe so. But I shall have to take my chances: Amaneen do not approve of drinking." Some were more observant than others, of course; but I did not want to give the wrong impression from the start by showing up with a case of gin in my baggage.

She inquired after my living arrangements, which I described; then she said, "Tents? Other gear for camping?"

"Lord Rossmere made it rather clear I am expected to stay in Qurrat and work on my assignment for the army."

Natalie regarded me with an ironical eye, and I laughed. "Yes, yes. I know. But if I should *happen* to go wandering out into the desert in search of things to learn, I am sure I can acquire suitable tents from a local merchant. Also the camel to carry them for me."

"Then you are prepared," Natalie said. "As much as you can ever be."

Which was to say, not half prepared enough. But I had long since resigned myself to that fact.

I could not help but think on the past when Tom and I met in Sennsmouth and looked out at the ship that would bear us to Akhia.

Fourteen years before, we had stood in almost this precise spot, preparing to depart for Vystrana. But there were four of us then: myself and Jacob, Tom and his patron Lord Hilford. Jacob had not lived to come home again, and Lord Hilford had passed away the previous spring, after many years of worsening health. I was pleased he had at least lived to see his protégé become a Colloquium Fellow, though I had not been able to follow suit.

Tom's thoughts must have gone along similar lines, for he said, "This isn't much like our first departure."

"No," I agreed. "But I think they both would have been pleased to see where we are now."

The wind was brisk and biting, causing me to think longingly of the desert heat that lay ahead. (I was somewhat erroneous in so doing: even in southern Anthiope, Acinis is not the warmest month. It was, however, warmer there than in Scirland.) If I felt a chill, though, I had only to cast my thoughts upon what lay in my future: the desert drakes of Akhia.

They are in many respects the quintessential dragons, the sort that come to mind the instant one hears the word. Scales as gold as the sun, giving rise to legends that dragons hoard gold and sleep atop mountainous piles of it, until their hides are plated with the precious metal; fiery breath that sears like the desert summer itself. I had seen many kinds of dragons in the course of my career, including some whose claim to the name was exceedingly tenuous . . . but the closest I had ever been to a desert drake was when I gazed upon a runt in the king's menagerie, so many years before. Now, at last, I would see them in their full glory.

I said, "Thank you, Tom. I know I have said it before, and likely I will say it again—but it bears repeating. This opportunity I owe entirely to you."

"And to your own work," he said defensively. But then he smiled ruefully and added, "You're welcome. And thank *you*. We got here together."

His tone was awkward enough that I said nothing more. I merely lifted my face to the sea wind and waited for the ship that would bear me to Akhia.

TWO

Arrival in Rumaish—Our welcoming party—Excluded from the smoking room—Upriver to Qurrat—Shimon and Aviva

Nature herself has provided the harbour of Rumaish with an awe-inspiring gate. Two rocky promontories rear pincer-like over a narrow strait between; in times of war it is easy to string chains between these to prevent the passage of enemy ships. The caliphs of the Sarqanid dynasty, however, felt this was not enough, and ornamented those two promontories with a pair of monumental Draconean statues taken from the so-called Temple of Silence in the Labyrinth of Drakes. The sea winds have taken their toll on the dragon-headed sculptures, and their features are now sadly all but indistinguishable; the effect of their steadfast presence, however, is no less impressive for that.

I stood at the ship's rail and sketched while we approached these two guardians, looking up frequently at their massive forms. Sentimentality for that ancient civilization had never been among my weaknesses, but my interest in them had grown by leaps and bounds after we discovered the temple on Rahuahane. What breed of dragon had they hatched on that island? For what purpose? Was that dragon among the types alive today, or had it gone extinct during the intervening millennia? Entering the harbour that day, I permitted myself a

The Harbour of Rumaish

moment of sentimentality, imagining those weathered stone eyes had seen the answers for themselves.

Then we passed through the gate and into the harbour itself. This is not so busy a place as Saydir, which lies at the mouth of Akhia's middle river; a more generous entrance makes that harbour better suited for commercial traffic on a large scale. Rumaish sees its share of activity, however, with ships from all over Anthiope. Even in those days, it was necessary to coordinate passage through the gate with a local official, so that the channel would not become clogged to the point of danger with too many ships at once.

Two men in Scirling military drab were waiting for us on the quay as we disembarked. One of them wore the cap and shoulder boards of a colonel. The other needed no insignia to identify him, for I recognized him immediately.

"Andrew!" My delighted cry was almost lost in the clamour of the docks. I dropped the bag I was carrying and hastened forward to fling my arms around my brother—the one sibling with whom I could say I was on good terms, rather than merely tolerable. "I thought you were still in Coyahuac!"

"I was, until recently," my brother said, swinging me around in a laughing circle. "But the rumour went around that you might be coming here, and so I asked for a transfer. Didn't want to say anything, though, in case it fell through."

"You mean, you could not pass up the chance to ambush me," I said reprovingly.

Andrew's unrepentant grin told me I had not missed my mark. Then a voice interrupted us: "Captain Hendemore."

The sound of his name caused my brother to stand bolt upright and tug his uniform straight, murmuring an apology to Colonel Pensyth. My own reproving look was put to shame by the colonel's, for he meant his a great deal more. I could guess at the conversation that had preceded this encounter on the quay: Andrew begging (with his best effort at proper military dignity) to be there when I arrived, Pensyth granting it on the condition that Andrew behave himself. My brother had idled away some time at university before deciding army life would suit him better, but the fit was still not ideal. I had loaned him the funds to purchase a lieutenant's commission—the highest I could buy without selling too much firestone at once—and he had gained a promotion to captain after his commanding officer was killed; I doubted he would ever rise higher, as he did not treat military life with the gravitas his superiors desired.

Tom distracted Pensyth with an extended hand and a greeting. "I take it you are here to lead us onward to Qurrat?" Tom asked.

"Yes, we've arranged a river barge," Pensyth said. "They'll be all day unloading your gear from the ship and loading it onto the barge, though, so Captain Hendemore and I have taken rooms at a hotel. After you've had a chance to clean up, perhaps you might join me in the smoking room."

This last was very clearly directed at Tom, not me. Ladies were not expected to smoke (though of course some of them did, and more of them do now); the smoking room was therefore an entirely masculine precinct. I could not help but wonder if Pensyth had intended to exclude me, or whether it was merely thoughtless reflex.

Either way, I would look quarrelsome if I pointed it out—especially since Andrew elbowed me in the ribs, grinning. "You and I will have a chance to jaw, eh?"

"Indeed," I said. Miffed though I might be at Pensyth, I could not deny that I looked forward to time with my brother. My relations with the rest of my immediate kin were not so bad as they had once been; the honour of a knighthood had at least partially mended the bridge with my mother, though from my own perspective it was more for the sake of familial harmony than because of any change of heart. And as well as I got on with my father, I had never quite discarded the childhood image of him as a minor pagan god, to be propitiated but never wholly embraced. Andrew was still the only relation with whom I felt truly warm—my son, of course, excepted.

Andrew stepped aside to chivvy a cluster of local men to their feet: dockside porters, who would undertake the labour of shifting our belongings from ship to barge. Then we went along to the hotel, situated up a very steep hill, which vantage allowed it to catch what cooling breezes were to be had.

The hotel, like many in the south of Anthiope, had separate women's quarters for the privacy of its female guests. I therefore left Andrew in the courtyard while I saw to my room. When I returned, he had arranged for cups of tea, of a variety I had not tasted before. It was delightfully warming on a day which, despite the sun, was rather more chill than I had expected.

"You know," Andrew said, with the air that could only mean he was about to say something appallingly blunt, "I can't understand why anybody thinks you and that Wilker fellow are having an affair. All it takes is one look to know it's utter nonsense."

Setting down my drink, I said wryly, "Thank you—I think."

"Oh, you know what I mean. He might as well be a eunuch,

for all you care. There are eunuchs here, did you know that? Mostly in the government. I swear that half the ministers I've met are missing their bollocks."

The army clearly had been a wonderful influence on my brother's manners. "Have you dealt with a great many people in government?"

"Have *I* dealt with them? No, not hardly. Mostly that's up to General Lord Ferdigan and his staff in Sarmizi, or sometimes Pensyth. People senior to me. I just trot along behind them with files and such."

Andrew's tone said he was glad to be at the back—a sentiment with which I could sympathize. I was unlikely to be invited to meetings with ministers here, as neither the Akhians nor my own countrymen would be eager to include me in matters diplomatic, and on the whole I was relieved . . . but I will admit there was a part of me that chafed at the exclusion, or rather at its cause.

It occurred to me that my brother had been present at a variety of meetings that might concern me. Whether he had paid attention, of course, was another matter. "Is there anything I should be aware of, before I go wading in?"

Andrew cocked his head to one side, considering. He had taken his hat off and was fanning himself with it, which was likely a breach of military protocol. Although I felt the day was rather cool, he had sweated through his uniform on the walk up to the hotel. "Everyone's annoyed. They didn't expect it to take this long—thought our superior scientific knowledge should make the problem easy, and never mind that people have been trying to breed desert drakes since time out of mind, with no success." He stopped fanning and leaned forward, propping one elbow on his knee. "To be honest—and not to put pressure on you or anything, but—I don't know how long this alliance will last. It's only this business with Yelang and their caeligers that has us and the Akhians working together. If there isn't *some* kind of progress soon, that may fall apart."

Nothing in what he said surprised me, but it was distressing all the same. Tom and I would undoubtedly be blamed for the failure, if we were left holding the baton when the end came. In fact, the dreadful thought crossed my mind that perhaps we had been chosen for precisely that reason. We made much better scapegoats than Lord Tavenor would have.

Well, if that was the plan, then I was determined to thwart it. And in order to do so, I needed information. Our predecessor's papers would be waiting for us in Qurrat, but I liked the notion of being well armed before we arrived. "Can you tell me anything about what Lord Tavenor was doing?" Andrew shook his head, and I remembered that he had only recently come into the country. "Have you at least met this sheikh? The one who is supposed to supply us with dragons?"

My brother brightened. "Yes! Only once, mind you, but Pensyth briefed me beforehand. Fairly important fellow, as I understand it. The Aritat helped put the current caliphate into power a few generations back, and he's their most recent leader."

"Why is he involved with the programme? Is it because of political influence?"

"No—or at least, not entirely. His tribe's territory is in the Jefi, and apparently that's where you find the most dragons." Andrew grinned. "He sends his nomad cousins to capture a few, and then they drag them back to Qurrat for you."

I could not help but perk up at his words. You may think

me mad for doing so: the Jefi is the southernmost portion of Akhia, the inhospitable desert valley between the Qedem and Farayma mountain ranges. It receives perishingly little rainfall; the nomads there survive by grazing and watering their camels at scattered oases. Even for a heat-loving creature such as myself, it cannot be considered anything like an attractive destination.

But it will come as no surprise to my readers that the prevalence of drakes there drew my interest. The Jefi was not so far from Qurrat—which made sense, as no one would wish to transport captive drakes any farther than they must. I was determined to see the creatures in their natural habitat before I left this country; now I knew where to go, and to whom I must speak.

Andrew clearly guessed at my thoughts, for he grinned widely. It lasted only a moment, though, before he sobered. "I wouldn't try to go down there without the sheikh's permission, Isabella. For one thing, you'll die. And if you *don't* die, the Aritat will kill you. They don't like trespassers."

Not to mention that my actions would reflect on Scirland. Trespassing would endear me to no one. "I understand," I said, and prayed for cordial relations with the sheikh.

The barge that took us up the river to Qurrat was not a swift vessel, but I did not mind, for it gave me opportunity to study the landscape around me.

The Zathrit, being the southernmost of Akhia's three major waterways, has its origin in the Qedem Mountains that separate that country from Seghaye and Haggad. An extensive network of irrigation canals spreads out from it like the branches of a tree; they were dry in this season, but come spring the farmers would knock down the mud-brick barriers at their mouths and channel the life-giving water to their fields of barley, millet, and wheat.

Along the banks of the river itself, the desert was far greener than I had envisioned. There were tall grasses and reeds, palm trees and other species I could not identify. Wildlife abounded, too, from fish to foxes to birds in the sky. But from time to time I would see the ground rising past the alluvial plain, and then I could see it desiccating into the distance, a dun colour not much different from my brother's uniform.

It was, in its own way, a landscape as lethal as the Green Hell. But whereas the jungle of Mouleen tries quite energetically to kill a person, with every tool at its disposal ranging from predators to parasites, the deserts of Akhia most often kill with indifference. Jackals may hasten one's end and then feast upon the carcass, but they rarely go to great lengths to hunt one down. Heat and thirst will do that work for them: one dies because the means of life are long since spent and gone.

That, however, was not my destination—not yet, and not (from the perspective of my military employers) at any point to come. Of course I did go out into the desert, more than once; but for the time being, I turned my attention to the settled lands of the river valley, and the city that ruled them.

Qurrat is a complex city, as many old settlements are. Unlike the Akhian capital of Sarmizi, it evinces little in the way of planned arrangements; there has been no equivalent to the caliph Ulsutir to knock down half the place and rebuild it in a grand style. There is no Round City at its heart, no sensible grid of avenues dividing one class from another. Like the central parts of Falchester, it simply *happened*, and people live in it as chance and circumstance dictate.

This does not prevent it from achieving a certain grandeur, all the more striking for its serendipitous distribution. The city is ruled by an emir or commander, one of the three who serve the caliph, and his palace overlooks the river from the vantage of a low hill, with gardens spreading like a green skirt down to the water's edge. Various plazas are decorated with stelae and statues taken from Draconean ruins, and these relics of the past alternate with Amaneen prayer courts, recognizable by their tall spires and elaborate mosaic tiling.

The area where Tom and I were to be lodged is not nearly so grand. The district known as the Segulist Quarter is one of the older parts of the city; and like many old neighbourhoods, it has long since been abandoned by the elite and given over to other segments of society. In this particular case, as the name suggests, the Quarter's residents are almost all Segulist (though they do not constitute the whole Segulist population of the city). It is a polite simplification to say that most of them are Bayitist, with a leavening of Magisterials. One might more accurately say the Quarter is a concatenation of a hundred Segulist factions, some of them borderline or outright heretical. To this day, for example, it contains a small enclave of Eshites, who seek the destruction of the Temple so that it might be rebuilt in what they view as purer form. Needless to say, this goal does not make them popular in Haggad; but they are permitted to live in Qurrat, so long as they obey the caliph's laws (and pay the caliph's taxes).

As Lord Rossmere had said, Tom was to be lodged in the Men's House, which some of the Quarter's residents maintain for the benefit of travellers and new immigrants. It meant sharing a room with three other men, but he did not expect to spend many of his waking hours there; when he was not asleep, he was likely to be at the compound which would serve as our base of operations.

Female travellers and immigrants being less common, there was no comparable Women's House for me to lodge in. I was instead to live with a local Bayitist family: Shimon ben Nadav and his wife Aviva.

Shimon was a merchant, dealing in fine linens from Haggad (as the intermittent hostility between those two nations does not preclude a certain amount of trade). They were an older pair, Shimon's first wife dead and their children long since grown and gone; most were married, but two unwed sons assisted in their father's business, accompanying caravans across the Qedem Mountains. They welcomed me in the courtyard of their house with a basin of water to clean my face and hands, and then dates and coffee to sate my hunger.

"Thank you so much for your hospitality," I said, and meant it quite sincerely. My previous expeditions had put me in a variety of housing conditions ranging from a Chiavoran hotel to a ship's cabin to a hut of branches in the middle of a swamp. Only the Chiavoran hotel had matched this for comfort, and I had not stayed there long.

"We are very pleased to have you," Aviva said in Akhian. It was one of her two languages; she and her husband spoke no Scirling, and I, being Magisterial, spoke almost no Lashon, as our liturgy is in the vernacular.

Despite the barrier posed by my fledgling Akhian, and perhaps a larger barrier of religious difference, she did not hesitate to carry out her duty. Leaving Andrew in the courtyard to talk with Shimon, I followed Aviva farther into the house. Their household was arranged in the southern style, with women's quarters not entered by male visitors, and a piercework screen looking out over the street, which permits the ladies to view the outside world without being watched in return. I expected to spend little more time there than Tom would in the Men's House, though, and so I fear I was perhaps less interested in what Aviva showed me than I should have been.

My attention was instead on the meeting that came the next day, when Colonel Pensyth and my brother took us at last to the compound where we would carry out our work.

THREE

Dar al-Tannaneen—The sheikh—Lord Tavenor's notes—Egg methods and results—Keeping dragons—Our challenge

Our destination lay a little ways outside the city, not too far from the Segulist Quarter. It had been the residence of a wealthy minister in service to the emir some ninety years before, but after his fall from favour it became the emir's property. That man being uninterested in an estate that did not benefit from river breezes, the site fell into disrepair. At his caliph's command, the current emir had leased it to Scirling interests, for the propagation of dragons.

Its semi-ruinous state was to our advantage, for we needn't concern ourselves with damaging the place further—always a concern when dragons are involved. The parts in decent repair served as offices or barracks for the small military garrison under Colonel Pensyth's command, while others had been gutted for scientific use. Tom and I would explore the entirety in detail quite soon . . . but first, we had to meet the sheikh who would be overseeing much of our work.

Hajj Husam ibn Ramiz ibn Khalis al-Aritati was not quite what I expected. Hearing that he was the sheikh of a Jefi tribe made me expect an aged nomad, of the sort occasionally depicted in romantic tales of the Anthiopean south: a headscarf and dusty robes, skin tanned to leather by the punishing sun and wind. Instead I met a man of about forty who appeared in every way to be a city-dwelling Akhian, from his clothing (turban and embroidered caftan) to his personal condition (soft and perfumed skin). My expectation was based on a misapprehension regarding the Akhian people; but I did not learn better until later.

He greeted us in the forecourt of the estate, along with an entourage of both Scirling and Akhian soldiers. Tom's hand he shook; mine I did not offer, replacing the gesture instead with a respectful curtsey. (As I was not yet in anything that could be called "the field," I was still in skirts, rather than the trousers which are my working habit. In truth I wore skirts a great deal in Akhia, or on some occasions robes after the local manner—though I did don trousers for certain strenuous undertakings.)

He spoke in Scirling, with a heavy enough accent that I suspected he had only begun to learn the language after our two nations formed their accord. My own Akhian being rather worse, I was grateful for the consideration. "Peace be upon you," he said. "Welcome to Dar al-Tannaneen—the House of Dragons."

"We are very glad to be here, Hajj," I said. It was, as I understood it, not merely a courtesy title; he had completed the pilgrimage to the holy city of Dharrib, and earned that mark of respect. "We are also very eager to get to work."

Speaking to him was peculiar, for I had drawn a corner of my own scarf across my face to form a veil. This was, I had been told, the way to show respect to a man of his eminence. But it muffled my words sufficiently that I was always concerned about whether I had spoken loudly enough, and in this case I was not reassured: the sheikh made no response to my words, instead turning and leading us through to a courtyard.

One of his underlings had prepared coffee and dates, the traditional materials of hospitality. None was offered to me, Akhia being one of the countries where men and women do not eat together in public. Since I have always been more partial to tea than coffee, especially as the latter is prepared in Akhia, I did not mind overmuch—not to mention that I would have difficulty managing the veil, and I did not know whether it would be an insult to lower it so soon.

Once enough time had passed to avoid a rude show of haste, the sheikh said, "If there is anything I or my tribe may offer to assist you, then you have but to ask. Everything we have is yours, for the good of both our peoples."

This was not, of course, to be taken literally. Generosity is highly prized in Akhia, but just because a man speaks the words as custom demands does not mean he is eager to share all of his wealth and belongings with strangers—even if his caliph has commanded it. Tom and I had no intention of imposing more than we had to. I said, "We shall first take an inventory of what is here, and familiarize ourselves with the work our predecessor did. Until that is done, we cannot possibly guess what else we might need. Your kindness is greatly appreciated, though."

He snapped his fingers, and one of the younger men with him leapt to his side. "Naseef ibn Ismail will take you to see the dragons," he said.

Had he spoken Akhian instead of Scirling, I would have known which "you" he meant. But in my language, we no longer differentiate between the singular and plural of the second person, much less the gender of the one addressed. All I had to go on was his body language, the angle of his shoulders and his head—and these told me that not only his most recent statement, but the one before, were directed at Tom, not the two of us together.

Such behaviour was of a piece with the snubbing Colonel Pensyth had given me in Rumaish, and the countless other snubs I have received in my life. My patience for such things has grown shorter by the year. "Oh, *delightful*," I said, and both Tom and Andrew knew me well enough not to take my bright tone for true. "I should be very glad to see the dragons—as they are, after all, the reason I have come all this way."

Pensyth would not have been given his post if he were deaf to the nuances of social interaction. He said hastily, "Dame Isabella, perhaps you would like to get started on Lord Tavenor's papers. Lieutenant Marton can show you those—that will get you out of the sun."

And out of the way. I wanted to object, for clearly, in Pensyth's mind, secretarial work was the best use for me. On the other hand, I did not wish to make a scene on my first day; and that hand was double, for our predecessor's notes were likely to be of more immediate use than the dragons themselves. The latter could only show us what was happening now. The former could show us what had happened up until now.

But for all that, it rankled to give in. I wanted to see the dragons, and I did not want to be excluded. Only a beseeching and sympathetic look from Tom persuaded me. Very well: I would play along, and prove my value in time.

The lieutenant delegated to be my handler led me through an arch to a smaller, dustier courtyard, and past that into a building that was fairly intact. "Lord Tavenor worked in the office here," he said, gesturing through a doorway to a larger room beyond. I peeked in to find a desk and various shelves, all of them echoingly vacant. The tiled floor was cracked, and the piercework shutters missing bits here and there. "The files themselves are down the hall. Shall I fetch them for you, miss—er, ma'am—er, my lady?"

"Dame Isabella will do," I said, lowering my veil. Lieutenant Marton did not deserve to be cowed, but for the time being I felt the need to stand on ceremony: if people would not accord me respect of their own free will, then I would enforce it where I could.

"Yes, Dame Isabella," he said. By the way his posture straightened, I think he almost saluted. Had I been so very commanding? I did not think so; and yet. "What would you like to see first?"

Lacking much in the way of information, I did not even know how to answer that question. "What are my options?"

"There are three major groups of files," Marton said. "Records of the dragon-breeding project, records of the egg-hatching project, and accounts."

Certainly not accounts . . . but the other two categories were quite broad. Ostensibly the breeding programme was the main endeavour here, but all the authorities on dragon naturalism agreed that success, if it were to happen at all, was more likely to come by way of dragons raised from the egg, and thus acclimated to human contact. Whichever choice I made, depending on how thorough Lord Tavenor had been in his record-keeping, I might be looking at mountains of paper.

Well, it could not possibly take me longer to read through his notes than it had taken him to write them, and I might as well start at the beginning. "Is there any sort of diary for the egg-hatching?" I asked. Tom would no doubt be learning something of the other project during his tour. Marton nodded, and I said, "Then bring me that—however many volumes it may be."

It was not so dauntingly many as it might have been. After all, in the progress of any given egg, there is a long stretch of time wherein nothing much happens. I could skim quickly past Lord Tavenor's meticulous daily notations of "no change" or weekly measurements, pausing only for the entries of greater substance.

Even so, I had not finished by the time Andrew came in, bearing an enormous tray of food. He looked sheepish and said, "The sheikh laid on a good picnic, but men and women don't generally eat together here—or so I'm told. Since I'm family, I volunteered to bring you your share."

I had encountered this kind of practice before, when we were stranded on Keonga. There, however, I had Abby Carew for company, and my son, who by dint of his youth was not yet considered a part of the male sphere. Furthermore, my own unusual gender status there had left me usefully ambiguous, so that I could dine with either sex, as I chose. Here it would be different: as the only woman in the House of Dragons, I would be eating alone every day, unless Andrew was present.

"For today, this will do," I said. "The sheikh will not be here every day, though, will he? I thought not. The Akhians may keep to their own customs, but I have no intention of separating myself from our Scirling companions going forward. It is too valuable an opportunity for us to discuss our work."

At least no one had stinted me on food. I persuaded Lieutenant Marton to join us, but even by our efforts combined, we could not finish what had been provided. "You're not expected to, Dame Isabella," the lieutenant told me. "It's a sign of generosity. What's left over goes to the servants. Most days we're less formal; we just send somebody to the market to bring back some nosh."

When the meal was done, I spent a few minutes writing out a list of the supplies I would need—which was virtually everything, as Lord Tavenor had not left so much as a blotter behind. I had brought my desk set with me to Akhia, but would prefer to keep it at the house, so that I could work in the evening if necessary. That done, I immersed myself once more in the records; and there I remained until Tom came in at last.

He must have poked his head in the door some time before; his polite cough had the sound of a man who has been waiting for the room's occupant to notice him without prompting. "Oh!" I said, putting my pencil in the latest diary as a marker and closing it. "I'm so sorry. Good heavens, is it that late already?" The light in the office had dimmed quite a lot, though I had not noticed it except to tilt the pages toward the window.

"There were a lot of formalities," Tom said feelingly. "Though it wasn't all a waste of time. I take it this room out front is meant for a secretary?"

"For Lieutenant Marton, unless we replace him. He asked if I wished to have a second office set up elsewhere in the building. For me, of course, though he did not say it." I rubbed the bridge of my nose, wondering if my headache meant I should look into getting spectacles. "I, er, may have said I would ask you if *you* wanted one. People are used to coming here; I do not like the thought of being shuffled off to some dusty corner where I can be ignored."

"Quite right." Tom came and perched on the edge of the desk, there being nowhere else to sit save the chair I currently occupied. "This room is big enough for us both; we're neither of us likely to fill it up with elephant tusks and Erigan masks. We can start out sharing it, and if that doesn't work, I'll move elsewhere."

I gave him a look of wordless gratitude. My eagerness to head off Marton's condescension had provoked me into taking advantage of my greater social status over Tom, which I ordinarily took care to avoid. Besides, it was he, not I, who was a Colloquium Fellow. If either of us was to have the main office here, it ought to be him.

Tom gestured at the piles of books on the shelves behind me. "What have you learned?"

"Quite a bit," I said, "alternately discouraging and frustrating. Were it not for this scarf, I might have torn half my hair out by now."

(Before I continue onward, I must issue an apology. There is no way I could conceal our predecessor's identity; it is a matter of public record who originally held the Akhian post, and many people remember his name. I fear that what I am about to say may border on the libellous, though, for I cannot tell this tale without being openly critical of Lord Tavenor's work. I may only hope to mitigate it by also saying that I have a great deal of respect for the man, and indeed his work—flaws and all—was the foundation upon which Tom and I built our own efforts. Without him, I do not know how we might have proceeded. Nonetheless, I *am* sorry.)

Tom waited while I opened my notebook and found the necessary pages. "The eggs," I said, "are delivered to Qurrat by the Aritat—the sheikh's people. But it isn't systematic: when they find a clutch of eggs, they collect them, regardless of their developmental stage. This means Lord Tavenor received everything from new-laid eggs to ones about to hatch." Indeed, one of them had hatched in transit, causing no little trouble for the tribesmen.

My description provoked a wince from Tom. "That explains one of the juveniles I saw, then. It was clearly not in sound health."

"It likely explains several of them, though ill health may not have been as obvious in the others." Our knowledge of dragon development was still scant in those days, but everyone with even a rudimentary awareness of the subject knew that dragon eggs were notoriously sensitive to handling. Transit from the desert to this compound had caused many to spontaneously abort, and those which did not often hatched bad specimens. The earlier in their incubation they were moved, the worse the prognosis.

If all we cared about was obtaining hatchlings, then we could have requested that the Aritat mark egg caches and return to collect them when they were nearly ready. But of course that would not solve our actual problem: presuming we could get our captive dragons to breed, we would need to be capable of incubating their eggs to a healthy finish, under artificial conditions.

The diary in front of me made a useful prop. I picked it up solely that I might drop it again on the desk with a dismissive hand. "He never went out into the field. Oh, he collected reports, and did his best to replicate the natural environment here—but it was all secondhand and guesswork. He didn't actually *know* what the usual incubation conditions were, not to the degree that is clearly necessary."

It was the way of the gentleman-scholar, which had once

been widespread. In some circles it still was, though the practice—or rather, the respect accorded to it—was on the decline. Our predecessors in all fields of science had once been content to work from the scattered observations of non-specialists and the unfounded declarations of ancient writers, rather than from empirical evidence. It was truly embarrassing to think how many centuries had passed during which even our great minds had believed, without a shred of proof, that a spider would not cross a line of salt—to choose but one particularly egregious example. The exact sciences had shed that mentality some time ago; the field sciences, such as natural history or anthropology, had taken longer, and were not yet done shedding.

Lord Tavenor was of the school of thought which said that a gentleman should not dirty his hands collecting data himself. His information came from travellers, sheluhim, merchants trading in various locales. In this case he had the reports of the Aritat, who undoubtedly were keen observers of the world in which they lived—but they did not deal in the sort of precise measurements that were necessary for scientific work. And Lord Tavenor, it seemed, had not asked them to.

"You want to go into the field," Tom said. "We can try—we always planned to try—but I get the impression the sheikh will not be in favour. It's possible Lord Tavenor asked, and was refused."

"If so, he made no note of it here," I said. Then I softened. "But you may be correct. These diaries are entirely devoted to the eggs themselves, not to conversations he may have had about them."

Tom picked up the diary, flipped through it (taking care to

leave my pencil in place as a marker), and laid it down again. "At the very least, we'll want to finish orienting ourselves here before we ask any favours."

Which in practice would likely mean sending Tom to ask, though the prospect galled me. To distract myself, I said, "What of the dragons themselves?"

He sighed. "More of the same, I suppose. Certainly neither the sheikh nor Pensyth had as detailed a description of their natural mating habits as I would like. Though in fairness, I very much doubt Lord Tavenor would have been able to replicate *those* conditions even if he knew them."

Nor would we be able to, however scientific our methodology. Among the dragons capable of flight, mating often involves an aerial dance. Allowing the same here would be a quick way to lose our captive dragons.

"What did he try, then?" I asked, for I had not yet touched those records.

I will spare my readers a full recounting of what Tom described—though interested parties can find the details in *Dragons of Akhia*, which has a chapter on the efforts carried out at Dar al-Tannaneen. Suffice it to say that Lord Tavenor was a keen horse-breeder (this being part of what had secured him the Akhian post), and he had applied both his knowledge and his ingenuity to the problem, searching for ways to bring together two desert drakes without them injuring themselves, each other, or their handlers. A great many restraints had been involved, and at one point he had even resorted to a process I will call "mediated by human assistance," and leave it at that.

When Tom was done, I asked, "The sheikh is gone now, yes?" He nodded, and I stood up so rapidly that my chair caught on a broken edge of tiling and nearly fell over. "Then there is no reason for me not to go see the dragons with my own eyes."

Tom stood as well, but with a marked lack of enthusiasm. "Isabella—I did not say." He hesitated, one hand tapping nervously on the surface of the desk. "You saw the dragons in the king's menagerie, all those years ago. They were runts, and easy to control. Some of the hatchlings here are defective, but not all of them, and not the adults that were captured for breeding. Lord Tavenor had to find a way to keep them. It . . . will distress you."

I stilled, laying my fingers flat against my skirts. "What do you mean?"

"He tried chains and muzzles," Tom said, clearly reluctant. "But the drakes developed sores on their hides, which became infected; he lost three that way. And two men died unmuzzling one of them for a meal—they got burned. He had to resort to other methods."

"Tom." I swallowed, and realized my throat had become very dry. "Delaying will not make it any more palatable."

"The supracoracoideal tendons," Tom said. "He cut them, so the dragons cannot fly. And he tested a method on one of the carcasses—a heated knife, to cauterize the organ that produces their extraordinary breath."

With one hand I felt behind me until my fingers met the arm of my chair. Then I sat down again, very carefully.

"If you do not wish to see them in person," Tom said, "then I will take those duties."

"No." The word came out of me of its own accord, a reflex as natural and unstoppable as breath. "No—I will see them."

It was not professional ambition that drove me to say so.

True, that was a consideration: to abdicate any portion of our scientific work to Tom alone would reinforce the very assumptions we both fought against. But that was not why I insisted on going.

I refused because I cared about the dragons too much to hide from their suffering.

Men commonly criticize women, and women scientists especially, for an over-abundance of sentiment. The reasoning goes that we feel too deeply; and our feelings, being unscientific, damage our scholarly detachment. Thus, by the logic of this syllogism, women are unsuited to scientific work. I have given this a variety of responses over the years, some longer and more elaborately constructed than others, but this being a memoir (and therefore by definition personal in tone), I will simply say that this is utter tosh.

Yes, I felt physically ill at the thought of what had been done to the dragons. I am indeed partial to their kind; I have not hidden that fact in these volumes, though for many years in my early career I strove to do exactly that, so as to establish some kind of credibility among my peers. I also recognized the pragmatic necessity that underlay Lord Tavenor's actions: it is simply not practical to keep healthy adult dragons captive, without taking *some* kind of measures to restrain their capabilities. But I do not believe that recognition of that necessity should mean abandoning all human feeling about our methods and their consequences. Indeed, a science which has no concern for such matters is a science with which I do not care to associate.

When I went to see our captive dragons, therefore, it was with a heavy heart; and I no longer shrink from saying so. What I saw did not make me feel better in the slightest.

The dragons were kept in large open pits within a perimeter wall that had been added onto the original compound. The edges were higher than they could leap without the assistance of their wings, and slightly overhung so the beasts could get no footing to climb out. Each had a small subterranean chamber adjoining, into which they could retire to escape the heat of the sun as needed; this was lined with stone, to mimic the rock shelters in which they often reside, and was pleasantly cool compared to the open sand.

But the dragons themselves were not happy. Beasts though they are, they are capable of feeling, and this can be read in their posture and behaviour. Our dragons were listless, dull-eyed, their scales dusty and neglected. Their crippled wings dragged in the sand; I saw that one had a bandage affixed to her left wing-edge, to protect a chafed spot from further aggravation.

In short, they were nothing like the dragons of the tales, great golden beasts soaring over their desert kingdoms, and the difference made my heart ache.

"No wonder they will not breed," I said to Tom. "An upset horse is less likely to conceive; I expect the same is true of dragons."

"Then we must find a way to please them," he replied. "Though how we will do that, I don't know."

Our stable at the time consisted of two females and one male; a third female had pined away during the gap between Lord Tavenor's departure and our arrival. Lord Tavenor, showing more education but little more imagination than I had when I was seven, had named them sequentially: one of the females was Prima, the male Quartus, and the other female Quinta. (Secundus and Tertia had perished some time ago, along with Sexta, Septimus, and Octa.) I walked the circuit of all three inhabited pits, and went down into the fourth to examine it from the inside. It was not all that much like the landscape in which they ordinarily roamed, but I could imagine the reactions of Colonel Pensyth and the sheikh if I asked them to create an enormous desert park.

Tom was leaning on the railing above, watching me explore. "Perhaps an enormous cage," I called up to him. "Two cages, one layered inside the other. We can measure the fullest reach of their flame, and make that the gap between the two cages, so that no one will be burnt. And build it high—a framework like the one they used for the Invisible House during the Exhibition. Forty meters would not be much for the dragons, but they would be able to fly at least a little."

I could see Tom smiling, even at this range. "With some kind of cart on rails to deliver their food. Though cleaning the interior might be difficult, I fear—we'd have to sneak in while they were sleeping."

If we could make the drakes reproduce reliably, the Crown might build a hundred dragon cages to our specifications, be they never so lavish. The creatures were unlikely to oblige us, though, if we could not better their conditions: and so my thoughts went around in circles. But there was value in imagining the possibilities, as that might give us notions of more feasible solutions.

I climbed up the ladder and stood for a moment, the dry wind brushing like silk against my skin. I felt utterly drained.

Tom put one hand on my arm: a gesture of support he did not often give where others might see. "We'll find a way, Isabella."

I nodded. "And if we fail, it will not be for lack of trying."

FOUR

Lumpy—Honeyseekers and the use thereof—In search of eucalyptus—A lack of hospitality—Messenger from the desert—A folded piece of paper

I made a point of visiting the dragon pits every day, including the smaller enclosures where the juveniles were kept. There were eleven of these, ranging from a hatchling barely six months old to one I thought would soon enter draconic adolescence.

The younglings were a good deal easier to keep than their elders, as desert drakes only develop their extraordinary breath when they reach physical maturity. Lord Tavenor had not named them, except with numerical designations; I suspect he felt they were not worth the effort, given how many of them emerged from the shell in poor form and died soon after. From another angle, one might say it was unwise to name them, for names create attachment, and attachment creates grief when a life ends. But it being winter, we were receiving no eggs, and I did not like calling them by numbers, so I gave them names instead.

I had a certain fondness for the eldest, whom I dubbed Ascelin, after the legendary Scirling outlaw: although Lord Tavenor had hoped that being in captivity from birth would habituate the drake to human contact, he was a feisty creature, not much inclined to cooperate with anybody. It was likely to doom him in the end—if he would not settle down in adulthood, he might well be slaughtered for his bones—but until then, he was the closest thing we had to a healthy wild drake. His wings had not yet been crippled, for fear it would send him to an early grave, but he was not permitted to fly.

The youngest of the lot, however, was the one with whom I formed a special bond. My sentimental choice of words may raise your eyebrows—as well they should—but my interactions with this creature were more like those between an owner and a pet than a scientist and her subject.

Our relationship began when I visited the juvenile pens and said to Tom, "That must be the one you were referring to earlier—the lumpy one."

He was thereafter known as Lumpy. His egg had been brought to the House of Dragons when it was quite new, and what hatched therefrom was obviously abnormal. Lord Tavenor had weighed the hatchling and confirmed his suspicions: the creature was much too heavy for his size, indicating that his bones had formed as solid masses, rather than acquiring the airy structure typical of the species.

My heart went out to him from the start. I knew from reading Lord Tavenor's records that our predecessor had considered having Lumpy put down: the little creature was nothing more than a drain on resources, being of no use to our scientific inquiry. The order was never given before Lord Tavenor's departure, though, and so Lumpy remained, crawling about his enclosure, occasionally flapping the undersized wings that could never hope to carry his adult weight.

I could not bear to have him put down, and told Tom as much. "I can make a scientific argument for it, if you like," I said while we ate lunch in our shared office. "I'm sure I could

LUMPY

come up with quite a splendid one, if you give me a moment to prepare. Something about understanding development by observing both successful and unsuccessful examples. If the abnormality is congenital, we might even have an advance in the captive breeding problem: after all, a dragon too heavy to fly need not have its tendons cut."

"But none of those," Tom said, "are your real reasons."

"Of course not. The truth is that I do not feel the poor creature should die just because someone bungled his care."

I meant to say more, but hesitated, wiping seasoned yoghurt from my plate with a scrap of flatbread. Tom read my hesitation correctly. "You wonder what kind of life it will be, though."

A heavy sigh escaped me. "He will never fly. I look at how the grown ones pine . . . though of course they have *known* flight, and lost it. Perhaps he would not miss it in the same way. But his health is not good; it is entirely possible that as he grows, it will become worse. Should we condemn him to an earthbound existence, laden with suffering, because of misplaced pity? Is that kinder than giving him a merciful end?"

Tom shrugged helplessly. "How can we judge? We have no way of knowing what *he* thinks."

"With a horse or a cat," I said, "one can tell. Or at least guess. But that is because we know their ways, and can recognize the signs of their moods. My father had a dog who drooped about the house as if she had three paws in the grave already, but she would curl up at his feet and whack her tail occasionally against his shins, and you could see she still took pleasure in his company." I wondered, but had never asked, what happened to that dog in the end. She had passed, of course—but had it happened naturally, or had the day come when the tail-whacking stopped? Had my father put her down, out of mercy? Had I not been a woman grown, thirty-three years of age, I might have written him to ask for advice.

"There is our answer, perhaps," Tom said. "Learn their ways, before we make a decision we cannot take back."

And so Lumpy lived. He never became a true pet; I did not let him out of his pen to follow around at my heels, for fear he might bite those heels off. But I visited him regularly, and brought him choice bits of meat, and did what I could to improve his health. When later events took me away from Qurrat for an extended period of time, I was told that Lumpy became quite dejected—inasmuch as we could discern such things by then. He did not live as long as his species might ordinarily hope for; a desert drake that survives its first three years (during which time many of them are killed by other predators) may hope to see as many as forty, and there are tales of some living far longer than that. Lumpy perished after a mere seven, as his increasing size exacerbated his physical difficulties. But that was a good deal longer than he might have had otherwise; and although I cannot read a dragon's mind, I believe he enjoyed the time he had.

Dealing with Lumpy put my mind on thoughts of life expectancy and maturation rates, which were of prime importance to any breeding programme. Indeed, if Lumpy's continued existence had scientific benefit, it was that he gave me an idea which ultimately proved to have revolutionary consequences.

The problem was this: desert drakes mate but once a year, near the end of the wet season, and lay ten or so eggs. The resulting offspring take approximately five years to reach sexual maturity; they ordinarily do not begin producing offspring until they are seven. Even if Tom and I met with success the moment we arrived and kidnapped every dragon in the desert for our needs, it would have taken years for the breeding programme to reach anything like regular production; and of course we could not be expected to succeed the moment we arrived. That much was understood, and allowed for. But each failed season would mean another year of delay.

In short, we needed to practice on something that bred a good deal faster.

We were making our morning circuit of the pens when the idea came to me. Lieutenant Marton was serving as our interpreter—Tom and I had both studied Akhian, but what one learns from a textbook and what a man speaks on the streets of Qurrat are rather different things—and we were taking notes on what the labourers could tell us of the dragons' health and behaviour. Before we could make any useful changes, we had to know the current situation inside and out.

But of course I could not stop myself from beginning to form theories and hypothetical scenarios. This put me to thinking about a draconic species that is far less finicky about its mating habits—which gave me an idea. In such a state of excitement that I nearly dropped my notebook into one of the enclosures, I said, "Honeyseekers!"

"What?" Tom said.

"My honeyseekers! Miriam Farnswood can send them to us!"

Tom frowned. Already his nose was peeling from the intense Akhian sun, even at the gentler angle of winter; his Niddey ancestry was simply not suited to this latitude. "And why should she do that?"

"Because they," I said triumphantly, "will breed like *anything*."

It was not simply that they would breed. The females lay a single egg at a time, but these are watched over by the male honeyseeker; he repeats his mating display until he has what he considers to be a sufficient number of eggs. By removing those eggs when his back is turned, one can persuade him to mate again and again, much more frequently than he would have under ordinary conditions. It is therefore possible, even with just a pair of honeyseekers, to produce a moderately regular supply of eggs—a fact I had discovered when I took one clutch away for dissection.

I had not made much use of this so far, as honeyseekers do not make such good pets that I wanted to send hatchlings to all of my friends. But the man who had gifted my pair to me was Benedetto Passaglia, the great explorer; and he had taken *extremely* detailed notice of their habits in the wild. Experimentation with those conditions might teach us valuable lessons about egg incubation in draconic species.

"It isn't going to be anything like a precise match," Tom said when I was done explaining this to him. (I fear I was somewhat less coherent in the actual moment, producing a great many fragmentary sentences which lacked vital bits of information.) "Honeyseekers aren't what I would call close cousins of desert drakes."

They were barely cousins at all, except in the broadest taxonomic sense. As my readers with an interest in dragon naturalism will know, they hail from the eucalyptus forests of Lutjarro, clear on the other side of the world from Akhia. "It would still be data, though," I said. "And more than we have now."

"True enough. Let's speak to Colonel Pensyth, and see if he will arrange for them to be shipped here."

Honeyseekers were far from the strangest things we might have asked for; Pensyth acceded to the request without a quibble. We ran into a difficulty, however, with our plans for keeping them.

"They are insectivores when the season requires," I told Andrew as he escorted me from Shimon and Aviva's house to Dar al-Tannaneen, "but their primary sustenance comes from eucalyptus nectar. I have a stand of trees in my greenhouse at home—do you suppose it would be possible to uproot one and ship it? Or would the shock of transition kill it?"

My brother laughed. Although an escort was (in my opinion) not necessary, I had come to enjoy these walks, passing through the bustle of the city to the estate outside the walls and back again at sunset. Andrew had always been my closest sibling, both in age and in our rapport, but we had not seen much of one another for years: he had joined the army just after I departed on the *Basilisk*, and his military assignments had kept us almost completely separate since then. Now I spoke to him morning and evening, on topics ranging from our respective duties to family to the places we had seen.

"You're asking *me*?" he said, in a tone that made it clear just how fruitless this line of inquiry would be.

I was forestalled from answering by our passage through the city gate. There were wider ones elsewhere, suited to the passage of carts two abreast, but those would take us too far out of our way; I went in and out of Qurrat by the old Camel Gate, so named because it was scarcely wide enough to admit one camel laden with goods. By the time we had squeezed through to the other side (Akhian propriety about contact between unrelated men and women bowing to necessity in such spaces), Andrew was looking thoughtful instead of amused. "Actually, there are a lot of gardens and parks here, and some of them are full of exotics. The ones belonging to rich people, of course. Marton would know more; he's a keen gardener. Maybe one of them has eucalyptus trees already."

That would be a good deal better than trying to transplant my own trees to Qurrat, or growing new ones from cuttings. "Thank you," I said, and we hurried on to the House of Dragons.

Marton did not know where eucalyptus trees might be found, but he promised to ask around. A few days later, he came to the office while both Tom and I were there, looking excited. "It's easier than I thought!" he said. "One of the Akhian fellows told me he thinks the sheikh has trees like that in his garden. Hajj Husam ibn Ramiz, I mean."

This was indeed fortuitous—perhaps. "I'll write him a letter asking if we can come look," Tom said, reaching for paper and pen as he spoke. "You'll know better than I will whether they'll be sufficient for your honeyseekers."

He dispatched his letter post-haste, and the next morning a reply was waiting for us when we arrived. Tom's brow creased in a frown before he had even finished reading. "What is it?" I asked.

"He says I can come tomorrow," Tom said, laying clear stress on the third word.

Tom alone. Not us both together. "You did mention us both, yes?"

"Of course I did." It came out with a hard Niddey lilt—a

sure sign that Tom was angry. "And his phrasing here is very clear. He doesn't say outright 'leave Isabella at home' . . . but that's what he means."

I was at a loss. I have been snubbed many a time for my sex, but rarely with such bluntness, under circumstances where my purpose is so solid. Nor could I think it some kind of misunderstanding—not after how I had been treated on my arrival here. Lieutenant Marton, who had delivered the letter, was hanging about in the doorway. I turned to him and asked, "Is the sheikh noted for being especially insulting to women?"

"No, Dame Isabella," the young man said promptly, his tone anxious. "He's got two wives, I think."

I forebore to say that a man may have any number of wives and still not be pleasant to them. "Then perhaps it is Scirling women he does not like," I said. "Or Segulist women. Or scientific women. Or women who are overly fond of the colour blue." The words were coming out with an increasing edge; I made myself stop and take a slow breath. Once that had been expelled, I said more quietly, "Then I suppose you will go, Tom."

He straightened up to an almost military bearing. "No. We'll go together. The Crown hired us both, Isabella—under duress, maybe, and none too happy about doing it—but they hired us both. I'll not be leaving you at home as if you were some mere assistant of mine, here only to file papers and make tea."

That had been precisely the grounds on which I accompanied our first expedition, to the mountains of Vystrana. My heart contracted sharply at his words, with the sort of pain that is very nearly sweet. To think that we had come so far: not only myself, from such trivial beginnings to my current position, but the pair of us together, from rivals circling one another like suspicious cats to this unshakeable alliance. I would not have predicted, so many years before, that we would end up in such an arrangement . . . but it made me more glad than I could say.

"Thank you," I said, very sincerely. Then I shook myself straight. "Tomorrow, you said? That gives us all of today to be useful. Let us not waste it."

The sheikh had asked us—or rather, Tom—to come by in the late afternoon, near the close of our usual working day. I brought a change of clothes to the compound that morning, and had a quick scrub with a rag and a basin of water before shifting into them. I could not prevent myself from accumulating dust on the way to the sheikh's house, as dust was inevitable in that climate . . . but I could at least make certain there were no drips of blood from Lumpy's breakfast on my skirts.

Hajj Husam ibn Ramiz ibn Khalis al-Aritati dwelt in a large and gracious estate on the bank of the river, with the main buildings situated on a low rise that would catch what breeze might be had. A servant greeted us in the forecourt of this compound and brought us through an archway to an inner courtyard. It was apparent even then that we had thrown them off their stride: the man clearly had been prepared to take Tom to some other, more masculine preserve . . . but it would not be appropriate to bring a woman there. (My Scirling readers can imagine this location as a gentleman's smoking room. I leave it to the invention of my readers in other lands to substitute an appropriate venue.) We sat on wickerwork chairs in the courtyard, without even coffee and dates to occupy us, and waited.

After a few minutes had elapsed, I murmured to Tom, "I imagine he is debating with himself whether to come down and greet us at all."

"He had better," Tom said. "I've got Pensyth's measure now. I can make quite a stink if the sheikh doesn't cooperate."

I did not like to think of us having to cause trouble just to get our work done. To distract myself, I occupied my time studying the courtyard. As I had not yet seen the caliphal estates outside Sarmizi, I thought this place the pinnacle of Akhian elegance; even by those standards, it was exceedingly pleasant. Detailed panels of stucco adorned the walls, some of them painted in bright colours, and *jardinières* edging the gallery above spilled a wealth of greenery into the air. The fountain at the center held a Nichaean figure that was either a reproduction or a relic in surprisingly good condition. Given the sheikh's apparent status and wealth, my bet was on the latter.

Tom, however, grew steadily more restless. I think he was on the verge of speaking again, or even getting up to leave, when the sheikh emerged from an archway to our left.

He was not pleased to see us—not pleased to see *me*, I suspected—and made very little effort to hide this fact. He neglected the usual greetings and said to Tom, "Is it customary in your land to arrive with an unwelcome guest?"

This was a *shocking* breach of hospitality on his part. Tradition there holds that no guest is unwelcome: an Akhian nomad may be starving in the middle of the wastes, and he will still be expected to share his last scraps with a visitor. At the time I did not know how egregious his behaviour was, but it still rocked me back on my heels, metaphorically speaking.

Tom took it in better stride than I did. He merely said, "I beg your pardon, Hajj, but we're here on a matter of business, and our duties to the Crown have to take precedence. I requested an audience for Dame Isabella and myself together because we're partners in our work. Even if we weren't, the idea we're pursuing right now is hers. She understands far better than I do what is required. If I came here alone, I would be wasting both my time and yours."

The sheikh looked as if he wanted to say we were *still* wasting his time. I wanted to cast subtlety to the wind and ask him what grievance he had against me; it was increasingly apparent that his animus went beyond the ordinary sort of prejudice I had dealt with before. But however much I boiled inside, I could not ignore the fact that I was representing the Scirling Crown, and that any action I took would reflect not only upon my own character, but upon that of my country. So instead I bit my tongue—literally, though only for an instant—and said, "Your pardon, Hajj. We will make this as quick and painless as we may."

Perhaps he had thoughts similar to mine. He was, after all, our designated liaison with the Akhian government; his actions reflected on his people as well. With bad grace, he sat in one of the wickerwork chairs and gestured for us to do the same. "What is it, then?"

Fortunately I had spent some time preparing my reply. In as concise a manner as I could, I related to him the potential value of honeyseekers as comparative subjects, and the necessity for feeding them upon eucalyptus nectar to maintain proper health. "We are told you have some here in your gardens," I said. "If I were permitted to see the stand for myself, I might judge whether it would provide enough sustenance for a breeding pair. Should that be the case, then we will have my honeyseekers shipped here, to supplement our research."

During this explanation, the sheikh had been looking fixedly at the centerpiece of the fountain, with an expression that said the sight did not bring him much pleasure, but was preferable to the alternative. As I came to a close, he opened his mouth to reply—but he was forestalled by the entrance of another visitor.

I had heard this one approach as I spoke: a clatter in the courtyard, as of a horse's hooves on the pavement, followed by a brief exchange of speech, too muffled for me to hear. But I did not realize the horseman was coming inside until the sheikh's gaze shot to the archway through which Tom and I had entered. From behind me a voice rang out in Akhian, saying, "Brother, I have bad news."

If Husam ibn Ramiz had disappointed my expectations of a desert nomad, this man fulfilled them. He wore the dusty, bleached-linen robe, the boots of worn camel leather, the dark cloak over it all. His headscarf flared behind him as he strode in, kept in place by its encircling cord, and he even had one corner of the scarf drawn up over his nose and mouth, to keep the dust out. He reached up to unfasten this veil as he spoke—but even before that covering dropped, I knew him.

Instinct alone kept me from whispering, "*Suhail.*"

He was in a bad temper; that was obvious from the jarring motion of his stride. Dismay overwrote this as he realized the sheikh was not alone: his momentum faltered just past the threshold, and he said, "My apologies. I didn't realize you had guests."

I had put my own scarf across my face in deference to the sheikh; now I turned my head, so that even my eyes were concealed. My heart was beating triple-time. Gears clicked together in my head, fitting together with the precision of clockwork. I no longer needed to ask why the sheikh detested me so, for I knew the troubles I had experienced with my own family, those members of it who disapproved of my life and my actions. And I knew that my behaviour in these next few moments—mine and Suhail's—would leave an indelible stamp on all that followed.

"You," the sheikh said in a tone fit to freeze water, "are supposed to be in the desert."

"I know," Suhail said. "The Banu Safr—Wait." He changed to Scirling. "Wilker, is that you?"

Tom rose awkwardly from his chair. "It is. I—did not expect to see you here."

I almost laughed. I had imagined that trying to find Suhail would be like looking for one grain of sand in the desert. He could have been anywhere in Akhia, or nowhere in the country at all. Instead he was the brother of the very man with whom our duties required us to work.

Suhail sounded baffled, as well he might. "Nor I. What brings you to Akhia?"

I could not continue staring at the tiles of the courtyard floor forever, however complex and fascinating their design. I lifted my head, gazing at a spot just to Suhail's right, and gave him a polite nod. "Peace be upon you, sir."

He stared at me. My face was half concealed, but surely he

must recognize my voice, as I had his. And what other Scirling woman would be sitting here with Tom Wilker?

I could read nothing from his expression, so blank had it become. Perhaps he did not recall me after all. Then he drew in a breath and gave me a brief nod, not touching his heart as he might have done. "And upon you, peace." He directed his attention once more to Tom. "Let me guess. You are Lord Tavenor's successor."

Whether Tom missed his choice of singular noun or simply chose to disregard it, I cannot say. All I know is that for once, I wished him to be less energetic in defending my status. "Yes, Isabella and myself both. We didn't realize you were involved."

"I'm not, really," Suhail said carelessly. "My duties are out in the desert." He reverted to Akhian, turning once more to the sheikh. "But I'm interrupting—I do apologize. Brother, when you have a moment, we should talk."

His disinterest in speaking with us was palpable. Tom cleared his throat awkwardly and said, "We are only here to see the eucalyptus trees in the garden. Hajj, if it pleases you, a servant could show us what we need. That way we won't keep you from your business any longer."

This suited the sheikh very well, who was calling for a servant almost before Tom was done speaking. Suhail did not wait around for us to be handed off, but vanished through one of the archways. I waited in my chair, with what I hoped looked like demureness, until someone came to guide us to the garden, but what kept echoing through my mind was: *Suhail ibn Ramiz ibn Khalis al-Aritati.*

It would have meant nothing to me three years ago, when I first met Suhail. I was not sufficiently *au courant* to name the influential families of Thiessin, let alone Akhia. But he was the younger brother of a sheikh, the scion of a tribe that had helped put the current caliph on the caliphal throne. Oh, I could imagine how his brother had seethed to hear the rumours about our conduct as we traveled the world together. Did anyone on the Scirling side of things know my archaeological companion was the sheikh's brother? Or had Hajj Husam kept that connection sufficiently hidden? The latter, I suspected, or someone would have thrown this in Tom's face when he insisted on the Crown hiring us both.

I saw nothing of the gardens as we walked through, though in hindsight I can say they were magnificent. Only my awareness of duty made me capable of focusing on the eucalyptus trees, when they were put in front of me. It was a luxuriant stand, capable of supporting at least a dozen honeyseekers, let alone my little pair. "Yes, this will do," I said, and then: "Let us get back to work, Tom. We don't want to distract the sheikh any more than we must."

He kept his mouth closed until we were well clear of the house. Finally he said, "That was surprisingly cold."

"It had to be." I stopped and leaned against the wall of a shop, because I could not face threading through the crowds while my thoughts were in such turmoil. "Duties in the desert, indeed. Tom, I believe the sheikh has gone to some effort to keep me from encountering Suhail, and vice versa. Now that has blown up under his feet."

"You think Suhail was pretending, then?"

The question put a chill in my stomach. That I had read the sheikh's intentions correctly, I was sure; it explained his animosity toward me, his refusal to acknowledge me except when necessity forced it upon him. But what if his fears were unfounded? What if his brother did not care that I had come to Akhia?

I could not believe that. Even if the warmth of our friendship had faded utterly from Suhail's mind, he would not have been so cool toward me. Indeed, the very fact of his coolness told me he had *not* forgotten: he would only act so if he needed to persuade his brother that nothing untoward would occur.

"He did not even ask after Jake," I said. My son had grown exceedingly fond of Suhail during our travels, the two of them bonding over a shared love of the ocean. "Yes, I am sure it was pretense."

Tom did not argue. "What now, then?"

A very good question. I had put more time than I should admit into imagining what might happen when I encountered Suhail again . . . but none of it had accounted for the possibility that our meeting would not be as free and easy as our previous interactions.

There was only one answer I could give.

"I will do my work," I said, and pushed off the wall. It would have been better had we been returning to the House of Dragons, rather than our lodgings in the Segulist Quarter. Then I might have distracted myself properly. "I will not give anyone cause to say it was a mistake to send me here."

But even as I spoke those words, I knew them for a lie. I had in my desk at Shimon and Aviva's house a folded piece of paper, and I would see it in Suhail's hands if I had to climb the walls of the sheikh's house to do it.

FIVE

A favour from my brother—Our routine—We lose Prima—A new arrival—Dragon wrangling

Alas—or perhaps I should say "fortunately"—climbing the walls of the sheikh's house would not have done me any good.

I had the sense to turn for aid to someone I trusted not to make the problem worse: my brother, Andrew. That he might laugh at me was entirely possible, but I could admit my conflicted position to him without fear of it rebounding upon my public reputation. (Tom I trusted even more, but any action he took would be read in light of the stories told about the two of us.)

When Andrew walked me home the next day, I invited him to the courtyard, where we might converse in relative privacy. "I was wondering if I might ask a favour of you," I said.

"Of course," Andrew said without hesitation. Then he grinned. "Am I going to regret saying that?"

"There is no reason why you should. It is not dangerous—oh, don't look so disappointed," I said, laughing. "It has to do with the sheikh's family. As it happens, his younger brother Suhail was our traveling companion during my time aboard the *Basilisk*."

"I see," Andrew said, and then: "Oh. I *see*."

As separate as we had been these past few years, he still

knew the rumours. No doubt he had some of them from our mother. "The tales are stuff and nonsense," I assured him. "Suhail is only a friend, and a respectable scholar. But it seems the sheikh disapproves of our association, and I do not wish to antagonize him by doing anything that might be seen as forward. I was wondering if you might carry a message for me—nothing inappropriate, you have my word. Merely that I have acquired a piece of research material, which I think would be of interest to Suhail."

Andrew forbore to mention that I referred to Suhail by his given name alone. It was habit, left over from our time on the *Basilisk,* when I had not known any more of his name than that, nor any title to gild it. "You want me to take the research to him? Or should I just tell him you have it?"

"I should like to give it to him myself, if I can," I admitted. "Though if that fails, then yes, I would like you to convey it on my behalf."

My brother shrugged. "Very well. I'll see what I can do."

What he could do, unfortunately, was to inform me the next evening that Suhail was already gone from Qurrat. "Back to the desert," Andrew said. "The sheikh doesn't go out there very often himself, so he's got his brother acting as his representative with the nomads."

And when, I wondered, had that practice begun? After Suhail came home following the death of his father? Or when word came that Tom and I would be assuming Lord Tavenor's duties?

Either way, it put Suhail quite neatly beyond my reach: a most frustrating situation. I could only hope that he came back to Qurrat soon, or Tom and I received permission to go out into the desert ourselves. As Andrew had said, he was the sheikh's representative to the Aritat, and they were the ones providing us with our eggs and live drakes. He should not be terribly difficult to find.

Neither of those things happened right away, however, and in the meanwhile I had my work to keep me busy.

Dar al-Tannaneen had its own rhythm, established under Lord Tavenor's oversight. The beasts must be fed, their enclosures cleaned, their health monitored. On Eromer the Scirling soldiers took up the burden of these tasks, so the Akhians could go to their prayer courts; on Cromer the Akhians returned the favour. (Our soldiers largely spent the resulting time idling about rather than reading Scripture. There were no Assembly-Houses in Qurrat, only Bayitist tabernacles; and Andrew told me the piety of his fellows varied in direct proportion to how much danger their lives were in.)

Tom and I spent those weeks familiarizing ourselves with things: the procedures of Dar al-Tannaneen, Lord Tavenor's records of what he had done there, and of course the drakes themselves, with whom I became acquainted to a degree wholly unlike any I had experienced before.

Always we had been chasing them in the wild, watching them from cover, ordinarily getting close observation only once our subjects were dead. In Akhia, by contrast, I came to know the dragons as individuals. Quartus was lazy, seeming content to idle about in his enclosure, some days rousing no further than the minimum necessary to gulp down his meal. Quinta was fretful, and the reason the enclosures had been deepened partway through Lord Tavenor's tenure, for she had almost escaped her pit on several occasions. The juvenile we called Sniffer had endless curiosity, and would play with objects we threw into his cage as toys.

None of that was immediately useful to our task, and I confined my notes on such matters to a private book, rather than the official records of Dar al-Tannaneen. This was the sort of thing Tom and I wanted to publish, separately from the business that had brought us here: it added to our store of knowledge about desert drakes, if not our ability to breed them. But we were not going to rush anything into print, regardless of military oversight. We needed to know more.

I knew perfectly well what was said about me around the compound. Tom had insisted I work at his side; this fed all the rumours that he and I had been lovers for years. I suspect, but do not know for certain, that Andrew got into fistfights in defense of my honour. Certainly Pensyth disciplined him for *something*, and more than once. I never asked why. Eventually the gossip among the Scirlings stopped. Whether it continued among the Akhians, I did not know, and did not want to.

Despite such vexations, it was a comfortable routine, and continued for nearly a month. And then, as they so often do, things seemed to happen all at once.

It began with Prima dying. She had been the first adult drake brought to the House of Dragons, and her health had been failing her for some time; but she was a tough old thing, and clung to life long after our assistants expected her to go. In the end, however, the trials of captivity won out, and she passed away.

The loss troubled me. It felt like a failure on my part and Tom's, even though Prima had begun to sicken well before we arrived in Akhia. It did, however, afford us a chance to examine her quite thoroughly, which was of great benefit. We dissected the carcass from muzzle to tail, handed off the bones to be preserved—nothing here would be wasted—and studied the remaining matter in detail. I spent an entire day doing nothing but sketching the intricate lace of blood vessels that covered the underside of her wing, which, along with similar structures on the underside of the ruff, assist in the regulation of body temperature.

Mere days after the loss of Prima, however, we received word that the Aritat had captured another dragon, and were in the process of bringing it to Qurrat. "Another female," Tom said with relief when he read the message. "Her tendons have been cut and her throat cauterized, and they say she's healing well." We had discussed more possibilities for keeping the dragons un-maimed, but the truth was that even if we could devise suitable pens for them—something the drakes could not melt their way out of—transporting them to said pens would still be problematic.

On the assumption that the scent of another dragon might cause distress, we put her into one of the enclosures that had not been used for some time, rather than Prima's recently vacated pen. Then we waited, and tried not to fret.

She arrived in late Nebulis, amid a cavalcade of desert tribesmen. They had bound her to a large cart, drawn on a long tether by a team of camels. The journey had clearly not acclimated the camels to their burden, for their nostrils flared with alarm every time the wind brought the drake's scent forward. Once they had dragged the cart into position near the enclosure, the beasts were unclipped and led away. I hoped they would be given some kind of suitable treat; the nomads are renowned for the care and affection they lavish upon their camels, and any creature which has been forced to serve as draught power for its own natural predator deserves a reward.

Tom and I watched their approach from atop the compound wall. "Dear God," Tom said when he got a good look at the chains binding the dragon to the cart. "We *have* to find a better system than this."

"A better system would be relocating our whole enterprise to the desert proper," I muttered. "Better for the drakes, better for the eggs, if we don't transport them as far." Of course, then we would have to transport everything else we needed, which would be costly. The desert can support bands of nomadic herders, but not a permanent base—not without a great deal of money and trouble.

Tom went to examine the drake while I hung back, sketching. This was in part for others' peace of mind: no matter that I had been around the world studying dragons, including rather publicly riding upon the back of one; nobody wanted to let Dame Isabella anywhere near a dangerous beast until it was properly confined. (There were some disadvantages to my social elevation.) But I also had an ulterior motive, which was that sketching gave me an excuse to observe the scene in detail. If I paused on occasion to watch the men moving back and forth, looking for a stride I recognized . . . well, my hand needed a respite.

I had spotted two potential candidates among the nomads by the time our own men were ready to pull the dragon down from the cart, but any action regarding either of them would have to wait. It was probably just as well: I did not even know what I intended to *do*. Better that I should attend to the business at hand.

Tom had injected the drake with a syringe of chloral hydrate, following guidelines laid down by Lord Tavenor. Despite the sedative, however, this was still a tricky process.

We were only beginning to guess at the appropriate dosage for a dragon, and had to walk a fine line between leaving the beast too lively, and inducing possibly fatal convulsions. Tom watched our new charge very closely, and finally gave the signal to move forward. Our men had tied ropes around the dragon's body; now they unfastened the chains that held her to the cart and began to drag her toward the enclosure.

This might have gone well had we kept the surrounding earth in better repair. But the ground outside the compound was quite rocky, and a large stone had begun to protrude from the soil. The ropes caught against this, halting all forward progress, and two of the men went to drag them clear.

Whether the drake was somehow roused by this movement, or had merely been biding her time until an opportunity arose, I cannot say. I know only that she strained with sudden violence against her bonds, long body writhing—and then one of her feet slipped free. She raked the soldier nearest, knocking him to the ground, and the other leapt back with a shout. This gave her more slack in the ropes; a moment later all four feet were loose.

This did not mean she was free. The ropes binding her legs were only part of the set constraining her, with the bulk holding her wings against her body and connecting her to the men pulling her along. But with her feet under her, she now had leverage to pull back against that restraint . . . and so she did, with great force.

Had Tom not gotten the sedative into her, there would likely have been a very angry wing-clipped desert drake charging about outside of Qurrat, and she almost certainly would have been shot. Instead a tug-of-war commenced, with many shouting men on one side and the drake on the other, swinging her bound muzzle back and forth in a manner that said she would have burnt them all to a crisp if she could.

She managed to get one foot up and over a draught rope, and the sudden downward yank brought half a dozen men tumbling to the ground. I dropped my sketch pad and hurried forward—to do what, I cannot say, for my slight weight would have made little difference in the equation. But I was not the only one leaping to assist.

One of the nomads hurled himself toward the rope now whipping loose. He caught it—skidded across the ground—then lost it a moment later when he stumbled on the hem of his robe, tearing the fabric with a noise that sounded almost like the drake's snarls. The words that came out of him then I could not translate, but the tone was recognizable: furious expostulation, in a voice I knew very well.

Suhail's headscarf slid from his head as he staggered to his feet. His jaw set in a determined grin, he leapt once more for the rope. The drake's foreleg came for him again; he kicked it away, then went swinging across the ground as she threw her head upward. But the men had regained their feet, and some of them came forward to help him. Suhail surrendered that cord to them and caught another one thrown by his fellow tribesman. This one had a loop in the end, and on his second try Suhail got that around the dragon's foreleg.

She went down heavily when he pulled her support out from under her. A frantic scurry commenced, and within a minute or two she was bound once again, sagging as if the exertion had taken all the fight out of her—or as if the chloral hydrate was finally doing its work. The hauling resumed, and soon she was confined to her pit, an exhausted lump underneath the inward-slanting edge.

Suhail saw me as he turned away from the pit. He could not have missed me; I was standing barely ten meters away, the only woman anywhere in sight. His lack of reaction said he knew precisely where I was, and had known for some time; but he did not meet my gaze, nor acknowledge my presence in any way. He merely went to reclaim his headscarf, shaking his head over the damage to his robe.

Surely there could be nothing wrong with approaching him and thanking him for his assistance. But I stayed where I was, silent and unmoving, until Tom returned to my side.

He had been on one of the ropes himself, and was soaked with sweat. Breathing heavily, he said, "We have to find a better way."

"Yes," I said, watching the nomads leave, Suhail in their midst. "We do."

SIX

Amamis and Hicara—Mahira's assistance—The garden enclosure—Proper conversation—A long-delayed gift

The death of Prima and the acquisition of Saeva (whom I named for her ferocity) were only two of the changes we experienced around that time. Not three days after that incident, my honeyseekers arrived on a ship from Scirland.

I had named them Amamis and Hicara, after the brother and sister who founded Spurena in myth. They were as hardy as their namesakes, surviving not one but *two* ocean voyages—albeit in far more luxurious conditions. I had been concerned that the rigors of travel would put them sufficiently off their feed that they would require special care upon arrival, but they fell with gusto upon the dishes of honey I laid out for them, dipping their brushy little tongues into the sweet liquid. When drab Hicara shouldered her brighter mate out of the way, he tried to spit at her—their defense mechanism, and arguably a form of extraordinary breath—but it did little good. The noxiousness of their spray comes from toxins in the eucalyptus itself, and my little dragons had been subsisting on clover honey during their journey.

They would have better soon enough. Despite the tensions between us, the sheikh had given permission for me to use the trees in his garden for the sake of our research. I had yet to determine, though, how that would be done. He would hardly wish me on his doorstep every day; and I had been very clear about not asking for that, lest he ascribe impure motivations to my presence. But that meant someone in his household would need to care for the honeyseekers in my stead.

Of course I hoped this might be Suhail. I had little expectation he would take it up, though, and was correct in that—but I could never have predicted who wound up shouldering the task.

I arrived at the House of Dragons one morning and learned from Lieutenant Marton that a woman from the sheikh's household was waiting in my office. "A woman?" I asked. "Are you sure?"

"Very sure," he said, as if my question were not entirely foolish. "Hajjah Mahira, her name is."

The woman sitting in my office was garbed like an Amaneen prayer-leader's wife. She wore the long cloak, and had veiled her face even though I was hardly a man to whom she need demonstrate respect. When I entered, she rose to her feet and said in Akhian, "Peace be upon you, Umm Yaqub."

"And upon you, peace," I said by reflex. "Umm Yaqub" was my appellation there: parents are commonly known as the mothers and fathers of their children, and "Yaqub" is the Akhian form of "Jacob." "You—were sent here by the sheikh?" He was not a prayer-leader, so far as I knew; but if one of his wives was extremely pious, she might dress in such fashion. And she, too, had completed the pilgrimage.

The woman gestured at the door and windows. "Will it bother you to close these?"

It would make the room stuffy, but I could endure that. I shut the door behind me and then crossed the room to tend to the shutters. Our privacy thus assured, I turned to find she had lowered her veil.

The line of her nose, the fine edge to her lips: these and other details were immediately familiar. The sheikh did not have such features, and I wondered whom Suhail and his sister took after, their mother or their father.

"I am Mahira bint Ramiz," she said, confirming my guess. "I live with my brother Husam, and when I heard of your research, I offered to assist. If this is agreeable for you, then you may show me what care these creatures require."

My time in Akhia had already done a great deal to improve my command of the language, but much of the improvement had been in the field of giving instructions to and receiving reports from our labourers, which left me less than wholly prepared for courteous conversation. I gestured for her to take a chair, wishing we had some kind of reception room in the compound, furnished in a more comfortable manner. It would be a useful thing overall, given the length of time this enterprise was likely to persist, and I made a mental note to inquire about the possibility. I did not even have coffee and dates on hand to offer her.

All I had were questions. "Are you a natural historian?"

It would have been a stroke of pure luck—and not entirely outside the realm of possibility, given Suhail's own scholarly tendencies. She shook her head, though, disappointing me. "No, I am studying to be a prayer-leader. For women," she added, when I showed my surprise.

That explained her mode of dress. I bit down on the urge to say I did not expect any sister of Suhail's to be so religious: like me, he followed his faith, but not with any particular zeal. Indeed, sitting with Hajjah Mahira made me feel like I was having tea with my cousin Joseph, who was a magister in Kenway. He never chided me for my lack of piety, but his mere presence always sufficed to make me feel vaguely guilty.

"I hope this is not a burden for you, or in any way detracts from your studies," I said.

"Not at all," she assured me. "I asked Husam to allow me to help. I often study in the garden, so it will be easy for me to do whatever is necessary out there."

The gears of my mind were clicking along, some of them weighing issues related to the honeyseekers, others performing calculations that had nothing to do with professional matters at all. If Mahira had responsibility for the honeyseekers, then I could deal with her instead of the sheikh. Indeed, I would *have* to deal with her, as it would be inappropriate for Tom to do so in my stead; and doubly so when she was so pious. The same rules of propriety that said I should not be conducting business with strange men might for once operate in my favour. And that, in turn, might open up certain possibilities.

Such considerations, though, had to wait. "They don't require a great deal," I said. "Honeyseekers are a good deal more cooperative in that regard than desert drakes! If you can arrange netting around the eucalyptus trees, to prevent them from flying away, that should be all the confinement they need—and really, even that may not be necessary. But I would rather not have to send all the way to Lutjarro for replacements."

When she smiled, her resemblance to Suhail grew even stronger. "Indeed. Will the eucalyptus trees provide all they need?"

"That and insects ought to be sufficient, but I will tell you what signs of ill health to look for. If they seem underfed, then you can notify me and I will investigate." I rummaged in a drawer and came up with the notebook in which I had begun to sketch out my plans. "The most important thing is the eggs. You will need to look for them every day; there will not *be* one every day, but I would like them collected at precise intervals after their laying, which means we will need to know when that occurs."

She cocked her head to one side, curious. "What do you intend to do with them? I understand this is for your research, but I cannot see how it relates to desert drakes."

"If all goes as I hope, it will teach us something useful about which environmental variations can be tolerated, and which ones cannot; also when such variations can be introduced without causing undue difficulty." I had an extensive outline of test cases in my notebook, the fruit of my association with other scientific members of the Flying University. Mine was not a field that often suited itself to laboratory-style experimentation, but in this instance a rigorous comparative approach was possible. Depending on how long I was permitted to continue the experiment, I might be able to test every significant variable in a wide range of degrees and combinations.

She followed my explanation with the attentiveness of an intelligent woman who does not know the subject at all, but is willing to give it the necessary thought. When I was done, she said, "Presuming that some of them are healthy . . . what will you do with all these honeyseekers?"

That was an excellent question. Their bones could be preserved, but they had limited use, on account of their minute size; even a full-grown honeyseeker is rarely more than fourteen centimeters long. "Distribute them as pets, I suppose," I said with a laugh. "You may certainly have a pair for your own keeping, if you decide you like them. We might make diplomatic gifts of some others."

"Eucalyptus trees are not so common," she said. "But we might grow more, and give those along with the animals themselves."

Mahira departed soon after, on the understanding that I would bring the honeyseekers by the next morning for them to be settled in their new home. I exited the office to find that our closeted state had excited a great deal of speculation around the compound, which I had to quell with actual answers. "The sheikh's sister?" Tom said when I told him. I could hear his unspoken question behind those words.

"Yes," I said, and smiled. What need climbing the walls, when I had a reason to walk through the front door?

I arrived the next morning to find Mahira in the garden, veiled, issuing instructions to servants who were fixing the last nets in place. They had shifted a trellis arch to serve as a doorway into the eucalyptus grove, and the whole effect was far more elegant than I had envisioned.

My honeyseekers were chattering in their cage, clinging to the bars and poking their delicate snouts out through the gaps. Once Mahira had dismissed the servants, she lowered her veil and bent to study them. "They are smaller than I expected."

"If they were not," I said, "they would be a good deal harder to keep." I opened the cage door and stepped back, beckoning for Mahira to do the same. Honeyseekers are inquisitive and relatively calm, but they would be more adventurous if we were not standing over them.

They crept out of the cage after a minute or two, and

Amamis and Hicara

quickly found their way to the nearest eucalyptus blossoms. Hicara buried her face in one straight off, as if I had been starving them for a month. "Little glutton," I said, smiling fondly.

We discussed their care for a time, and were nearly finished when I caught a glimpse, through the nets and eucalyptus leaves, of someone approaching. "Are we expecting company?" I asked Mahira.

She did not reach for her veil, nor did she look surprised. "I was beginning to think he would not come."

The newcomer ducked under the nets of the arch and straightened up: Suhail.

My heart thumped in my chest. I had hoped this arrangement might give me an opportunity to speak with him, but I had not expected it to occur so promptly. "Oh dear," I said involuntarily, looking about like a guilty thing. "Are we going to get in trouble for this?"

He laughed, though I noted a strained edge to it. Mahira said, "Why should there be trouble, when you are so well chaperoned?"

I supposed if she did not suffice—a woman, related to Suhail, and studying to be a prayer-leader—then no one would. "Thank you," I said, and tried not to give away how heartfelt it was.

She shrugged. "Husam is being excessively cautious. That will excite far more rumour than allowing you two to behave like rational adults. If anyone needs me, I will be studying over here." She took a book from the pocket of her cloak and went to sit on a small bench in the corner of the grove, near to where Amamis and Hicara were exploring.

Which left Suhail and myself standing near the entrance,

awkwardly not looking at one another. He spoke first, in his lightly accented Scirling. "I am sorry I did not write."

"Oh, it's quite all right," I assured him. The words came out too loudly. Moderating my tone, I said, "I am glad to know you are well."

He nodded; I saw it out of the corner of my eye. His hands were locked behind his back. "My family—my tribe as a whole—we have been having some difficulties of late. For a while now, I should say. Years. I've been rather occupied dealing with that."

I searched for something to say that would not sound inane, and failed. "Your family seems to be doing well now."

"Well enough." He reached out and touched one of the eucalyptus leaves, tugged it free and inhaled its clean scent. "Husam has kept me busy seeing to business matters, mostly here in Qurrat, while he goes to the caliph's court. Until he sent me to the desert, that is."

I could not repress the urge to ask, "How many months ago was this?"

His smile was ironic. "Not long before your predecessor left."

Meaning the sheikh had probably learned of Lord Tavenor's impending departure, and the likelihood of me coming in his place—or if not me, then at least Tom, who was thoroughly tainted by association. But I could not say that, and so I turned to what I thought would be a lighter topic. "What have you been doing in the desert? Seeking out Draconean ruins?"

It was the wrong thing to ask. Suhail's expression became shuttered. "No. Fighting the Banu Safr. One of the rebellious tribes."

The phrase meant nothing to me at the time, and I did not pursue it; Akhian politics were not what interested me just then. "I am sorry. I hope there has not been much bloodshed."

"Not until recently."

I thought of the bad news that Suhail had brought with him on his first arrival, and felt sick at heart.

"What of you, though?" Suhail asked, with the air of a man making an effort to be less grim. "It seems you have done well."

I gave him an abbreviated version of the events that had brought Tom and myself to Akhia, and spent a pleasant moment in tales of Jake's exploits at Suntley. Suhail seemed more like himself as I went on, and even laughed at an incident involving the school fish-pond. He was the one, after all, who had taught my son to improve his swimming—though I doubted he had intended it to be put to such ends.

But I recognized the look in Suhail's eyes. I had seen it in the mirror for two long years when I was growing up: the period I referred to as the "grey years" in the first volume of my memoirs. For the sake of my family, I had sworn off my interest in dragons, and the lack of it had leached all colour from my life. As it happened, my good behaviour was ultimately rewarded, and I did not regret the path I had taken to my present point. Suhail, on the other hand . . .

I could not say this to him. I knew too little of his situation; it would be the height of arrogance for me to barge in, thinking I knew what was best for him simply because I had once experienced a similar thing. Perhaps a marriage was being arranged for him, with a wife of good family who would not mind her husband gallivanting off to study ancient ruins. Or perhaps Suhail did not begrudge his brother the aid their tribe required. His circumstances might be of limited duration, a thing for him to endure for a little while before returning to the life he loved. All of these might be possible—and none of them were my business.

One thing *was* my business, though, and it had been tucked into my sleeve since that first encounter in the courtyard, waiting for the moment when I might deliver it. And if it brought a spot of colour into Suhail's own grey years, that would ease my mind a great deal.

I pulled the paper loose from my sleeve and tried to smooth it out into a more respectable-looking packet. "Here. This is for you." When Suhail eyed it warily, I said, "It is nothing inappropriate. You could post it in the town square and no one would think anything of it." Indeed, most of them would have no idea what it was.

He took the paper and unfolded it the rest of the way. This took a fair bit of unfolding; it was thin tissue, and quite a large piece when stretched to its full extent. Out of the corner of my eye, I saw Mahira watching in curiosity, and not bothering to hide it.

Suhail saw what I had given him, and his hands trembled. "It is the stone."

The Cataract Stone, as it is known these days, though it had not yet been given that name anywhere outside of my own head. I found the engraved slab during my exploration of the Great Cataract of Mouleen, but had not known its significance at the time. The stone, as most of my readers no doubt know, contains a bilingual inscription: the same text, rendered in both Draconean and Ngaru. The former was at the time unintelligible to us, but the latter could be translated; the Cataract Stone therefore served as a key to the code, a way to decipher the Draconean language and unlock its secrets at last.

"Someone went back to the waterfall," I said, forgetting that I had not told Suhail where the stone lay. "He took a rubbing for me. I wanted you to have it."

He looked at me, startled, and then studied the paper more closely. "This is an *original.* Isabella—" He caught himself. "Umm Yaqub. Even now, I would have heard if this had been published. How long have you been sitting on this?"

My cheeks heated. I almost dug my toe into the ground, as if I were a child caught out in a prank. "A little while." Suhail waited. "All right, I've had it for more than a year."

He made an inarticulate noise: half laugh, half horrified roar. "For the love of—you know better than that! To keep private something this important—"

"I haven't been a *complete* fool," I said tartly, well aware that I had been at least a *partial* fool. "There are several copies of that, and my will contains instructions that they should be released to the scholarly community if I die. I would never let such important data be lost! But . . ." My face was still hot. I looked away, and found myself meeting Mahira's eyes, which did not help at all. She was staring at us both with open curiosity. "You are the one who made me see the importance of the inscription. Without that, I would never have known to ask someone to go back and take a rubbing. And I cannot translate it; I can barely learn languages spoken today. There are other scholars of my acquaintance who have worked on the problem of Draconean, but none with your dedication, and none with any connection to the discovery of this stone. I thought it only right that you should be the first to work on the text."

He stood silent through my explanation. I finally dragged my gaze back to his, and lost my breath when I did. Yes, these had been grey years for him—and I had just poured a torrent of colour into them. He looked fully alive, as he had not since he strode into the courtyard that first day.

I might have cast my professionalism to the wind when I kept the rubbing secret, hoping someday to give it to him . . . but I did not regret the decision at all.

Suhail folded the paper carefully along the original lines, cautious lest he smear anything. It had been painted with a fixative, but care was still warranted. "I cannot bring myself to complain any further," he admitted. "This is a gift beyond price—thank you. But promise me you will make the text public now."

"I will." (A promise, I should note, that I fully intended to keep. But having given Suhail the original, I could do nothing without one of the copies I had left in Scirland. My duties to the Royal Army meant I would not have much leisure to prepare it for publication, and my employers would not be pleased with me if I spent my time on something so irrelevant to the task at hand. All of which sounds like a justification, I know—but upon my honour, the delay in ultimately publishing the text was not intentional.)

At that point Suhail noticed Mahira staring at us, and spoke in Akhian rapid enough that I caught barely one word in four. I could at least make out that it was an explanation of the paper, and his reaction to it. Rather than try to follow the words, I watched Mahira. She looked pensive, giving little away; but I thought she might be pleased. If she was as fond of Suhail as I suspected, she must be glad to see him receive a gift of such personal value. And she did not seem to disapprove of me giving it.

Suhail tucked the paper into a pocket of his embroidered

caftan and laid his right hand over his heart. "I will not forget your generosity," he said. "But . . . I should go."

"Of course," I said—and then, without thinking, I extended my hand to him.

He retreated a step, smiling regretfully. "You are not *ke'anaka'i* here."

It was a reference to our time stranded together in Keonga. There I had been considered neither male nor female, but something else entirely: dragon-spirited, the soul of an ancient creature reborn in a human body. Neither Suhail nor I believed in the metaphysical truth of the concept, but the social aspect had been real enough, and it had given us an excuse to bypass many of the constraints of propriety.

But only for a time, and that time was now ended. "Yes, of course—forgive me." I folded my hands against my stomach and gave him an awkward little curtsey. "I do hope I will see you again. Tom and I will need to go out into the desert, I think, if we are to improve matters here; it would be very valuable to have your assistance with that."

"All things may be possible, God willing," Suhail said. It was a ritual phrase, and for all his sincerity, I did not think he was optimistic.

Then he was gone, leaving me with Mahira, who laid her book aside and rejoined me. With surprising candour, she said, "He wanted very much to speak with you."

And I with him. "Thank you for arranging this," I said, and was surprised to hear my own words come out melancholy. It was that as much as any sense of duty which made me say, "I should return to my work now. Please do let me know how the honeyseekers fare."

PART TWO

In which we venture into the desert,
where someone takes an
unexpected interest in our work

SEVEN

Plans for the desert—Colonel Pensyth is concerned—Akhian politics—Riding camels—My introduction to the desert

"If we are to go into the desert," Tom said, "we will need a flawless case for doing so. Not just what good it might do here, but an actual plan for how we are to conduct our research."

Such plans are more common nowadays, but at the time it was a startling change from our usual mode of operation, which involved wandering out into the field and seeing what we might discover. (That mode worked far better when the body of existing knowledge was small enough that all one had to do was hold out a hand for new data to fall into it.) Tom and I worked long hours for a full week constructing our plan, for we knew any failed request would only make the next one more difficult: if we wanted to succeed, our best chance would be on our first try.

We might also have stood a better chance if only one of us tried to go. The truth was, however, that the House of Dragons did not require much attention from us on a daily basis. Lord Tavenor had done a good job setting up the procedures there; Tom and I were needed only when crises arose (which they did not often do), or when we altered the standard arrangements. We were reluctant to do much with the latter until we had data to guide our alterations, and so I saw little reason why we both should not go to the desert—except that Colonel Pensyth would not approve. "We shall tell him the truth," I said. "You know anatomy far better than I, but I am the one who can record it best, with my drawings."

"And you're the better student of behaviour," he agreed. "What if we marked this up—made it clear who will be doing what tasks? Some of them could be either of us, but if we divide it all very carefully, we can make it so that the two halves can't possibly be pulled apart."

When I came home from Dar al-Tannaneen to Shimon and Aviva's house, I sat up for hours more refining my plans for the honeyseeker eggs. The creatures lay these in nests made of leaves, and cement them into place with a mixture of saliva and nectar, which dries to a sticky consistency. I would be leaving some eggs *in situ* as a comparison—a "control," as it is properly called—and placing the remainder in different situations. Each nest would have an attendant thermometer, and Lieutenant Marton would record the temperature at regular intervals. I even prepared tags for the legs of the resulting hatchlings, with instructions that any who perished or failed to hatch should be preserved for later examination.

"It would be best for all involved if I went away for a time," I said wryly to Andrew after showing him my plan. "I am starting with the smallest variations, and working my way up to more significant ones; it will be months before I have enough data to draw conclusions. In the meanwhile, I imagine Lieutenant Marton would prefer to have me not looking over his shoulder every five minutes."

My brother shook his head, browsing through my outline. It went on for pages. I had thought I was being thorough when

I conducted the Great Sparkling Inquiry, fifteen years previously, but I had been a mere novice then in scientific methodology. Now that I had a better grasp of the subject, I could be very thorough indeed.

"I never would have thought," Andrew said, "when you had me steal books out of Father's library for you, that it would lead to *this*."

That was peculiar, for it seemed to me that my life had drawn a fairly straight line from that beginning to my current position. All the same, I supposed Andrew had a point: it is one thing to think your younger sister may eventually study dragons, and another thing entirely to find her conducting a breeding programme in a foreign country, with the threat of impending war driving her work.

"I hope it will lead me a good deal further," I said with a smile. "I am not nearly done yet."

The day after Tom submitted our proposal to Colonel Pensyth, Andrew arrived in the morning with the news that I was to report to the building that housed the soldiers, rather than going directly to my office as usual. I went with him readily enough, assuming that Tom would be joining us there. In this, as it happened, I was wrong.

"Dame Isabella—please, have a seat," Colonel Pensyth said, gesturing me to a wicker chair in front of his desk.

I did not miss the fact that his adjutant had closed the door behind me. "Are we not waiting for Tom?"

"He is not coming," the colonel said. "Tea?"

"Yes, please," I said automatically, my thoughts awhirl.

This much I will say for Pensyth: he did not waste much time on the niceties, which would have only given me anxiety.

"I read the proposal Mr. Wilker sent me, and it seems quite sound. But there is one issue, which is the . . . social situation with the Aritat."

I sipped my tea, buying myself time to think. By the time I had swallowed, I had not found any reason to be other than blunt; and so I was. "Are you speaking of the unfriendliness between myself and the sheikh?"

"I'm more concerned with his brother." Pensyth settled back into his chair. I had never gone to school, but I had heard my brothers' stories; I felt like a boy up in front of the headmaster for some transgression. But I was a woman grown, and reminded myself of that fact. I had nothing to be ashamed of in front of Pensyth, nor was I required to accept his judgment in all things.

He said, "Before you came here, Dame Isabella, I read your account of your voyage. Hajj Suhail ibn Ramiz is the man you traveled with, isn't he?"

"Yes, he is." I sighed and set my teacup on Pensyth's desk, so I could lace my fingers together and grip them tight without being obvious. "Shall we get to the point? You are afraid that I will disgrace Scirland by carrying on with an unmarried man."

"I would never suggest that."

No, he would only imply it. I ground my teeth, then said, "Colonel, do you make a habit of querying your men about their involvement with every woman they meet? I assure you that many if not most of them have done far more to merit censure than I have. I know it may be difficult to believe, but dragons truly are my concern here. I have not undertaken their study in the hope of attracting a new husband; indeed, such a thing would be an inconvenience rather than a benefit, as there are few husbands who would accept my life as I have become accustomed to living it. As for scandal outside the bounds of marriage . . . that would be even more inconvenient, as people question my professional integrity quite enough without such justification to encourage them. So you may lay your mind at ease, sir: I have no intention of disgracing our nation. Not when there are dragons to be studied."

By the time I reached the end of this increasingly frosty diatribe, Colonel Pensyth was staring wide-eyed at me. He even looked embarrassed, which perversely softened my feelings toward him. (I expected him to be angry.) When I finished, he shut his slackened mouth and seemed determined not to open it until he was absolutely certain what was going to come out of it.

"Well," he said at last, shifting in his chair with a creak of wicker. "That is good to know. Because I agree with you and Mr. Wilker: it would be very good for you to gather more data, and that means going to the desert. Since that is where the sheikh's brother is . . . well." He cleared his throat, and an uncomfortable silence followed.

Given what I had just said to Pensyth, I took great care not to show any excitement at the prospect of seeing Suhail again, out from under the eye of his brother. "I am very glad we are in agreement, Colonel. When should Tom and I be prepared to depart?"

"As soon as I can get you out there, I suppose. But that may be a while yet." Pensyth rose, locked his hands behind his back in the military manner, and began to pace. "Dame Isabella . . . how much do you know of Akhian politics?"

I blinked, not following his change of subject. "Within the country? Very little, I fear."

"Do you know what I'm referring to when I say 'rebellious tribe'?"

That was the term Suhail had used, in the garden. I had forgotten, and not inquired about it after. "I have heard it, but nothing more."

Pensyth said, "There are two kinds of Akhian—in a manner of speaking. They divide themselves into 'the people of the towns' and 'the people of the desert.' City-dwellers and nomads, essentially. But they're all of the same stock: trace the city lineages back, and you find they all come from the desert. Call themselves by the same tribal names; those in the towns send their boys out to the sand for a few years so they won't forget their roots. That sort of thing.

"But over the last century or so, those two groups have begun to split farther apart. So when the current caliphate got into power, they decided to tie city and desert together. The tribes are all ruled by sheikhs in the towns, now—people like Husam ibn Ramiz. They get some benefits in exchange. But there are tribes that don't like the arrangement, and refuse to be ruled by city men."

"The rebellious tribes. I see." I thought back to what Suhail had said in the garden. "And one such group is the . . . Banu Safr, I believe?"

Judging by the sharp look Pensyth shot my way, I might have been better off concealing my knowledge. He no doubt wondered where I had obtained it. "Yes, the Banu Safr. Old enemies of the Aritat, and therefore enemies of the caliph, because his dynasty took power with Aritat support."

All of this was information Tom ought to know—but I feared that if I said as much to the colonel, I would lose this moment of agreeable candour, in which he was speaking to me like a human being rather than a female-shaped problem. And since I had already shown some awareness of the topic, I might as well continue. "There's been trouble with them, I understand."

"A hell of a—Your pardon, Dame Isabella. Quite a lot of trouble. Which is why I bring this up. I read what you and Mr. Wilker submitted, and I understand that you think you can make a valuable contribution in the field. But the Banu Safr have staged several raids on the Aritat in the last few months, and men have died. You must see my concern."

I was busy biting my tongue over his phrasing, that I merely *thought* I could make a valuable contribution. I had to collect myself to say, "I have been in the middle of armed conflict before, Colonel. More than once."

"All the more reason for you to exercise caution, I should think."

"And I so shall." I rose and crossed to the wall, where he had hung a large map of Akhia. "Can you show me where we are talking about? I know that Aritat territory is in the Jefi, but not its specific borders."

Pensyth exhaled sharply. "Borders, I can't give you. I'm sure they have them—they defend them very strenuously against their enemies—but it isn't the sort of thing that gets marked on paper. At least not any paper I've seen. But here." He came and pointed to a part of the basin between the Qedem and Farayma ranges. "This section, roughly speaking, is Aritat territory. And here is where the Banu Safr run."

"Where have our dragons been coming from?"

This time his exhalation was more of a snort. "You have the records of that, Dame Isabella—not me. If it isn't specified there, I don't know. But I do know that this—" He tapped an area at the foot of the Qedem. "This area is absolutely lousy with dragons, so I would guess around there. They even call it the Labyrinth of Drakes."

I liked the sound of that very well indeed. "There is your answer, then. The Labyrinth is farther removed from Banu Safr territory. We shall go there, and be safe."

"You'll go wherever the Aritat are." Pensyth went back to his desk. "Even in winter, Dame Isabella, the desert can kill you very quickly. But once you find them—then yes, by all means ask them to take you as far from danger as you can."

He had, clearly without realizing it, slipped into speaking as if I would be going along after all. I hid my urge to smile. This tactic can work very well with certain people: divert them with practical matters, logistics and such, and they will forget they meant to send you packing. By the time they recall, it is too late; backtracking will only make them appear foolish. "The sooner we depart, then, the better," I said. "Our work depends heavily on the season, and I do not want to waste any of it."

Pensyth jotted down a note. "I'll talk the sheikh around. We'll arrange kit for you, out of our own gear, though if we can get him to supply animals that would be ideal."

"Thank you, Colonel," I said—and then fled before he realized he had lost the argument.

Andrew was dispatched with us, ostensibly to provide a military presence in what was, after all, a military undertaking, but also—I suspected—as my chaperon. Although such measures would ordinarily have irritated me, in this instance I did not mind. In fact, our departure had something of the feel of a holiday: I was setting out with two of my favourite people in the world, away from the strictures of society, and I was going to see dragons.

I behaved myself, though, as we assembled at a caravanserai on the outskirts of Qurrat. Our traveling party was small, consisting only of myself, Tom, Andrew, and a quintet of Aritat men who would guard us and see to the animals. That latter was quite necessary, for the animals outnumbered the humans by more than two to one; the sheikh was taking advantage of our departure to send new breeding stock of both camels and horses to his people.

Tom, Andrew, and I were all on horseback, being wholly unfamiliar with the alternative discipline of camel-riding. "We should learn, though," Tom said, eyeing the ungainly-looking camels with disfavour. "They're hardier than horses, out there."

We did not trouble with this for the first two days, being more concerned with sorting out other logistical matters. But on the morning of the third day, Tom approached one of the Akhians, a fellow named Yusuf, and asked whether teaching us to ride camels would slow us down too much.

Yusuf looked us over with a dubious eye. "It can be hard on the back, if you aren't used to it."

"The only way to become accustomed is to practice," I said, in my most utterly sensible voice.

I was still dressed in skirts, but this was no obstacle to that day's grand experiment. The nomads of the desert go about in long robes all the time, often with nothing at all on underneath—as I found out during my time among them. One has the option of a number of postures in a camel saddle; the truly skilled can sit almost cross-legged, with each foot on the opposite side of the camel's neck. I opted for a more common posture in which one hooks a leg around the horn of the saddle, tucking that foot beneath the other leg.

The arrangement thus produced bears some resemblance to riding sidesaddle on a horse, which one might expect would mean I was good at it. In truth, however, I had not used a sidesaddle for years, preferring to dress myself in divided skirts and sit astride. Furthermore, a camel's gait differs from that of a horse in certain ways . . . not to mention that their greater height and humped back leaves one feeling perched atop a very unstable hill, sure to fall at any moment. In counterpoint to this, I must say that although camels have a reputation for evil dispositions, the one I rode was quite agreeable. I will not go so far as to call her sweet or affectionate; she was clearly a creature with a mind of her own, and a somewhat unpredictable mind at that. But I have ridden horses that are far more intractable, and I appreciated her inquisitive nature.

Camel-riding was indeed hard on the back, but we adapted and made acceptably good time. This far from the river, the terrain was scrubby farmland, agriculture being scratched out of soil so dry it is startling it will bear fruit at all. One early afternoon, halfway through our journey, we entered a narrow valley with suspiciously straight walls. Much later I learned this may have been a canal, during the height of Draconean civilization. Archaeologists have found signs that the area around it used to be rich farmland, which of course requires more water, and there is a place that may be where the canal was breached and destroyed.

But at the time it was merely yet another bit of uninspiring terrain that stood between me and dragons. I chafed at the length of our journey, wishing with all the fervor of a young girl trapped in a carriage with a least favourite aunt that we might be at our destination already. Which is unfair to my companions—I liked all of them a good deal better than my least favourite aunt—but all the same, the days dragged by.

We might have made better time had we taken a barge upriver and proceeded from there. Doing that, however, would have taken us through the lands of the Taaruf, who are not on the best of terms with the Aritat. I began to appreciate that, although on paper Akhia is a single country, it is not unified to the degree that I had assumed. The current arrangement binding town and desert together has gone some way toward changing that, but the tribes still control their own territory, answering more to their sheikhs than to the caliph on his throne.

Instead we struck out overland, first through territory belonging to the Banu Zalit, then through the lands of the Isharid. As the days went by, farmland gave way to drier and drier terrain until, by imperceptible degrees, we arrived in what was unquestionably the desert.

It did not consist entirely of sand dunes. Indeed, though this is the common image of deserts, there are relatively few places in the world where it is true. Much of the landscape is stony and hard, supporting thorny plant life here and there, and lusher vegetation—if anything can be called lush away from the main rivers—in wadis and oases, in nooks and crannies of the barren ground. The trick of surviving in the desert is to know where these nooks and crannies might be, and to conserve water in between.

What amazed me the most was the realization that we were seeing the desert at its most verdant. The winter rains were drawing to a close, and everything was in full flower. But this greenery was still intermittent, with long stretches of hard soil in between where nothing at all would grow; and then we would come over a rise and find a carpet of wild lavender or red anemones had sprung up in the lower ground between two ridges. In a few months these would be gone as if they had never been, devoured by camels or burnt to crisp straw by the sun. For this brief span of time, however, the desert alternated between sterility and wonder.

The nights were bone-chilling, and all the more so because the days were still acceptably warm. The sun was also strong; I wore both hat and scarf so as to shield my face and neck, and we non-Akhians daubed our exposed skin with a paste intended to prevent burns. It did not work as well as Tom in particular might have hoped, but we fared better with it than without.

In retrospect, I feel as if I ought to have seen the smooth course of our journey out into the desert as a sign. It is not true that all great deeds must be attended by hardship and privation, and that any expedition which begins without trouble must inevitably go awry . . . but such has been my experience more often than not. Superstition therefore says that I should have known I would either accomplish little, or find myself in difficulty very soon upon arrival.

EIGHT

The Aritat—Desert mother, desert father—The Ghalb—
A dead camel—Fire in the night

The tents of the Aritat spread out along the edge of a wadi, dark shapes above the green, with camels moving all around. I was astonished at their number, tents and camels both: I had envisioned the nomads as existing in small bands, perhaps as few as two dozen individuals. This is not at all the case, and the Aritat at that time claimed more than three thousand tents (the customary method of counting the population), with tens of thousands of camels to their name. What we came upon was not the entirety of the tribe—they almost never gather in a single location—but this particular group alone boasted in excess of fifty tents, each one home to several people.

We dismounted when we drew near, and the Akhians with us threw handfuls of sand up to form clouds in the air, which is how one signals peaceful approach. In response, two men mounted their camels and loped out to meet us.

As usual, my limited aptitude for linguistic matters hobbled me in this initial encounter. My command of Akhian had been improving, but people in rural corners always speak differently from their urban counterparts, and it was decidedly urban Akhian (not to say scholarly) that I had been mastering. Yusuf spoke that dialect better than his companions, which was why we communicated with him the most—but among the nomads, he lapsed into what almost seemed like another tongue entirely.

The men seemed to be directing us to a tent some distance away. We dismounted and led our camels there, while all around us men, women, and children emerged from their tents to watch us go by. We were not the first Scirlings they had seen—a detachment of soldiers had come out here at the beginning of this enterprise, to scout out the situation—but I was the first Scirling woman to visit them, and very exotic in my khaki dress.

Our destination stood out from all the others by virtue of its size: whereas many of the tents had only a single central pole to support them, creating one "room" within, and few had as many as three, this tent had five. The man who waited outside it was more finely dressed than the others, in white robes as snowy as the environment would allow. This was the sheikh of the local clan, Hajj Nawl ibn Dawwas—a man who, in different times, might not have been beholden to any superior authority. Since the imposition of unified governance between the towns and the desert, however, he answered in some matters to Husam ibn Ramiz. Between that and our status as guests, he showed great deference in greeting us.

We were soon seated upon fine cushions and plied with coffee and dates, while a man sat cross-legged in the corner playing upon the stringed instrument called a *rebab*. Outside, men slaughtered a camel for our supper—and not one of the camels used to bear burdens on the march, either. The meat was therefore very tender, and a sign of great esteem. (This accrued to us not on our own merits, of course, but those of Husam ibn Ramiz. To feed us a tough old camel—or worse, to feed us no camel at all—would have been an unforgivable insult to him.) Certain notables of the clan joined us, while others listened at the flap, hanging on every word of our conversation.

For once we did not meet with the polite (or not so polite) disbelief that so frequently greets our work. People often have difficulty understanding why Tom and I would risk ourselves in pursuit of mere understanding . . . but tell them your purpose is war, and no one questions your sanity at all. Nawl ibn Dawwas was not a particularly warlike man, the Aritat having lived more peaceable lives since the ascendance of the current caliphate; but it was still a thing he had been brought up to value above almost anything else. He knew this business with dragons had a military purpose, and he approved.

Encounters with powerful people have always made me uneasy, and so I was grateful that I took my own supper with the sheikh's wives and other female relations rather than the men. I was even more grateful when at last we escaped the sheikh's tent. By then it was full dark, with scarcely a sliver of moon to light our way, and I could only follow blindly in Yusuf's wake as we crossed the encampment to another tent. This one was not exceptional in any way, being woven of dark goat hair, with one side open to catch the wind, and light spilling out across the ground.

A guard dog began barking as we approached, but fell silent when someone came out and touched the top of its head. Even in the dark, with nothing but a silhouette to go by, I recognized Suhail.

It was my turn to halt in my tracks, as he had halted when he found us in the courtyard of his brother's house. I knew, of course, that he was out with the Aritat—but that tribe consisted of many clans, scattered across many camps. No one had told me he was with this one.

Likely because no one here had reason to think I would care. It seemed the rumours concerning my conduct had not reached this far.

Tom greeted him with surprise, and received an apology in return. "I only just returned to camp," Suhail said, "or I would have come to find you in the sheikh's tent. We did not expect you to arrive so soon. Please, come in."

This was directed at all four of us: Tom, myself, Andrew, and Yusuf. I took a moment to straighten my dress and the scarf over my hair, then followed the men into the tent.

It seemed Suhail had been out hunting. A splendid falcon sat on a perch in one corner of the tent, and a woman near the fire was plucking the feathers from one of several small birds, which I presumed were the fruits of Suhail's labours (or rather his falcon's). She cleaned her hands off and rose to greet us, along with another man.

Both were older and much weathered by the sun. Suhail, making introductions, said, "These are Umm Azali and Abu Azali—my desert mother and desert father."

This he said in Scirling, so there was no chance of misunderstanding him. "Desert mother?" I repeated, my gaze slipping to the woman. She did not look much like Suhail, nor did the father—even allowing for the way desert life had thinned their flesh. Suhail was not a fat man, but we all looked plump next to the nomads, who seemed universally made of rawhide.

"They raised me during my fosterage," he said. "It is custom, for many of us in the city. A way of making certain we do not forget where we came from."

Pensyth had mentioned this, after a fashion. I wanted to inquire further, but felt it would be rude. The couple urged us to sit and fed us more coffee and dates, eager to share their hospitality; Umm Azali joined in, despite the mixed company, which meant I had to do the same. (I did not manage sleep until quite late that night; it has not generally been my habit to drink coffee after sunset.)

The conversation was pleasant, if largely inconsequential or else incomprehensible. It is incumbent upon any traveller to share news from the territory he has passed through; Yusuf had spoken to other nomads on our way here, and now he related what he had learned from them, little of which meant anything to me—when I could even understand his words. I mostly looked around the tent, which was made of goat-hair panels and surprisingly sparse in its furnishings. I felt as if I were among the Moulish once more, as in a sense I was: these, too, were a migratory people, for whom material possessions were often more of a burden than a luxury.

As you may imagine, I also watched Suhail, as covertly as I could. He seemed more like himself out here, which pleased me, but also surprised me a little. After all, I knew him largely as a man who loved the sea: I half expected him to pine in such an arid land. But it was clear that he was more comfortable and relaxed in the tent of his desert mother and desert father than he was in the house of his brother. And if he spoke to me but little, nor looked in my direction much—well. I had promised Pensyth I would behave myself; it helped that he did the same.

I was recalled to the conversation when Suhail spoke in my own language. "Tomorrow," he said to Tom; I had missed the question he was answering. "It's too late tonight. Besides, there was an argument over who would be your host. If I weren't here, you'd stay with the sheikh—but since I am, Abu Azali won the argument."

He was referring to our sleeping arrangements. Of course it was much too dark out to pitch the tent we had brought; but I had not thought about what that would mean. I was simultaneously relieved and alarmed: relieved that we would not be in the sheikh's tent, and alarmed at the prospect of word reaching anyone that I had slept under the same roof as Suhail.

But it was also the same roof that sheltered Tom, Andrew, Abu Azali, Umm Azali, and Yusuf. The most inappropriate deed either of us could have performed in such crowded quarters was to accidentally tread on someone if we got up in the night. No one seemed to think there was any reason for concern, and so I went along.

The next morning we undertook the task of setting up our own household. Using the phrases Suhail taught him, Tom formally begged leave on behalf of our Scirling trio to become the "protégé" of Abu Azali, which is to say a guest under his protection. This is an extension of hospitality among the nomads, and meant that we would pitch our tent next to Abu Azali's in the line, as if we were members of his family. Furthermore, they dispatched a girl—Shahar, daughter of their son Azali—to see to our domestic needs. This was reckoned good practice for her, as she was fast approaching the age at which she might marry, and thus become mistress of her own tent.

In this she reminded me a great deal of Liluakame, the Keongan girl who had been my "wife" during the time of our shipwreck. Here no such pretense was needed, nor was I providing an excuse for Shahar to delay marriage until her prospective husband would be ready. My household was, however, serving once more as a training ground for a future wife. Shahar was quite determined in her practice, and firmly halted any effort on the part of either Tom or myself to take on some of her duties; whether this was owing to her zeal or the status we had as associates of Husam ibn Ramiz, I do not know.

Indeed, for once we had no responsibilities at all save the pursuit of our work. To this end, Tom and I asked the very next day who might be able to guide us to the dragons.

We had to inquire of Abu Azali, because Suhail was nowhere to be found. Even conveying our point was something of a challenge—Yusuf had to assist—but once he understood, he responded with a flood of words that made Yusuf grimace. "The man you want is one of the Ghalb," he said. "Al-Jelidah. He is not here, and no one knows when he will be back."

"Who, or what, is a Ghalb?" Tom asked.

Yusuf spat into the dirt. "Filthy carrion-eaters. But they know the desert."

This was, of course, not the most useful answer he might have given. Further questioning elicited that the Ghalb were a tribe—"If they even deserve that name," Yusuf muttered—unlike any other in Akhia.

Indeed, some have questioned whether they are Akhian at all, or whether their ancestors hail from some other land. Certainly their way of life differs from that of the other nomads. They have no fixed territory, but pay a fee to the other tribes for protection and the right to pass through their lands. By law they are forbidden from owning horses, and most do not even own camels, instead making do with some sheep, and a breed of donkey that is esteemed above all others in the region. They survive largely by hunting, and by dispensing their skills in medicine and handiwork to the other tribes; for this reason, and because they are barred from raiding or making war, the nomads despise them as mere craftsmen. (Their reputation as carrion-eaters arises from the fact that they do not slaughter their meat according to either Segulist or Amaneen law.)

But the Ghalb, as even Yusuf admitted, know the desert. Because they do not engage in warfare and are permitted passage throughout Akhia, they are sometimes employed as guides by the more conventional tribes, directing them to good pasturage or hidden sources of water. It seemed the Aritat had been making extensive use of Ghalbi aid in seeking out caches of eggs; and this man al-Jelidah was the one who had been assisting this camp.

Tom, asking around, learned that al-Jelidah had gone to share his wealth with his family—or possibly to bury it, which the Ghalb sometimes do if they have no immediate need of the money. (The Scirling traveller Saul Westcombe wrote a sensational tale fifty years ago about the secret treasures of the "Gelbees," for which he hunted fruitlessly through the mountains until a rockfall did him in. Likely he would have been sorely disappointed had he found the pittance of coins al-Jelidah had received.) But the men in camp assured Tom that Ghalbi assistance was not needed, not in this season; there were no eggs for us to find right now, only dragons. And for those, all we needed was our eyes.

Among the Moulish we had needed to delay our work, for not participating in the life of the camp would have marked us as inexcusably antisocial. Here, however, we had the imprimatur of the sheikh, and therefore were expected to carry out our duties post-haste. As it happened, we had an opportunity to begin our work the very next day—or rather, the very next night.

Andrew and I had gone in search of Suhail. Having given us into the care of his desert mother and desert father, he seemed to have vanished. I gathered from Umm Azali that he might be found in the tent of the local sheikh. This I approached with trepidation, not knowing if it would be an offense for me to stroll up unannounced—but one of the women there (the sheikh's younger wife, Genna) came out to greet me. From her I understood that Suhail was elsewhere in camp.

We found him eventually between two rows of tents, surrounded by a quartet of sleek, graceful hounds. These were the salukis, a breed almost as renowned as the horses and camels of the desert: sighthounds, deep-chested and narrow-waisted, like cheetahs or the savannah snakes of Bayembe, with feathery tufts of hair down the backs of their legs. They frolicked about him, tongues lolling in canine grins, while he ruffled their ears with a gentle hand. At our approach, they went still and watchful, until Andrew and I both offered our fingers for a sniff. Even then, however, they remained wary, and did not return to their play.

"Umm Yaqub," Suhail greeted me respectfully, rising from his crouch and dusting his hands off. "Captain Hendemore. I hope you have been settling in well?"

I said, "Yes, very much so. Your—does she count as your niece? Shahar bint Azali. She has made our tent comfortable with laudable speed. We are lucky to have her assistance."

It was not the most graceful small talk I had ever made. Fortunately we were soon rescued by a sudden commotion. There were shouts at the edge of camp; turning, I saw a boy galloping in on a camel, looking as if he might slide off the hump at any moment. But he kept his seat, steering toward us, and nearly tumbled over the camel's head in his haste to rein it in and dismount. I could not follow his breathless report, but had to wait for Suhail to translate. He listened, then turned to us and said, "A dragon has taken one of the camels."

"Damnation!" I said, then winced. Andrew had not been a good influence on my manners. Fortunately, Suhail had heard salty language from me before (when I was too much in the company of sailors, who were just as bad as my brother). In a more moderate tone, I asked, "Would it be troublesome if I went out with the herdsmen in future days? If I wait in camp, I will never see a drake hunt."

I saw a brief flash of Suhail's smile, before it faded once more into reserve. "You've missed only one part of it. If you are brave—if you do not fear the lion and hyena—you may see more."

He knew very well the measure of my courage, not to mention my foolhardiness. "Do you mean—" I stopped, eyebrows rising. My heart began to patter like that of a young lady at her first public dance. "The stories are true?"

He answered with more levity than I had heard from him since arriving in Akhia. "How am I to know what stories you've heard? But you will see with your own eyes what is true."

Suhail took us to meet another man, a fellow called Haidar ibn Wajid. His age was difficult to judge; the desert is not kind to human skin, and his weathered face might have belonged to a man anywhere between thirty and sixty. He was a hunter rather than a herdsman, riding out often with a falcon on his glove to bring down bustards, sand grouse, and francolins, rabbits and foxes and more. At Suhail's request, he mounted his camel and rode out. In the afternoon he returned and pointed at black specks in the sky, some distance off. In a careful approximation of city Akhian, he said, "Vultures. That is where we must go . . . but not *too* close."

Six of us rode out shortly before dusk: myself, Andrew, and Tom, with Haidar and two of his comrades leading us. Suhail himself stayed behind, much to my regret. Our Akhian companions found a rise overlooking the vultures' target, and when I fixed upon it with the field glasses, I saw the carcass of the camel, already somewhat torn by scavengers, but far from entirely consumed. Of the drake, there was no sign.

We waited for several hours without result. This was my first time sitting out in a desert night, rather than sheltering inside a tent; the experience, apart from the penetrating cold, was both breathtaking and eerie. The stars above were brilliant beyond compare, and the waxing crescent moon gave some light before it set . . . but all around us the desert was composed of silver and shadow, and sounds carried across it for miles. I heard the coughing roar of a lion and tensed, until Haidar shook his head. "A long way off," he said. "He will not come here."

Of greater concern—and greater promise—was the unnerving laughter that came from much closer by. The Akhians held their weapons close when they heard it, while I tried and failed to pinpoint the origin of the noise. "What was that?"

"Hyena." Haidar's voice was barely more than a whisper. "They will find the camel soon."

In the darkness I could barely make out the carcass, but I remembered more or less where it had been before the light faded, and after a bit of searching fixed its dim silhouette in my field glasses. Before long I saw dark shapes slinking about it, and heard more of that strange, cackling sound, so disturbingly like a human laugh.

Haidar, who had seen this before, was not looking at the carcass. Instead he watched the sky, waiting for the stars to go out.

"Now," he murmured, and I lowered the field glasses just in time to see.

The flare was shockingly bright, after hours in the dark. Howls came from the desert floor, and there was a scrabbling of nails against the dirt as the surviving hyenas attempted to flee. But the drake wheeled about—I could barely see it, tracking its movement by the blackness that swept across the sky—and stooped again, blazing once more at its fleeing prey. A frantic search through the glasses showed me hyena corpses strewn about, some of them still burning, especially around what was left of the camel. Then the dragon settled to the ground and began its feast.

Some of the stories told about desert drakes are pure fancy. Among these I count the jinn, the spirits said to be born from the "smokeless fire" of a drake's breath. But seeing those bursts of flame in the night, I can understand how such legends begin. And it is no fable to say that drakes are cunning hunters, clever enough to kill one beast and then use it as bait, luring scavengers who will become the main course.

A drake, hunting in this manner, can often gorge itself on enough meat to sate it for a week or more. Having done so, they are often too heavy to fly; they will lair where they can, or if no immediate location offers itself, walk ponderously back in the direction of their home caves, making short, gliding flights when the terrain permits. Once ensconced in a safe place, they will remain inactive until hunger begins to pluck at

Night Hunt

them again, rousing only to shift between shade and sun as their comfort requires.

I was shivering uncontrollably by the time we regained the comfort of our own camp, but the experience had been thrilling. During the course of our research I went out several more times to observe what I could of this nocturnal hunt, wishing that I, like a cat, could see in the dark. Even once I learned to watch the stars, I often missed the drake's initial approach, for it glides down on silent wings, lest it frighten off its prey.

It was a promising start to our work. But, unfortunately, it was all too soon disrupted—by those long-standing enemies of the Aritat, the Banu Safr.

NINE

Stolen camels—Suhail rides out—The trouble we bring—A breeze upon my cheek—Our dreadful journey—The Banu Safr

I missed the attack of the Banu Safr, as I had missed the drake taking its initial prey, because I was not out with the camels in their pasture. But even at a distance I heard them: the shrill yells, the bellowing of the camels, the crack of gunfire.

At the time I was sitting in front of our tent, with one of the scruffy guard dogs (so different from the graceful salukis) sniffing around my feet. I was attempting to sketch the night hunting of the drake, as much from imagination as from the few visual observations I had been able to make. At the sudden outburst of sound I twitched in my seat, nearly dropping my pencil. "What is that?" I asked no one in particular—for everyone who spoke Scirling was elsewhere.

Shahar came outside to stare in the direction of the noise, biting her lip. I repeated my question in Akhian, but did not understand what she said in reply until she mimed shooting a gun, grabbing something, and running away. The Akhian government has made great strides in curtailing the raiding ways of their nomadic tribes, but they have not stamped them out entirely; and the rebellious tribes are the most prone to breaking that edict.

I made an abortive move toward the camel tethered alongside our tent, but Shahar grabbed my sleeve to halt me. From her flood of words I understood that I was being an idiot—and she was right. What good could I do, riding unarmed toward a battle? But Suhail had gone out to view the herds, and Andrew had gone with him, for curiosity's sake.

Certainly I was not the only one lunging for an animal to ride. Virtually every man in camp was mounting up, with weapons in hand, and they quickly thundered out to join the fray. But a raid is, by its nature, over very quickly: before long men were flooding back into camp, the remaining camels in tow, minus the ones that had been taken.

Suhail and Andrew were among those who returned. My relief, however, was short-lived. "We're going after them," Andrew said breathlessly as he dismounted. "If we can get the camels back before the thieves reach their own territory—"

"*We?*" I repeated, my voice sharp. "Andrew, you are not going with them."

"Why not?"

My foremost reason was that I did not want to risk him, and did not trust him not to risk himself . . . but I did not say that. (I do, however, write it here, which I suppose means that now Andrew will know the truth.) "Do you think Colonel Pensyth will thank you for involving yourself in a matter of internal strife between two Akhian tribes?"

"Fine words, coming from you," Andrew said with a snort.

I gave him a quelling look. "Besides which, you cannot keep up with them. On a horse, yes; but they are saddling camels, which you barely know how to ride. Do you know their tactics? The tricks raiders use to conceal their trail? Will you be anything more than one more gun, when they catch the thieves at last?" Softening, I added, "I know you are a soldier, Andrew. And it chafes, sitting idle while others deal with a problem. But look—they are not taking everyone, not even all of the fighting men."

Indeed, the group that was collecting supplies and loading them onto their camels was quite small, barely a dozen riders. One of them, I saw, was Suhail.

I did not properly hear Andrew's first, muttered response. Only when he raised his voice and said, "Very well, Isabella—I won't go," did I turn and take his hand in mine. "Thank you," I said. "I have quite enough to worry about as it is."

Tom appeared then, a rifle in his hands and two more slung under his arm. "Dear God, not you, too," I said involuntarily.

He ignored me, going to where Suhail and the others were preparing. I drew close in time to hear him say, "These may be of use to you."

Looking about, I saw that most of the pursuit party were armed only with bows and lances. Some had rifles, but less than half; and Suhail was not among them. He looked at the gun Tom was proffering and said, "Your colonel sent those with you for your own use."

"And today my use is to give it to you," Tom said. "You've bloody well got more need for it than I do at the moment. Just bring them back when you're done." He extended the rifle further, almost forcing it into Suhail's hands, then leaned the other two against the side of Suhail's camel, which gave him a grumpy look.

"Your ammunition—"

The word was not even out of Suhail's mouth when Tom

dug two cardboard boxes out of his back pockets and handed them over. Suhail grimaced. "I was going to say, you have a limited supply, and should conserve it. We don't need guns to deal with these Banu Safr dogs."

"But they'll help," Tom said. "Good hunting."

Suhail did not argue further. I watched, hands knotted tightly about each other, as the retaliatory party mounted up. Of course he had to go: he represented his brother here, and would lose a great deal of face if he hung back from battle. But I worried all the same.

The camp was quiet after they left. Several men had been injured during the raid, but they bore it stoically as their wives cleaned and bandaged their wounds. I tried not to pace as I calculated how rapidly the party might return. There were too many variables I could not account for: it depended on how determined they were, and whether they caught the raiders before they passed into Banu Safr lands. Our group might turn back at that border—or they might not, carrying their counter-raid into enemy territory. It would be brave, but a good deal more dangerous.

Either way, they would not return by nightfall. Andrew offered to help stand watch over the camel herds, lest a second party of raiders strike while the best warriors were gone; this was apparently a tactic employed by the more cunning nomads, though no one thought it likely here. I dressed for bed on my side of the tent we shared with Tom—an arrangement I had thought would be decried as inappropriate, given the absence of any other woman. (Certainly it had attracted censure during our previous expeditions, even when we were *not* sharing a tent.) But so long as the tent was officially Andrew's, he had the right to give shelter to any guest he liked, even with his unmarried sister present.

Through the curtain that divided us, I addressed Tom. "Thank you for giving him the rifles."

"You're welcome," Tom said. After a moment he added, "I would have given my left arm to go with them. These raids have been causing no end of trouble for the Aritat, and I suspect it's because of us."

The enmity between the two tribes went back a long way . . . but from what I could tell, it was not always so active as this. "I fear you may be correct."

"I don't know what to do about it, either," Tom said. "This is about more than just our scholarly curiosity; there are governments involved. The caliph is the one who told them to gather dragons and eggs for us."

I nodded, even though Tom could not see me through the thick goat-hair fabric of the curtain. "All the more reason for us to reach a point where we no longer need supply from the desert."

Then I paused, thinking. My thoughts were interrupted shortly thereafter by Tom saying, "I recognize that kind of silence. What are you thinking about?"

I smiled ruefully. "I am thinking that we ought to have had this conversation before I dressed for bed, so that I could come to the other side of the curtain without being completely scandalous. But I am also wondering why the Banu Safr should *care*."

"About the dragons? I've been considering that myself. They supported the old caliphate, you know, before the Murasids came to power. They may just be eager to interfere with anything the caliph is trying to do."

Unlovely though it is to admit, I hoped Tom was right. That would mean Scirland's involvement here was peripheral to this conflict, rather than central. We would merely be an excuse: the spark that lit the bonfire, not the fuel itself.

These thoughts, combined with worry for Suhail, made sleep difficult that night. Ordinarily I sleep like a very tired log in the field, but all I could seem to manage was a fitful doze, from which I was roused by every little sound: a camel grunting, men laughing around a distant fire, Tom turning restlessly in his own bed. I had just made up my mind to call out and ask if he, too, was still awake, when I felt a breeze across my cheek.

Had I resided for longer in that tent, I might have understood more quickly. As it was, I thought Andrew had finished his watch and lifted the flap to come in. Then my sluggish brain pointed out that the breeze was coming from the wrong direction for that.

I rolled over just in time to meet a hand bearing a damp piece of cloth.

This hand reacted quickly to my movement, clamping itself over my nose and mouth, muffling all sound. Someone was kneeling over me, almost invisible in the darkness. I shoved at his arm, trying to dislodge his hand, and kicked with my legs, hoping to hit something that might topple over and make a sound. All I caught was air, and my fiercest efforts made no mark on his arm; I cursed the way fieldwork destroyed my fingernails, leaving me without claws.

But it was not failure that made my struggles subside. My mind was lifting free of my body, floating into the night sky on a dragon's wings; and then I had no awareness of anything at all.

* * *

I awakened on the back of a camel, galloping through the darkness.

My immediate response to this was not heroic in the slightest: I vomited. An intense nausea wracked me, and it was not made any better by the swaying motion of the camel, when night gave me no stable point upon which to fix my gaze.

The man in front of me growled under his breath. I had, on instinct, turned my head aside—but this had not entirely spared him. As my senses returned, however, I felt no guilt whatsoever for this. For I realized that he had drugged me (or if not him, then one of his comrades); and having accomplished this, he had kidnapped me.

My voice answered but weakly when I tried to shout. Even that feeble croak, however, made my kidnapper pull a curved knife from his sash and hold it up so that it caught what light was to be had. The message was clear, and I fell silent.

Shouting would not have done much good anyway. I could tell by the terrain—flattish desert, quite unlike the wadi I had gone to sleep in—that we were no longer anywhere near the Aritat camp. Sound carries far across the open desert, but at this distance, the best I could hope for was to be mistaken for a hyena.

What other options did I have? I tried to force my disoriented brain into motion. Even my best efforts, however, turned up little. By wiggling I might have unbalanced myself enough to fall from the back of the camel; this would have earned me only bruises and perhaps some broken bones. I could not hope to overpower the man in front of me, and even if I did, there were others around us who would subdue me rapidly enough.

The thought of others made me look about. I soon spotted

Tom, bare-chested and still unconscious, riding pillion on another camel. Far too late, it came to me that the sound I had taken for restlessness on his part had likely been another kidnapper drugging him. Were it not for that blasted curtain . . . no, even then matters would not have ended well. They would simply have synchronized their attacks more precisely; or matters would have become violent. I took some minor solace in knowing they did not wish us dead. It would have been far easier to slit our throats than to spirit us out of camp.

Did the men of the Aritat follow us? With my hands lashed to the saddle, I could not turn to watch our trail. It depended on whether our captors had gotten us out quietly, I supposed. It might be that no one even knew we were gone. Once they did . . .

I slumped, trying not to lean against the man in front of me. (Oh, if only propriety had compelled them to put me on my own camel.) The best warriors of the clan were gone, pursuing the raiders. Had that been a diversion? Either way, I was not sure how many men could be spared for a second pursuit. Andrew would not be held in camp, of that I was sure—but alone, he could not do very much.

Such calculations were not cheering, but they gave me some minor distraction from the bone-deep chill that soon robbed me of all feeling in my bare toes. I tucked my feet against the camel's warm sides, curled in on myself, and endured. Dawn came as a blessing, even though we did not stop; we rode on until it was nearly midday. Then we halted amid some rocks that offered shade for a few, while the remainder propped up their cloaks to form miniature tents and huddled inside.

By then I was tormented with thirst. The day was not hot, but the air was terribly dry, and I had not had anything to drink for hours. Pride made me want to refuse when my riding partner offered me a waterskin; I knew I would be grateful to him for it, and did not want to give him such influence over me. But I would need water eventually, and the longer I delayed, the more precious the gift would seem. I took it and drank: one swallow only, after which he pulled the container from my hands.

They kept Tom separate from me, in the shade of a different rock. Unprotected though I might be in my nightgown, he had it worse, fair as he was; his shoulders and back were already painfully red. "Please," I said to my captor, in my very best Akhian, city-inflected though it was. "Have you any robe or cloak that might shelter us from the sun?"

He made no reply, but only scowled at me. Then he got up and went to a man I promptly marked as their leader. Hope rose in my heart—but when he came back, the only item of clothing he bore was a gag, which he stuffed into my protesting mouth. Tom was similarly gagged soon after; and so we remained for the rest of the journey, except when freed to take water and food.

(I wondered at the time why they had not gagged us from the start. I cannot say for certain, but I believe they knew the drug they had used—later identified as ether—would cause vomiting after we roused; to gag us would have been to risk us choking on our own spew. Which raised any number of interesting questions about how they had obtained ether, and learned the use of it. The chemical was first discovered by an Akhian chemist, Shuraiq ibn Raad al-Adrasi . . . but that does not mean it is commonly found in the middle of the desert.)

Once a little time had passed, we mounted and rode again.

By nightfall it was apparent to me that any pursuers were unlikely to catch us before we reached enemy territory. It was not merely cold that made me shiver as I tried to sleep.

Long-time readers of these memoirs may recall I had been kidnapped in the night once before, during the expedition to Vystrana. The difference between the two situations, however, could not have been more stark. There it had been my own foolishness that put me at risk; here I had been doing nothing more foolish than trying to sleep in my own tent. There my captors had been relatively decent men: smugglers, to be sure, but more interested in making a living by illicit means than sowing mayhem. Here it was apparent that my captors only needed me alive, and any suffering I might endure along the way was of no concern to them.

I did not think I could talk my way out of this one.

I lay on the hard ground and stared up at the sky, watching the stars swim back and forth. When I blinked the tears away, my gaze lit upon a constellation I recognized: Kouneli, the Rabbit. The sight was so unexpectedly comforting that I almost broke down in a mixture of sobs and laughter. *There,* I thought. *At least* one *thing here is familiar to you.*

It also gave me a notion of which direction we traveled in. Our path curved back and forth somewhat to follow the terrain, but overall we had been heading southeast. That might prove useful, and so I filed the information away.

We rode throughout the next day, with the usual pause when the sun was at its height, and arrived at another camp just before sunset. By then Tom was in a wretched state, his skin blistered from overexposure to the sun. I had unbraided my hair during that first halt and used it to shelter my neck as best I could, but my feet were almost as badly off as Tom's back. Any plan for escape would have to account for those injuries, or we would not get very far.

I was half afraid they would leave us in a heap on the bare dirt. But no: we were dragged into a tent, and after one of the men gave us water, he left our gags off. I supposed there was no reason to fear noise now.

It meant we could talk at last. "Tom," I said urgently. "Are you all right?"

An inane question, of course—and yet one asks it all the time, in such moments. He tried to sit up, and made the most extraordinarily unpleasant noise when his movement brought part of his blistered arm into contact with the ground. "Stay still," I said, and looked about for anything that might help. The tent was very bare, but there was a jar not too far away that proved to contain more water. I conveyed some to Tom in a cheap tin dipper, then drank my own fill. Then I found a nearby rag—it looked as if it had once been a man's headscarf—and soaked it before laying the fabric across the worst of the blisters. Tom hissed through his teeth when it touched him, but then he sagged and said, "That helps. Thank you."

"I assume these are the Banu Safr," I said, as much for distraction as because I thought it needed saying. "If Suhail and the others went out to get a few camels back from their enemies, we can only hope they will do as much for us."

"One hopes. Yes." Tom shifted position, wincing. "Isabella, if you have a chance to get free, then go. Don't wait for me."

"Don't be absurd," I said, my heart beating so strongly I could taste my pulse. "I would not last two hours out there." But he was not the only one thinking of escape. Two days and a night: a camel could go that long without water, easily, and a person might survive it. That assumed, however, that we could find our way back as efficiently as we had come. Under the circumstances, leaving without a supply of water would be suicidal.

Nor would I leave without Tom. They had not killed us . . . but if one vanished, who was to say the other would remain safe?. (If I may be permitted the exaggeration of calling our situation there "safe.") I said, "Now that we are here—and no longer gagged—we may be able to talk to someone. Negotiate a trade, perhaps. There must be something they want."

"Ransom," Tom speculated. "It will take them a long time to write to Pensyth in Qurrat, or Lord Ferdigan in Sarmizi. Longer to hear back. We may be here for a while."

On that cheering note, we fell silent.

I had time to re-wet the rag twice before they came for us. One of the men cursed when he realized we had taken water from the jar; I presumed that meant we were in his tent. But not for long, as they dragged us upright and took us across camp to another shelter.

A woman waited for us there. The sight of her startled me: I had been thinking of the Banu Safr only as our enemies, and had therefore conceived of this as a military camp. But of course that was absurd; they were a tribe like any other, and had women, children, all the elements of ordinary life. I would have noticed them sooner, had I not been so concerned with the simple task of walking. I had pressed my feet often against the sides of the camel to keep the soles from being burnt, but the tops were in poor shape, and the rocks on the ground were sharp besides.

She took me behind a curtain to inspect me, while someone else presumably did the same to Tom. "My name is Isabella,"

I said quietly to her as she moved around me. "What is your name?" She made no answer. I tried again, my Akhian broken more thoroughly than usual by the tension of my circumstances. "Please, water? My feet—pain. Cool is good." But it seemed she was not there to treat me, for no help was forthcoming.

The inspection done, I was pulled back out into the main part of the tent, where a man waited. Tom soon joined me, and was pushed onto his knees at my side. I mentally identified the man as their sheikh; his clothing was finer than the others', and he stood as one who is accustomed to wielding authority. To us he said, "You speak Akhian?"

Tom nodded, swaying on his knees with exhaustion. I said, "A little."

"You are *sojana*," he said. "Do you understand this?"

"Prisoners?" I said in Scirling, which of course did no good at all. Thinking of the words we had used for our dragons, I shifted to Akhian and said, "Captive."

He nodded. "Please," I said before he could go on, "what do you want? From us, or from others. Money? Camels?" I did not know the word for "ransom," and could not assemble a good enough sentence to explain that I would be happy to negotiate.

The sheikh shook his head. "Someone else will come for you. Until then, you stay."

Someone else? I doubted he meant the Aritat. Some unknown party, perhaps? The Banu Safr were rebellious; they did not have a city sheikh this man might answer to. But there could be a sheikh of greater renown, someone leading a different clan of his tribe. Or perhaps I was wrong, and he was not the sheikh. That man might be out even now with the raiding party that had stolen the camels, and this one waiting for his return.

"If we—" I stopped, frustrated with my linguistic limitations. I did not know how to ask whether there was any practice among the nomads that amounted to a white flag, a signal of peaceable parlay, under which we might be permitted to communicate with our friends and prevent them from doing anything foolish. I was not even certain I *wanted* to prevent them: as much as I feared the consequences if they staged a counter-raid, that might be our best chance at freedom. Once we were transferred to that unknown third party, who knew what would happen.

The sheikh did not wait for me to sort out what I wanted to say, much less how to say it. He left the tent, and Tom and I were alone with our captors.

TEN

Kidnapper, Brother, and Wife—Oddities in camp—The first attempt—Another breeze—A less dreadful journey—Suhail departs

I was able to guess some things about our captors. Based on physical resemblances and the way the woman behaved, I surmised that the two men who slept in the tent were brothers, and she was the wife of one. The husband had participated in the kidnapping, but the brother had not. I never did learn their names for certain; I thought the brother *might* be called Muyassir, but they were taciturn around us and addressed one another rarely. I thought of them as Kidnapper, Brother, and Wife.

Tom and I were tethered to the two central poles of the tent, with tough leather cords we could not easily break nor unknot. These gave us some freedom of movement, but not much; and in any case neither of us was in a hurry to go anywhere. Tom spent most of his time lying facedown on the rugs that covered the ground, protecting his burned skin as much as he could. Despite his care, some of the blisters broke; any time I was given water, I used some of it to rinse the sores, hoping to prevent infection. When I moved about the tent, I did so on all fours, with my feet up in the air to keep them from scraping against anything. I could only do this in the brief periods when we were alone: to show the soles of the feet is a terrible insult in Akhian society, and the first time I put mine up to protect them, Brother retaliated with an immediate blow. This almost led to disaster, as Tom lunged to stop him from striking me again, and was himself struck in turn. I threw myself to the ground, babbling apologies in a mixture of languages, and learned my lesson.

I did achieve one minor victory early on. Our kidnappers had dragged me out of my tent in my nightgown, and I was exceedingly aware of this fact at every turn. I soon hit upon the tactic of huddling under one of the carpets, demanding in a loud voice to be provided with suitable covering against the eyes of all these strange men. Before long Wife took up my cause; it was the one point upon which we were united. I do not think back on the woman with any fondness, and I doubt it was my well-being which motivated her to speak; but I am grateful to her for that small measure of support, whatever the reasoning behind it.

So I was given a proper robe and headscarf, and even a belt—which Wife threw at me with a comment whose words I could not understand, but whose tone implied that a woman who went unbelted might engage in any sort of impropriety. The items were tattered and less than clean, but I counted them as a trophy nonetheless.

We gained another minor respite from the steps they took to secure us. The Banu Safr moved camp the very next day, to a different area with fresh pasturage, and Tom and I were loaded into a howdah on the back of one of the camels. With the sides tied shut around us, we could neither see where we were going, nor be observed by any scouts; but we were also sheltered from the sun. As stuffy as it became in there, I preferred it to the alternative, which might have killed Tom outright.

We were two days in transit to the next site, and Tom predicted that the Banu Safr would attempt to hide their trail, making it difficult for our companions to find us. By then I was fairly certain we had been taken in a different direction from the stolen camels, increasing my suspicion that the raid had been a diversion from this, their true mission. But who were the Banu Safr waiting for?

If I could not escape, then I might at least hope to answer that question.

Escaping would not be easy, and I hesitated to rush into a poorly planned attempt, for fear that doing so would only make matters worse. No one ever left sharp objects within our reach, with which Tom and I might cut our tethers. Even once we were free of those bonds, we would have to leave the tent without anyone noticing, or else overpower our guards without a disturbance. We ought to steal two camels: we could ride double, as we had on the way here, but that would tire our mount and make it easier for pursuers to catch us. I had grand visions of sending the entire herd of camels stampeding off into the wilderness, forcing the Banu Safr to choose between their captives and their livelihoods; but I did not know if camels were prone to stampeding, and even if they were, it would be impossible to drive off enough of them at once.

Hunting for openings we might exploit, I found myself noticing other things. The rugs that carpeted the floor of the tent, for example, were clearly new: their nap was still thick, their colours unstained and undimmed. When Wife cooked meals, she used brass pots that lacked the scrapes and small dents of older tools. She wore quite a bit of gold jewelry as well—cheap stuff, as even I could tell, but she seemed very proud of it, and during our move to the new campsite I saw her displaying it to another woman, in the manner of one showing off a new acquisition.

All of it pointed toward wealth recently obtained. It might have been a reward to Husband and Brother for their valour; I rather thought most of it predated the kidnapping, but the Banu Safr had been causing trouble for a while, and sheikhs are supposed to be generous with their followers. But where had the sheikh gotten that wealth? This tribe lacked the city connections that helped enrich their brethren. They might have been extorting "brotherhood" from villages in settled areas; that is the term given to the protection money that was once common, before the current political arrangements came into being. (Indeed, one could argue that the tax money the city sheikhs now receive and distribute to their tribes is still "brotherhood," just given a different name. But that is neither here nor there.) Their rebellious status meant the Banu Safr scraped by in marginal territory, however, and I could not imagine the villages within their reach had any great wealth to offer. Where, then, was the money coming from?

"Perhaps," I muttered to Tom when I had the chance to share this with him, "it is coming from whoever is coming for *us*. Whoever has put them to the task of interfering with our work." There was no longer any question in my mind as to whether the raids had been solely a product of tribal enmity, or spurred by the attempt to capture and breed dragons. If the Banu Safr only hated the Aritat, they would not have bothered kidnapping Scirling naturalists.

"I've seen a surprising number of guns, too," Tom murmured back. "All throughout the camp. They don't look very new . . . but where are these people getting them?"

He and I did not have many opportunities to talk. Our

captors became angry when we conversed in Scirling—or, for that matter, in any language they did not understand—and in Akhian, of course, they could supervise everything we said. But there were times each day when Wife stepped out to fetch water or handle some other domestic matter, and then we could whisper briefly. We debated trying to leave during one of those absences, if we could break our cords. Even with clothing, however, I would not long be mistaken for an Akhian woman; and Tom, of course, was still clad in only the trousers he had worn to sleep. (They gave him a robe and a headscarf when he went out; but with his burns, this was not a mercy.) At night, we might stand a better chance outside the tent . . . but inside the tent, night meant three enemies sleeping at our elbows.

Unfortunately, we could not afford to wait for a good opportunity to escape. Several days after our arrival in the new campsite, Tom overheard a snatch of alarming conversation.

"We're to be handed off," he whispered to me when he came back to the tent, the words harsh and quick. "I don't know who's coming for us, but—"

But whoever it was, we almost certainly did not want to be in their clutches. I bit my lip, thinking. "Tonight—"

Tom shook his head. "Sooner. Make them take you out, and run."

They never allowed us both to leave the tent at the same time. Tom had already made that calculation, though, and put a finger on my lips when I would have refused to leave him behind. "I'll distract them," he said, and then we could say no more; Brother was coming back into the tent, and he already looked at us with suspicion.

I wanted to argue with Tom. Even with a distraction, I stood very little chance of escaping. But I recognized the set of his jaw all too well. Even if I had the freedom to say everything on my mind, I would not persuade him. All I would do was squander this opportunity, slim as it was.

To allay Brother's suspicions, I waited a short time, quelling the urge to fidget. I could not delay long, though, for fear Wife would return; if she did, my semblance of a plan would fall to dust. Ordinarily she accompanied either Brother or Kidnapper when they took me out to attend to biological necessities, which I then performed under her watchful eye. I had no desire, and likely insufficient skill, to subdue her. Seeing opportunity in her absence, I spoke up, indicating an urgent need to leave the tent.

Brother did not want to take me without her supervision. But I insisted, until finally he spat what sounded like a curse and unknotted my tether, leading me out into the morning sunlight.

He took me out past the edge of camp, to the area used for such matters. I gave him a freezing glare when it seemed he might stay by my side; he looked disgusted and turned his back. It was not enough. If I tried to send him out of sight, though, over the low rise that separated us from the camp, he would become suspicious. I found myself eyeing a rock on the ground a little distance away, and thinking very unpleasant thoughts.

Shouts from the camp stopped me before I could decide one way or another. Brother took a step away, listening; then he ran to the top of the rise and a short way down the other side, his attention fixed on the commotion. That, no doubt, was Tom at work, and my heart ached to think what he might have done to cause so much noise.

But I would not let it be for nothing. Hiking up my borrowed skirts, I ran.

There was broken ground not far away, studded with scrubby trees, which might afford me sufficient cover to hide. Brother would search, or call for help; in time they would bring the salukis to run me down. I must make it to a camel or a horse before that happened, or my escape attempt would not get me even a half mile to freedom.

When I saw movement up ahead, I knew even half a mile had been sheer optimism.

There was a man among the rocks, armed and veiled against the dust: a guard, I presumed. I veered to the right, wincing as my bare feet slammed into the hard ground. Behind me I heard more shouts, Brother noticing my break for freedom. I ran for all I was worth, but it was not very much. I had not gone a hundred meters when Brother slammed into me from behind, knocking me down and driving all the breath from my lungs.

What followed was unpleasant. Brother dragged me back into camp—and I do mean dragged; he did not even permit me to regain my feet. Tom and I were both beaten soundly for our disobedience, him worse than me. When that was done, they threw us once more into the tent. I suspect that were it not for the security the tent offered, they would have staked us out in the dust, like the guard dogs.

Lying sprawled on the carpet, Tom spoke in a voice barely more than a whisper. "I'm sorry. But we had to try."

"Quite right," I said, trying to sound resolute. One of his eyes was swollen nearly shut. "Tom . . . do you think you can ride? Tonight?"

He lifted his head just enough to look at me, then put it

down before anyone could notice. We had no chance to speak after that, but we knew one another well enough that we did not need to. The last thing anyone expected was for us to try to escape a second time, so hard on the heels of the first. There was good reason for that—we were in dreadfully bad shape to be attempting anything—but what could they do if we failed? Beat us a second time? It seemed they would not kill us, even when provoked. And while I did not relish the prospect of pain, I was more and more certain I did not want to be handed off to whomever had ordered our kidnapping.

Our second plan was no more complicated than our first, for we had nothing with which to complicate it. While Wife stood in the opening of the tent, calling out to a friend of hers across the way, I unhooked the lamp from its place on the central pole for long enough to spill a bit of oil on the knots of our tethers. That, I hoped, would speed the process of unknotting them, which we must try to do in the dark.

We had to wait until they were fully asleep. When at last their breathing evened out and stayed that way for a time, Tom and I turned our attention to the cords. He was better with knots than I, and had watched how Brother and Kidnapper undid our bonds; his slid free first, and then he bent to work on mine.

In the grand scheme of things, it was not much of a victory. Getting ourselves loose from the tent pole was only the first of many steps that must be completed before we could escape, and far from the hardest. But I took heart from it anyway as I stood, biting my lip when my abused feet took my weight.

Once more I felt a breeze upon my cheek.

This time I had no confusion as to the cause. The sensation was not from the direction of the front flap, and I was wide awake; I could see the paler spot where the back wall of the tent had opened, its seam cut apart, and someone was crawling through.

I did not know until much later that the nomads tell tales of this sort of thing; indeed, it is one of their favourite genres. I only knew that I thought, *He is a madman.*

The Aritat had indeed come after us, and Suhail had led them himself.

He paused just inside the slit, allowing his eyes to adjust to the greater darkness within. Tom took a step forward. Fearing he had not recognized that dim silhouette, I gripped his wrist to stop him. Tom's breath hissed between his teeth, and for a moment all three of us froze, for fear he had roused our captors.

They, however, were quite accustomed to Tom's small sounds of pain in the night. No one spoke or sat up, and after a moment Suhail parted the slit in the tent wall again. It may have been to confirm what he thought he had seen, or to usher us out. I took it as the latter.

Suhail stayed put while Tom and I crawled through the gap, then followed us out. His clothes were dun-coloured and his face whitened with ash; on a night like this one, with the moon bright in the sky, that was better camouflage than darkness would have been. Tom blended in a good deal better than I did in my borrowed clothes.

Leaving that camp was one of the most terrifying things I have ever done. The Aritat had not come in sufficient numbers to stage an assault—and any such attempt might have had dire consequences for Tom and myself. Instead we departed by what I presumed were the same means the Banu Safr had used to kidnap us, the chief difference being that Tom and I were on our feet.

Suhail led us, crouching in the shadow of one tent until he saw that the way was clear, then running for the next. Our path seemed tortuous, angling first one way, then another, in order to avoid guard dogs and camels couched alongside the tents. Partway through this I realized we were not alone: two other men of the Aritat were paralleling our path, and judging by the knives and rifles they held, both were prepared to kill anyone who stumbled across us. After that I could scarcely breathe.

Only when we left the final row of tents did my lungs begin to work properly. I knew we were not yet clear; if someone noticed us missing the camp would give chase. But we were past the point at which someone might accidentally stumble upon us—or so I believed.

He was not a guard, I think. I do not know who he was. He carried no rifle, and seemed utterly startled when we scrabbled up a narrow wash and came face-to-face with him.

The tableau lasted for only an instant. He stared at us, mouth open in surprise. Then a hand clamped over that mouth, for someone had risen up behind him; another hand passed over his throat, and blood fountained out in its wake, black in the moonlight.

Andrew held on a moment longer, until the man had stopped thrashing. Then, breathing quickly, he lowered the body to the ground. "Come on," he whispered. "Before someone wonders where he's gone."

The sudden violence of it paralyzed me. But Suhail took me by the arm, heedless of propriety, and pulled me forward. Their camels were not far away. We mounted up, and were gone before the Banu Safr knew we had escaped.

* * *

I will not say much of that ride. It reminded me far too vividly of another desperate flight, which some of my readers may recall. (Tom was not half so badly injured as Jacob had been, but he could not stay on a camel without riding double; the resemblance was more than enough to upset me.)

Andrew stayed close beside me. My relief at seeing him warred with the unpleasant realization that my brother had indeed become a soldier; and this meant more than simply putting on a uniform and idling about in foreign countries. His clothes were stained with blood, which of course we could not stop to wash out. The man he killed belonged to an enemy tribe, one that had kidnapped and mistreated me in an effort to stop my work . . . but it was a long time before that memory no longer made me shake.

We rode pell-mell for Aritat territory, and if you have never been atop a galloping camel, you will have a difficult time understanding what that was like. When it moves at a trot or a pace, a good camel may have a remarkably smooth gait; at a gallop, it is about as stable as a bucking horse. We did not gallop the whole distance, of course, as that would have been a good way to kill our mounts. But we did so often enough for it to be exhausting—because of course we had to assume the Banu Safr were pursuing us. Suhail's companions assured us that the enemy camels were poor creatures, with no chance of catching Aritat camels in the chase; but this was not so reassuring as it might have been.

Our Akhian rescuers were in good spirits overall, even when the skies opened the next night and drenched us in chill rain. They laughed and clapped one another on the back, showing a gaiety wholly at odds with my usual impression of the nomads. I gathered that nobody of the Aritat had carried out that sort of secret, nighttime raid in generations; their enemies thought them incapable of it. Such efforts were not deemed as glorious as the more public sort of raid, charging into battle atop a spirited horse—but there was a romance to the activity that could not be denied. One of the fellows seemed to think this would impress the girl he hoped to marry, and preened as he rode.

It certainly had impressed me, to the point where it robbed me of anything resembling eloquence. When I attempted to thank Suhail for the risk he had taken on our behalf, it came out pure stammering incoherence. He fixed his gaze between the ears of his mount and said, "I should have moved more quickly. When you ran . . ."

Startled, I turned to stare at him. That figure I had seen in the distance—in my fright, I had not looked properly, had not recognized him as I ordinarily would. Not a Banu Safr guard after all.

"Perhaps it was for the best," I said, swallowing. "Had you come to my aid then, who knows what would have happened to Tom."

"*You* would not have been beaten," Suhail answered, gaze still fixed. "But the attempt showed us which tent you were being kept in, which we hadn't known. I am grateful to you for that."

The robe and headscarf they put on Tom when he left the tent had not merely been for propriety; the clothing was a security measure, designed to conceal him from watching eyes. "How long were you out there?"

"Since the day before." He straightened his shoulders and

managed something like a smile. "And hardly needed, it seems. You were halfway out of the tent by the time I got there. All we did was provide camels for the ride home."

That came far short of the mark—but I could not find the words to say it. Instead I asked, "Has anyone been told that we vanished? Outside of the camp itself, of course."

I had not meant to make him look at me, but I succeeded. His head whipped around, the damp ends of his scarf swinging loose. "*No.* What could they do in time? I knew we could get you back."

This last was said with more than a little bravado—but as he had indeed gotten us back, I could hardly argue. It was a relief to know the Scirling cavalry would not soon go thundering across the desert to start a war that was no longer needed . . . or at least, I hoped it would not be. "We'll have to tell them now," I said with a sigh. "If only because I'm certain there is more going on here than a few raids born of traditional grudges." I told him what Tom and I had observed in camp: the signs of wealth, the unusual quantity of guns.

He frowned especially over the guns. "I thought they had too many," he muttered, twisting to glance over his shoulder as if he could count the firearms from here. "Who could be paying them? The Muwala? Or—" He stopped himself, shaking his head. Such names would mean nothing to me, ignorant as I was of Akhian politics. What mattered was that we had evidence of conspiracy; others would be better positioned than I to investigate it.

The Aritat camp was not where we had left it. I was grateful anew for our rescuers, who saved us not only from the Banu Safr but also from wandering in the desert like something out of Scripture. I nearly lost my composure when I saw that

Umm Azali had pitched our tent alongside her own, so that it was ready and waiting for Tom and me to collapse into it. She inspected our burns and other ills, pronounced them not so serious as to need Ghalbi attention, and doctored us as necessary, while Suhail reported to Hajj Nawl.

He returned to us just before sunset, when Tom was asleep and Andrew was in the tent next door obtaining our supper. I met him outside, so as to avoid waking Tom. "You will both be well, I hope?" he asked in a low voice.

"Yes, with a bit of rest," I said. "A few of the blisters need care, but we will heal."

"Good," he said. "It will help if I can say that to my brother and your colonel."

The words caught me unprepared, though they should not have. "You mean—you are going back to Qurrat?"

Suhail shrugged, looking away. The tents cast elongated shadows across the ground, and I could not help but think how much this camp resembled the one I had just fled. Nomads can tell the difference between the tribes based on little more than camel tracks, but such skill is well beyond me. "I have to," he said. "I can't write a letter saying, 'misplaced your naturalists, so sorry, but got them back mostly in one piece.'"

When he put it like that, I supposed he could not. "I see."

He hesitated, then said, "I do not like to abandon you, though."

I could imagine what was going through his head. He went off to chase raiders, and came back to find us missing; now he proposed to leave us again. Who knew what might happen in his absence? "Do you think the Banu Safr will attack again?"

"Yes. We killed one of their own; they'll want revenge for that. But we alerted the Firiyin when we were chasing the camel thieves—they're another clan of the Aritat, and they're nearby. They'll keep an eye on the Banu Safr, and send warning if they see a force headed this way."

How the nomads remained so aware of each other's locations and movements in the vast expanse of the desert, I could not comprehend. I trusted his trust in them, though. I therefore said, "You would not be abandoning us. Your duty is to your brother, not to Tom or myself. And as you said, people in Qurrat need to know what happened here."

During our previous travels, I had often thought of Suhail's expression as being open and sunny. That was less true in Akhia, however, and now it closed off into a polite mask. "If you are certain."

"The language is a difficulty," I allowed, "but we have dealt with that before. Your responsibility lies in the city: I would not keep you from it."

"Very well," Suhail said—and he left the very next morning.

ELEVEN

Moving camp—Al-Jelidah—In search of dragons—A "love note"—The differences of my life—Dragons in flight—On the edge of the Labyrinth

It took two weeks and a pointed comment from my brother before I realized I had made a mistake.

Those two weeks were rather busy. We moved camp soon after our return, heading farther from the Banu Safr, even though the grazing to the south was not as good. (I later learned that the other Aritat clans mustered a force of fighting men, and these kept their enemy usefully occupied while we got away.) Our status as guests meant that Tom, Andrew, and I would not have been expected to assist, even had Tom and I not been recuperating from our injuries—but I chafed more than I expected to at the idleness. "At least there are camels to carry things for us," Tom said wryly. He remembered as well as I did the challenge of shifting our gear through the Green Hell of Mouleen, with nothing more than our backs (and those of the Moulish we could persuade to assist us) to bear it.

I was exceedingly glad not to have to carry everything this time. I had packed few changes of clothing; in the field I am often resigned to wearing the same garments long after I would have considered them unacceptably soiled at home. We had one saddlebag loaded with field glasses, thermometers, and other scientific equipment; another contained books and empty notebooks, pencils for my sketches, Tom's dissection tools, and so forth. On the whole, it was not so very much. But there was also the tent and all its furnishings; and Husam ibn Ramiz had not stinted us there. We lived in a style matched only by the local sheikh.

Because of the duty laid upon them, the Aritat took our needs into account, choosing a wadi that might afford us a better chance to see dragons. Tom said, "I get the impression that's why they were sent the new breeding stock. The work they've been doing on our behalf has lost them more than a few camels and horses along the way."

I remembered well the camel that had served as bait during the nighttime hunt. "Then I am glad they are being compensated. They will likely lose more before this enterprise is done."

Tom and I, however, had come to the desert to observe life, not death. It was mating flights we needed to see, rather than hunting flights, and those lacked vultures to serve as a signal flag. To achieve our goal, we had to exert much more effort.

Mating flights did not take place over the hospitable wadis where the nomads pastured their camels. True to their name, desert drakes preferred to conduct their displays over the stony, barren ground in between regions of relative bounty.

I owe a great debt to al-Jelidah, the Ghalbi man we had been told about upon our first arrival. He had returned to the Aritat camp while Tom and I were captive, and we met with him at the first opportunity, to recruit his help in seeking out dragons.

As I mentioned before, I lack the encyclopedic knowledge that permits the nomads to distinguish between one tribe and another based on small details: the shape of a camel's footprint, the way they secure their headscarves, the roofline of their tents. Even I, however, could tell at a glance that al-Jelidah was not of the Aritat. He wore a long shirt of gazelle skin, and covered his hair with a tied cloth rather than the more usual scarf-and-cord. Where most of the Aritat wore woollen socks in winter, or else boots of camel leather, and sandals in the summer, al-Jelidah went barefoot regardless of season, and the soles of his feet were as hard as horn.

He often travelled alone in the desert, which is almost unheard of. Even in these days of relative peace, conflicts often arise between the tribes, and a man alone is easy prey for enemies. But the Ghalb are the enemy of none: many despise them as beggars, but they are permitted to travel throughout the region, and few bother to trouble them. Their camps are small, rarely more than an extended family in total, and individuals may be found in the oddest places—such as the depths of the Jefi, chasing dragons.

I do not know what he made of our work. To him it hardly seemed to matter; he had been hired as a guide for us, and would have guided us in search of anything we wanted, be it dragons, locusts, or the truffles which liven up the nomad diet in winter. He made no complaint when the sheikh insisted we take Haidar with us, the man who had led us to watch the dragon hunt at night. To the best of my recollection, I never heard al-Jelidah complain about anything. He was as phlegmatic as stone.

Haidar came with us as a guard, and made no secret of that fact. (He would have brought nine more of his fellows, too, had we allowed it, but such a party would make our work all but impossible. Tom persuaded the sheikh that Haidar, Andrew, and himself constituted sufficient armed force.) His presence was a great boon to us, for we spent more time out of camp than in it, and his hunting both extended our rations and gave us a welcome respite from the tedium of dates, coffee, and unleavened bread.

This was the group we took into the field proper. They saw me in trousers, as few others did; al-Jelidah did not seem to care (as per usual), Haidar frowned in disapproval but said nothing (I made sure to don a belt, so he would not think my morals suspect), and Andrew clapped one hand over his eyes, proclaiming loudly that he took no responsibility for my behaviour. But if I was to ride throughout the Jefi in search of dragons, I did not want a skirt or robe hampering my ability to move at speed.

The first drake we found was male. I noted him on the map I was creating, but we spent little time in his vicinity, for we were interested not only in the flight but its fruit. Female drakes, as we learned from al-Jelidah, will not lair within a ten-kilometer radius of their male counterparts, and so we rode a circuit at that distance from the overhang in which he sheltered, hunting signs of a female. It took days to locate one, for that region has many rock formations that can serve as lairs; but, having found it, now we knew where to watch.

We made a meager bivouac in a sheltered nook from which we could easily venture forth to watch the site. We took it in shifts to do this latter, for our quarry had hunted with great success just before we arrived; we saw her dragging her full belly up the scree to her home, and then had to wait for hunger to drive her forth once more. Indeed, we were altogether more than a week in that location, twiddling our thumbs and hoping for profit—which left us a great deal of time for other occupations.

For the most part Tom and I spent our energy on recording desert life more generally, so as to create a picture of the environment in which the drakes thrive. There is a surprising amount out there, at least in winter: everything from large mammals like the onager and oryx down to beetles, scorpions, and an abundance of spiders. But nomads are accustomed to filling their idle moments with conversation, and so we spent a great deal of time talking, whether around the fire at night or during our shifts watching the female's lair. It was during one of the latter, when I had only Andrew for company, that he enlightened me as to my error.

I did not think I had mentioned Suhail much. From what I could recall, my work had occupied the bulk of my attention, as it ordinarily does; I only mentioned Suhail at that moment because I was discussing the possibility that the Draconeans had successfully bred dragons. Andrew said—out of nowhere, or so it seemed to me—"You know, Isabella, if you wanted that fellow here, you should not have sent him away."

"I—what?" I stared at my brother in complete perplexity. "I don't know what you mean. I did not send Suhail away."

Andrew had been fanning himself with his hat while he leaned in the shadow of a tall rock. Now he gestured with it as if to wave off my words. "All right, all right. I should have said, you ought not to have told him to *stay* away."

Indignation was rapidly overtaking my perplexity. "I did not do that, either. I merely said—"

"That his duty was in Qurrat. Translation: you didn't want him to come back."

Nothing could have been further from the truth. But I could not say that to Andrew. "What ought I have said, then?"

Andrew rolled his eyes heavenward. "How about 'hurry back'? Or 'we'll be waiting for you here'? Except that one isn't true, I suppose; we've moved camp again. You might have tried 'I left something in Qurrat; would you be a dear and fetch it for me?' "

"Suhail is not a dog, to fetch my slippers on command. And I can hardly go calling him 'dear,' when—" I clamped my mouth shut, breathing out through my nose. "Andrew, I am *trying* to keep my behaviour above reproach. I do not need you encouraging me to do otherwise."

"Oho." Andrew sat forward, folding his legs like a tailor and putting his elbows on his knees. His gaze, above the reddened skin of his cheeks, was more piercing than it had any right to be. "Is *that* how the wind lies."

"Don't use nautical metaphors; they make you sound ridiculous." But I was needling him in the hope of distracting him from the topic, and we both knew it.

Andrew let me squirm for a long moment. Then he said, "I should have guessed, when you asked me to carry that love note to him."

My outraged squawk startled lizards back into the rocks. "It was not a love note!"

"From you? 'A piece of research material' is as good as a lock of your hair, tied up in a scented ribbon." He laughed.

For once I blessed the lingering effects of my sunburn. It made my skin peel disgustingly . . . but it also meant no one could see when I was blushing. Andrew had been there when I met Jacob in the king's menagerie, standing at the edge of the dragon enclosure. He knew that courtship had proceeded along unusual lines. It was true that if I *were* minded to seek a new husband, an intellectual gift would show my esteem far more sincerely than a more conventional token of love.

All of that, however, was neither here nor there. I had not come to the desert for personal reasons, but professional ones. "Andrew, I have other things on my mind. You are in the army; you know as well as I do how important this research is. Your work in Coyahuac—were you securing mines there? No, do not answer that; if you were, you likely are not permitted to say." In theory it was possible to synthesize dragonbone. We had not yet mastered the process; but if we ever did, we would need the raw materials, some of which were abundant in Coyahuac. "Right now, this programme here is our best hope. We must have caeligers to face those of the Yelangese, or we will lose ground to them all around the world. If Suhail staying in Qurrat helps me concentrate on my work, so much the better."

"But it doesn't." Andrew climbed to his feet, knocking dust and pebbles from his palms. "I can see your thoughts drifting, a dozen times a day. Besides—it doesn't have to be one or the other."

I felt weary, as if I were ten years older than my brother, instead of a year his junior. "Yes, it does. You and I are not held to the same standards, Andrew. People will forgive a slip, a weakness, a minor personal folly—when it comes from a man. They may click their tongues at you, even gossip about your behaviour . . . but at worst, it will only reflect on *you*.

"If I misstep, it goes far beyond me. Errors on my part are proof that women are unsuited to professional work; they are evidence that the Crown should never have assigned a woman to this post. My flaws are not merely my own. And so I cannot permit myself to indulge in anything that might validate the assumptions people have already formed—about me, and all my sex."

Andrew scowled and kicked at a small stone, which ricocheted off into the dust. "Bollocks. Sorry, Isabella, my language—you aren't like other women. People know that."

"Ah, yes," I said ironically. "I have made myself exceptional. It is a wonderful game, is it not? Because I am exceptional, anything I achieve does not reflect on my sex, for of course I am not like them. Strange, though, how that division seems to vanish when we are speaking instead of my shortcomings. Then I am a woman, like any other."

I had never seen my brother look so uncomfortable. The last time we had been in the same country, I would never have said such things. I did not even know what provoked me to say them now: sibling trust, the constant irritations I had suffered in Qurrat, or—yes—my wish that Suhail had not gone away. I had not even spoken this angrily to Tom, who knew more of my feelings on the matter than anyone save Natalie.

Andrew retreated from the awkwardness by returning to our original topic. "Suhail, though. I saw his face, when he was packing up to go back. I think you hurt him, Isabella."

Now it was my turn to flinch from his words. But fortune smiled upon me: at that moment a scraping sound drifted on the desert wind, and I turned to see the drake at the mouth of her lair.

She yawned prodigiously and lay down just beyond the edge of the shade, basking in the sun's warmth. Her scales brightened gold where the breeze wisped dust away, and her broad ruff rose from time to time, catching the air and,

I thought, cooling her slightly, by means of the blood vessels that laced its underside, akin to those on her wings. Apart from that movement, she was so still that a fox ran near her jaws; she was not yet hungry, for she let it pass with no more comment than one opened eye.

None of this was especially noteworthy, but observing it ended my conversation with Andrew. He said nothing further then, nor when he and I returned to the camp, leaving Tom to keep watch until dark.

As my readers may well imagine, though, his words stuck under my skin like burrs. Had I done wrong by Suhail? I had only meant to assure him that we would not perish if left alone for a time . . . but reviewing my words, I saw how they could be interpreted in quite another light. From that perspective, I sounded ungrateful and cold, eager to be rid of him at last.

Surely he did not think that—not when I was so grateful for his aid. And not after I had given him the rubbing of the Cataract Stone. I blushed to remember what Andrew had said regarding that, but clung to the thought nonetheless. Although calling it a love note was a great overstatement, I would not deny it was a token of friendship. Suhail had understood that, had he not?

Without him present to ask, I could only speculate. And, of course, plan what I might say when he returned.

In the meanwhile, I had my work; and it kept me very busy indeed.

When desert drakes rise to mate, they must signal to one another their readiness to entertain callers of the opposite sex. This is accomplished in dramatic fashion, by the female ascending to the peak of the tallest hill, dune, or rock formation she can find and roaring in a powerful voice that, it seemed to me, must carry to the farthest edges of the desert. She accompanies this with many gouts of flame; and for this reason, the display customarily takes place just before dawn, when her flame will be visible at a great distance.

Male drakes who wish to present themselves for her consideration travel to this location and array themselves around the base of her perch. They make a great presentation of their ruffs and wings, stretching both as far as they can go so as to make themselves appear large; they are of course smaller than their female counterpart, and a male who is too dainty will rarely win the attention of his lady-love.

The female, having attracted her suitors, will snarl and breathe flame at those she finds unacceptable. I am told, though I did not witness it with my own eyes, that a particularly stalwart male may weather this abuse and keep his place; but most who are thus spurned will depart, leaving behind three or so that have gained her favour. These are the dragons who participate in the mating flight itself.

With a great sweep of her wings, the female leaps into the air. Her suitors follow, but as they start without the advantage of height, it takes them longer to become airborne. This gives the female a respectable lead, and she uses it shamelessly, wheeling and soaring above the desert floor. Here a smaller male may sometimes fare better than expected, if he is especially nimble. But a drake who relies on such tactics must succeed quickly, or not at all; otherwise the flight becomes a contest of endurance, and his larger brethren will win out. They maneuver for position in the sky, lashing out at one another as circumstance requires or allows. It is not uncommon for a male to be wounded in this struggle, and to quit the field on account of his injuries. This happened in the very first flight we observed, and the beast in question was not able to hunt for some time afterward. I suspect he did not survive the summer, for a drake that does not feed well in the wet season will lack the bodily resources to last when food becomes scarce.

This drama enters its third and final act when one of the males succeeds in attaining a position above the female. Now he may attempt to stoop upon her; she ordinarily permits this, though I did see one female drive off her would-be paramour in no uncertain terms. (I can only speculate as to why, and none of my guesses are terribly scientific.) Here there is a countervailing pressure against the desire of a female to seek out a large mate: she must sustain them both in gliding flight while the copulation takes place. This is a brief matter, but the strain upon her must be enormous, and more than one flight has ended in failure because the participants had to separate early to avoid crashing.

The airborne stage of the process poses quite a challenge for the landbound audience. Drakes have been known to travel kilometers while conducting their aerial dance, and often the only good perch from which to observe is the one upon which the female began her display. Tom and I opted for a more active approach, which is to say: we threw ourselves into the saddle and set out to see just what Akhian horses were capable of.

Our mounts responded magnificently. On more than one occasion I was charging hell-for-leather after the drakes as they soared away, only to wheel my mare about on her hindquarters when they came swooping back in my direction.

Mating Flight

At any time other than during a mating flight, Tom and I would have made irresistible bait, easy prey for a drake to claw up or burn to a crisp. But all their attention is on the dance; and so we raced madly about beneath them, crying out observations to one another that often became lost in the roaring.

This was exhausting work, and by the time the flight ended I would gladly have collapsed in the nearest bit of shade—but I could not stop there. The most vital data was yet to come.

Andrew had been waiting in the shelter of a small cliff, safely distant from where the female made her initial display. Tom and I rode to his side, and I dismounted at a trot—a stunt I had not tried since I was fifteen, but I did not want to lose a single moment. Our camels were already kneeling in the sand, and lurched to their feet almost before we were in the saddles. For rapid changes of direction at speed, horses were the most effective choice; but only camels could do what we needed now.

We set off with al-Jelidah, first at a gallop (to make up the ground we had lost), then slowing to the pacing gait the camels could maintain for an extended period of time. The drake coasted ahead of us, sometimes ascending or making leisurely sweeps from side to side, looking for a good nesting ground. The sun climbed high overhead, and I had not had a drink of water in hours. But ahead of us the land rose steadily, and I whacked my camel with my stick, urging her up the slope.

Just as I reached the crest, al-Jelidah's borrowed camel surged forward to join mine. As soon as he came within range, he leaned forward to seize the halter, pulling me up short. "What are you doing?" I exclaimed.

He gestured ahead, and spoke a word I did not know.

This has happened to me more times than I can count, in the course of my travels. I had a list in my head of possible translations: dangerous, forbidden, cursed, and so forth. But Tom, pulling his camel to a halt on the other side of me, said, "Isabella, remember the map."

Our pursuit of the drake had gotten me entirely turned around. I had to work to recall the geography of the area, and every second I delayed, our quarry's lead grew. The sun was no help, being too high overhead to provide much sense of direction. But when I turned to the ground ahead of me, I saw that it was increasingly broken; and then I remembered.

I stood at the edge of the Labyrinth of Drakes.

This is a curious geological formation, nestled at the base of the Qedem mountain range. Millennia of floods from the higher peaks have carved the sandstone into a maze of canyons and gullies, some of them exceedingly narrow, so that one seems to be riding through a corridor without a roof. There are oases within it, but little space to farm, and no one lives there today.

Thousands of years ago, of course, it was quite different.

The Draconean ruins there are famous, and have been since they were rediscovered by the Haggadi outlaw Yoel ben Tamir while he was fleeing from his pursuers. Whether they constituted a city or merely a ritual site was a matter of long-standing scholarly debate. Giorgis Argyropolous, the Nichaean antiquarian who made the first comprehensive survey of the place, gave fanciful names to each of the structures he found, and termed many of them temples; those appellations have endured, even though in most instances there is not a shred of evidence to support them. It is the natural response of the human imagination, when confronted by the silent, monumental remnants of the past: we assume that surely they were special, that the awe we feel is a sign of their hallowed nature.

That these ruins remained lost for so long is a testament to the hazards of the region. It is not safe to wander long in the Labyrinth: apart from the predators that lurk within, there are rock slides, and one may easily become lost in the winding passages. Furthermore, during the winter and spring there is great risk of sudden floods from storms at higher elevations, which can easily drown the unwary. In ancient times it is thought the Draconeans maintained dams which reduced this risk by channeling the flow in a controlled manner to where it was needed—but these are long gone. The peril of the Labyrinth remains.

Perilous or not, that was our drake's destination. "We have to watch her nesting behaviour," I said, trying to pull my camel free of al-Jelidah's grip. "And take measurements once she is gone—temperature, the depth in the ground—"

Al-Jelidah cut the air with his free hand. "No."

Tom chivvied his camel until it came around to stand in front of mine. She snapped her teeth at Tom's mount, as if to express my own mood. "There will be other flights, Isabella," Tom said. "And drakes who nest somewhere we aren't liable to drown."

I gestured at the canyons ahead. "They're bone dry!"

"At the moment, to be sure. But how much has it rained in the mountains recently?" We did not know the answer to that . . . which was part of the problem. "The water could be on you in a heartbeat. And how are you going to chase her, when she can fly over the things you have to ride around? I know you aren't afraid of risk—but this would be a damned stupid way to get killed."

A damned stupid way to get killed might have described any number of incidents in my life, had my luck been only a little different. Tom's steady gaze, though, reined in my impulse to give a defiant answer. A past history of reckless decisions did not oblige me to behave recklessly every time the opportunity arose. He would not mock me for showing caution; I had no reputation to maintain here.

And *that* thought—the notion of what other people might say—robbed me of all my momentum. Had my increasing notoriety gone that thoroughly to my head? The account I had written of my travels on the *Basilisk*, the speaking engagements I had taken after my return . . . despite my intentions, they had often skewed toward the sensational, rather than the scientific. A headlong charge into the Labyrinth of Drakes would have made a splendid story to tell. But my purpose here was not to increase my fame as an adventuress; it was to study dragons, not merely for the benefit of natural history, but for the future well-being of my nation. Risking my life, in a situation where I stood very little hope of success, would do nothing to further that goal.

Buried beneath that was something even less admirable: the realization that I wanted to go in simply because al-Jelidah had said no.

I released my camel's rein and lifted my hands, relinquishing any intention of going forward. Tom nodded, looking relieved. He and I both lifted our field glasses and watched the drake for as long as we could; but she soon dropped down behind a promontory and was lost from sight. I imagined her digging the pit for her eggs, somewhere the intense desert sun would find and heat them, and vowed I would see it with my own eyes before long.

TWELVE

Observing a clutch—Umm Azali—Suhail's youth—The poem—Young drakes hunting—Plans for return

As Tom predicted, there were other flights. We developed quite a good system for observing them, too, stationing ourselves and Andrew at various points and dividing up the terrain so that we need not all race to watch. And very few of the dragons were as inconvenient as our first; most laid their eggs in more accessible locations.

I had an especially splendid chance to observe one of these, by dint of scrambling to the top of a large, rocky outcropping and peering down on the drake from above. She dug a shallow pit, scraping the earth sideways with her claws, rather than between her hind legs as a dog does. This done, she crouched over it and laid her eggs—six of them in total. Then she tossed sand back over them, and lowered her head to the ground to blow across it, blurring the marks of her activity. (They do not breathe fire over their eggs, whatever legend says. Doing so would vitrify the sand, and the resulting plate of rough glass would tell any interested predator that tasty treats lie below, ready to be tunneled out.)

We marked the spot and came back the next day, when we were sure the drake had gone. She would, we were told, revisit her clutch periodically, and rebury the eggs if necessary; but desert drakes do not brood, which gave us leisure to examine the site. Careful excavation netted us a great deal of data, from the depth at which the eggs are buried (fifteen centimeters or so: enough to keep them covered if the wind is not too fierce, but not so deep as to be entirely insulated) to the temperature of the ground (easily thirty degrees at the surface during the hottest part of the day; perhaps ten degrees cooler where the eggs lie). Standing by the egg pit, I could feel for myself how well the drake had chosen her spot. It lay in a shallow bowl, reasonably protected from the wind, but fully exposed to the sun. If our guesses about the role of heat were correct, then such conditions were vital to the successful incubation of the eggs.

"Do you want to take them?" Haidar asked when we were done, gesturing at the pit.

"No, definitely not," I said. "By all means remember the location—but if we take them now, we will likely have nothing to show for our efforts but dead eggs. We do not know nearly enough yet to interfere so early in the process."

Tom did take one egg, not to incubate, but to dissect. We had only rudimentary chemical equipment with us, but he analyzed the albumen and yolk as best as he could, and I packed the pieces of shell carefully in sand for later study. Their texture was very different from that of mature eggs, and the comparison might tell us something.

"Even if we can't breed them," he said to me one night, over the last scraps of our supper, "at least we'll have learned a good deal about them."

"We will figure out how to breed them," I said. But having watched the mating flights in their full glory, I spoke with a good deal more assurance than I felt.

* * *

I have not yet said much about Suhail's desert mother and desert father, and should remedy that now.

As with many of the relationships I recount in my memoirs, what I am about to describe came together over an extended period of time, through many small conversations and moments of rapport. I did not learn everything in one fell swoop (a phrase which, I note in passing, originated in the description of dragons hunting). For the sake of convenience, however, I will condense matters here—not to mention smooth over the inevitable linguistic difficulties—so that I might not tax my readers' patience overmuch.

Umm Azali I came to know far better than her husband. This has generally been the pattern in most of the places I have gone: with the exception of Keonga, where my primary ally was considered to be neither male nor female, I have generally been on closest terms with my own sex. It is an extension of the same segregation I experience at home, which says that the conversation of women is primarily of interest to other women, as men's is to men, and rarely do the twain meet. I had made concerted efforts to overcome this in the Flying University; but each expedition put me into a new social world, and I lacked both the time and the energy to pursue such ends except where necessary to my work.

(I did not realize until long after I had left the desert that the nomads of the Aritat treated me in some respects like a man. This is a thing that happens sometimes with widowed or divorced women, or those who are too old to go on bearing children: their disassociation from the primary marker of womanhood, which is to say motherhood, reduces the assumed distance between them and the world of men. I shall refrain from extended commentary on this, except to note that my own widowed status and lack of attendant child put me once more into something of a grey area—albeit not to the extent that had pertained in Keonga.)

Umm Azali and I never became what I would call close, largely because I spent so much time out in the desert pursuing dragons, rather than in camp. She was unfailingly friendly, however, which I attribute to my association with Suhail. It was therefore natural that I should talk to her about him.

"How long have you known him?" I asked her one day.

"Since he was a boy," she answered. "Four years he was with us—for his fosterage. His nephew Jafar will come to us next year, for the same thing. No one would follow a sheikh who does not know the desert!"

I was mending a great rent I had torn in one of my dresses when it caught against a thorny bush; she was baking bread. Many of my conversations in the field have been conducted thus, with one or both of us engaged in some useful task; it is often more productive than when I try to question people too directly. "Was Suhail with you for more than just his fosterage, then?"

Umm Azali shrugged, kneading the dough with tough, efficient hands. "Off and on. Not always with us, not once he began to explore the ruins. More than he had as a boy, that is. But he visits often."

Of course it would be out here that Suhail had cultivated his fascination with Draconean ruins. Although al-Jelidah had stopped me from going into the Labyrinth, I had seen any number of fragments during my own work: everything from a statue carved into the side of a cliff to the shaft of a stela, abandoned in its quarry after it cracked in half. Their fingerprints were all over the desert, worn down by the ages. "How old was he? During his fosterage, I mean."

"Eight? At the start." Umm Azali's grin cracked her face. "Braids flapping as he ran about."

I had noticed that the Aritat boys often wore their hair in two long braids, dangling down their chests. I forbore to mention that in my homeland, that style belonged exclusively to little girls; I was too busy reeling at the image of Suhail arrayed thus.

It was on a later day, I believe, that I asked her about the Draconean ruins, and his interest in them. Umm Azali clearly did not share that interest, for she merely shrugged again. "He used to imagine himself as an ancient prince. Lord of the desert—all sorts of foolishness, as children do. But mostly it was the language. Every time we rode past one of those carvings, he wanted to know what it said."

We might soon have an answer to that, I thought, if he could translate the Cataract Stone. I wondered if he was working on that even now, back in Qurrat.

Umm Azali talked a great deal about her family: not merely Suhail and his brother Husam, whom she and her husband had fostered a few years before Suhail himself, but their son Azali and all his children; their daughter Safiyya, married to one of Abu Azali's nephews; even their son Abd as-Salaam, who had, as Umm Azali put it, "grown his beard." It took me some time to realize this was a colloquial way of saying he had become a prayer-leader, i.e., one who no longer cut his beard or hair. He lived now in a town on the edge of the desert, in the area where the Aritat would go once the rains ended and the desert became too dry to support the herds. (As nomad tribes go, the Aritat were of middling piety: they prayed, but only twice a day, and they observed the month of fasting according to when circumstance allowed, rather than the dictates of the calendar. Some of the tribes are very nearly heathen; for example, I did not recall seeing anyone among the Banu Safr pray during my captivity. Though admittedly, I had not seen much outside that tent.)

All of this was fascinating to me—but not, I must confess, because I had any great interest in their children and grandchildren. (Apart from Shahar, I had very few dealings with Umm Azali's kin.) Rather, I prized the way these stories built up my sense of Suhail's world and his past: the boy he had been when he came to the desert; the ways he had become a man here; the role he had among the Aritat, as his brother's representative in the matter of the dragons. Knowing that he had once strutted about as an imaginary Draconean prince changed my understanding of him—and I will not relate some of the other stories Umm Azali told, on the occasions when we were sitting privately with other women and the conversation became distinctly improper. He had said so little of himself when we knew one another aboard the *Basilisk*; all I had known was that he was estranged from his family. To meet a woman who was kin of sorts, with whom Suhail appeared to have a warmer relationship, gave him a very different appearance in my mind.

In time I reached a point where I felt safe inquiring about that estrangement. I began by asking, "Do you know how I met Suhail?"

"During his travels," she said.

"Yes. We encountered one another by chance, not once but twice. Very happy chance indeed, from my perspective. I was sad when we had to part company—when he received word that his father had died."

Umm Azali made a noncommittal noise. We were not in public then; we had gone into the shade of the tent, for it was the hottest part of the day, and very few people were moving about camp. Abu Azali was out with his son's herd, and Tom and Andrew were in the sheikh's tent, enjoying his hospitality and the masculine company to be found there. It was as good a time as any to press.

"I know very little of Suhail's father," I said, "save that he was sheikh before Husam ibn Ramiz, and that he and Suhail were not close." I hesitated for a moment, considering, then added, "You have no doubt noticed my familiarity in calling Suhail by his given name alone. It is because when I knew him, he used no other; and he said once that his father would not thank him for using his name."

This time her noise was less noncommittal—rather more of a snort. Umm Azali said, "Hajj Ramiz ibn Khalis would not have wanted his name attached to what his son was doing."

"Why not?" Scandal had attached itself to me, and by association to Suhail; but that came well after we met. If Suhail had done anything worthy of his own scandal before our first encounter, I had not heard of it.

"Those ancient ruins," Umm Azali said. "Abu Husam wanted his younger son to grow his beard—he was a pious man. He did not like anything associated with idolatrous pagans."

Idolatrous pagans? The Draconeans, I presumed, once I sorted out the Akhian words she had used. "When you say he did not approve . . ."

Umm Azali's lips thinned. "He threatened to lock his son up until he renounced all connection with the blasphemies of the past. Suhail ran away."

My mouth was very dry, for reasons that had nothing to do with the desert air. I remembered once, at the age of fourteen, being tempted to say "damn the cannons" and chase after my dreams regardless of consequence. I had not done it; I had endured my grey years and gone obediently in search of a husband, with fortunate results. Suhail, it seemed, had done otherwise—for a time.

I wanted to ask whether the occasion of Suhail running away had been the same journey on which I met him—and if so, how on earth Suhail had come to be as well funded as he was, for certainly he had no shortage of money when I knew him. I doubted his father had given him coin when he ran away, especially not for the purpose of digging up Draconean ruins. But Umm Azali was clearly becoming uncomfortable with this line of conversation, and so I let it rest there for the time being.

From Abu Azali I got a rather different impression of Suhail. I should pause here to explain that among the nomads of Akhia, poetry is a highly developed art; it has the virtue of requiring no material resources and posing no burden to carry from one camp to the next. One cannot go a day among them without hearing a poem, for children recite them in their games, and men and women alike share them during work and leisure, as a distraction from their labours or a pleasant pastime. They use it to remember history, to argue about disputed points, to elicit shocked giggles when in suitably private company . . . and they use it to tell stories.

I said before that actions like Suhail's—creeping into an

enemy camp in the middle of the night to carry off some theft by stealth—are a thing told of in desert tales. In the more prosaic cases, it is a camel or sheep the raiders go to steal; in the more romantic ones, it is the kidnapped son of a sheikh. Such poems had not been recited much in recent times, I think, for no one among the Aritat had done anything of the sort in many generations; but they became exceedingly popular following Suhail's exploit. It is only natural that someone would undertake to compose a new poem in honour of the occasion.

Abu Azali missed no opportunities to recite that poem. He was so proud of his foster son, I thought he might burst. It made me regret that I did not understand the nomad dialect well enough to appreciate the poetry firsthand; I gathered that it compared Suhail to a desert drake, moving in stealth through the night, with only the wink of the stars to signal his passage. (I learned rather later that it was just as well I could not understand the poem, for its description of *me* would have left me unsure whether I should squawk in indignation or burst out laughing. There were descriptions of my beauty that likened me to a camel—a high compliment in that society, but in my case both unfounded and not at all an aesthetic I could comprehend—and a good deal of swoony behaviour that would have been very pleasing to my childhood friend Manda Lewis, but bore very little resemblance, I hoped, to reality.)

This, then, was my second image of Suhail: a noble warrior, the son of a sheikh, esteemed for his learning and his courage. It struck me as both accurate and not, for while I knew Suhail's courage very well, I did not see him as a warrior. We had ridden sea-serpents, stolen one caeliger and crashed another (by means of a sea-serpent, no less), and I had once seen him cut a man's arm off with a single blow—but that had been done to save the man's life, and the effects of that action had haunted Suhail for some time after.

The truth, I knew, was neither the brave raider of the poem—who owed more to the conventions of the genre than to Suhail's own actions—nor the fanciful boy Umm Azali remembered. Nor, indeed, was it the man I had known on the *Basilisk*, for that man had been without context or a past. The reality of Suhail ibn Ramiz lay somewhere at the intersection of those things, and other byways besides, which I had not yet begun to discover.

In short, I did not truly know who Suhail was. But I did know this much: whatever obstacles propriety might pose, I did not want him to become a stranger to me again.

In addition to pursuing mating flights and marking every cache of eggs we could find, Tom and I spent some time observing juveniles. "After all," Tom said, "once they hatch, we still have to keep them alive. And it may be possible to train them out of some of their most inconvenient habits, if we know how they're trained *into* them in the first place."

We had of course missed the first window for this. The eggs hatch at the height of summer—a most unusual timing, biologically speaking, for that is when food is at its most scarce. Furthermore, we knew that desert drakes estivated, which is of course the summer equivalent of hibernation. It is not so deep a slumber as hibernation, and includes periods of wakefulness; but it rather suggested that the adults were not closely engaged with nurturing their offspring. (Indeed, a female desert drake makes me look like a doting mother by comparison.)

We could, however, learn something from last year's crop, who were then approximately six months old. They did not hunt in the dramatic fashion of their elders, for they lacked extraordinary breath; instead they subsisted on lizards, rabbits, and the largely terrestrial bustards that form such a significant part of the nomad diet. We soon discovered that the majority of conflicts between humans and drakes occur with juveniles: the nomads will hunt an adult drake if they must, but avoid that whenever possible, owing to a justified fear of being burnt alive. The immature beasts, however, are merely competition, and are fought as such.

It was comical to watch the youngest drakes attempt to hunt. Their flight is not exceptionally well developed at that age; they will launch themselves into the air and sink down again quite rapidly, hoping to land on prey, but often failing. "If their parents are asleep when they hatch," I asked Tom, "how do any of them survive?"

He shook his head, not taking his gaze from our current subject. "They may cannibalize one another after the hatching. If not that, then *something* else kills them; otherwise the desert would be overrun with ten thousand starving drakes."

Cannibalism seemed plausible, given what we knew of swamp-wyrms and their immature form. "Even a nest full of siblings, though, would only feed them for a short time."

"True." The juvenile staggered on landing, then steadied itself with outstretched wings before sauntering onward, for all the world like a cat attempting to persuade onlookers that no lapse of grace had occurred. Tom turned to me, a grin creasing his sunburnt features. "The only way to answer that will be to come back out here again later."

We both knew we would have to go back to Qurrat soon. The Aritat themselves would be retreating; the winter rains that made the desert briefly verdant had ended, and pasturage would rapidly become scarce. Most nomads would move to the fringes of more settled areas, to oases and the periphery of rivers, where they could wait out the dry months. The heart of the desert would be left to the drakes.

But our work was no respecter of personal comfort. To understand the drakes properly, we had to see them in all seasons—even if it meant walking into the furnace.

Tom and I planned it out in the shelter of our tent. "We'll go back to Qurrat for a time," he said. "Pensyth will want us back; and besides, there won't be much we can do here until later. We'll come out again in . . . early Caloris, do you think?"

"Late Messis would be better. It will depend on how matters are at the House by then. Well before the eggs are expected to hatch, so that we can take notes on estivation and such." I did not say that I desperately wanted to sneak into the cavern of a sleeping dragon, but judging by Tom's wry smile, he knew my thoughts regardless.

In the meanwhile, the Aritat would bring us eggs at regular intervals, rather than the system that had prevailed under Lord Tavenor, wherein they shipped their finds as their hunters encountered them. That way we could make reasonable estimates of the eggs' maturity, which would allow us to experiment more precisely with their incubation conditions, as I had arranged with the honeyseeker eggs.

Our thermometers we left with Haidar, who promised to take measurements of every cache before it was dug up. Our tent we left as a gift to Umm Azali and Abu Azali, who promised it would be Shahar's when she wed. The Aritat were moving in the same direction as our group, but far too slowly for our purposes; we therefore rode ahead, with a well-armed escort the sheikh had provided.

The morning we departed, I cast one glance over my shoulder toward the Labyrinth of Drakes. I knew I would return; but I had no idea what would happen when I did.

PART THREE

In which civilization poses as many dangers as the desert

THIRTEEN

Back in Qurrat—Enemies of the Aritat—Caeligers in Va Hing—Honeyseeker results—Improving conditions—I feel unwell

The journey back to Qurrat was blessedly uneventful. Shimon and Aviva welcomed me back without much fanfare—or perhaps it would be more accurate to say they accepted me back. I was not living with a family; the contrast with our circumstances in the desert made that clear. I was essentially staying in a very small hotel, where both my virtue and my religious integrity could be suitably chaperoned. As this oversight placed no real constraints on me, and my hosts had no objections I could discern, it worked out well for all.

A message was waiting for me at their house, encouraging me to take a day or two of rest before returning to Dar al-Tannaneen. Tom, arriving at the Men's House in the Segulist Quarter, received a message saying Pensyth wanted to see him the following morning. "Concern for my delicate constitution, which has no doubt been wearied by my trials," I said. "Very touching, but I think I can find it in me to rub along."

"I wish *I* could take your holiday," Andrew said with a melodramatic sigh. "But that is army life for you."

He and Tom collected me first thing the next morning, and together we all went to the House of Dragons. Pensyth made no comment upon seeing me there, but was very solicitous of my comfort, to the point of holding my chair for me—a thing he had never done before. I soon gathered that he thought me still in need of recovery from the ordeal of my kidnapping. I sat on the urge to ask whether he had forgotten that Tom, too, had been subjected to that indignity, or whether he merely did not care about Tom's condition. (Neither, of course, would have been the case; but I wanted to needle him by asking. I was not twenty-four hours back in Qurrat, and already my prickliness was reasserting itself.)

"Did you receive our report about the Banu Safr?" Tom asked. "The guns, and the other signs of wealth? Not to mention where they got the drug that knocked us out. I don't think that was any herbal tincture."

"Our surgeon thinks it was ether," Pensyth said. "Based on the symptoms you described. And no, they wouldn't be making that in the desert—not unless they have a lot of chemical apparatus you didn't see. Damned if I—my apologies, Dame Isabella. I have no idea where they got it from. There isn't much hope of finding out, either."

Tom frowned. "No one even has a guess?"

"Oh, they have guesses. Too many of them. It could be any tribe that doesn't like the Aritat, or the caliph. More than enough of those to go around." The colonel shrugged, leaning back in his chair with an air of resignation. "I know the Akhians are looking into it, and I know they aren't bl—aren't likely to tell us what they find out."

This was frustrating, but hardly surprising. They would have no desire to tell us about their internal conflicts; those would only open up gaps my own nation might exploit. I said,

"Without information, though, we can't do much to stop them in the future."

By the scowl on Pensyth's face, he did not need me reminding him. "If it were up to me, I'd march a company into the desert and teach the Banu Safr a lesson they won't soon forget. It wouldn't get at whoever is behind this, but it would rob them of one tool, at least. Unfortunately, there's no chance of the caliph allowing that."

I imagined not. Doing so would be tantamount to announcing he couldn't keep order in his own country. Tom said, "The Aritat did what they could on that front. It kept us safe enough, after the initial trouble."

"Well, you're back here now, and well away from the Banu Safr." Pensyth linked his hands and leaned forward, adopting the posture of a man getting down to business. "I hope you have something useful to show for all the time you spent out there."

"I could share our notebooks with you, if you like," I said.

It must have come out too sweetly, because Tom shot me a quelling look. He said, "We have a good deal of data, where before we had only guesswork. It will show its value, I'm sure. The current breeding season has passed, but that gives us time to prepare for next winter's effort. Isabella and I have some thoughts for how to change the drakes' environment so they'll be more inclined toward their natural habits."

He was better at saying that with a sober face than I was. Our thoughts ranged from a kind of overhead sprinkler that might induce them to believe it was the rainy season in midsummer, to a set of harnesses into which we might strap the drakes and then swing them about to simulate flying. The only one that was even faintly practical was a special breeding enclosure, with a pedestal for the female and space enough for all our captive males to gather around her. Without a flight to follow, though, we were not at all certain how much good it would do.

The only way to find out was to test it, and as Tom said, we could not do that right now. The prospect of delay, however unavoidable it might be, clearly irritated Pensyth. "In the meanwhile," I said before he could complain, "we've made arrangements for a more systematic approach to the eggs. Once we have a chance to study the data from the honeyseekers, we'll be able to make alterations that will, I believe, greatly improve our success rate there."

It only mollified Pensyth a little: after all, our purpose here was to breed dragons, not merely to hatch them. I wondered what he had expected, when he heard we would be taking up Lord Tavenor's duties. Was our reputation so tremendous that he believed we could achieve instant success? Or was he simply so impatient for results that any failure to produce them was unacceptable?

The latter, it seemed. "The world didn't stop turning while you were off in the desert. The Yelangese have unveiled an entire fleet of caeligers in Va Hing—thirty of them. And our observers say the design is different, more refined. How many caeligers do we have? *Five.* It isn't enough."

When I last heard of it, our own fleet had numbered four: one largely reconstructed from components fished out of the Broken Sea, and three built from material acquired since. I surmised that Prima's bones had been put to quick use. "Have the Yelangese done anything with their caeligers yet? Aside from unveiling them."

Dar al-Tannaneen

Pensyth gave me an unpleasant stare. "Would you prefer we wait for actual war to begin, Dame Isabella? The threat is enough."

I had not forgotten the Battle of Keonga, where the raking fire of a single caeliger had wreaked havoc on the defenders below. Such tactics would be of limited use against an enemy that had artillery with which to respond; but Andrew had already speculated in my hearing about other applications. A caeliger might drop bombs on ships or fortified positions—or even if it were not used to fight, it could scout the movements of the enemy, giving generals much more accurate knowledge for their own maneuvers.

It was not always reassuring, having a brother in the army.

"We are doing our best, sir," Tom said.

Pensyth sighed wearily, nodding. "Yes, of course. I should not keep you from it."

Five minutes more or less would make no difference to our success—but I was glad to escape his office and return to the (in my eyes) more comfortable world of dragons and their needs. Lieutenant Marton had managed things effectively in our absence; Sniffer had died, but he had been in poor health when we departed, and I was not surprised to see him go. "I tried to get ice to keep him in, so you could examine the carcass," Marton said apologetically, "but it didn't work out."

Tom thanked him, and we began our rounds. Lumpy was still alive, I was pleased to see, as was Ascelin, the eldest of the juveniles, the fierce one for whom I had a liking. Saeva, the adult brought to us in Nebulis, had developed an infection in her tail, but the men had managed to restrain her enough to wash and bandage the wound on a regular basis, and it had healed well.

Once we had inspected the place and found all in order, Tom set about instituting the changes he and I had planned—changes based on our desert observations—while I turned my attention to the records of the honeyseeker eggs.

Not enough time had passed, of course, for me to have anything like definitive results. Even honeyseekers do not breed so quickly as to supply me with the hundreds of eggs I would need to test their tolerances in full; and of course I would ideally repeat the process later, or have someone else do so, to see if the second set of data matched the first. (As some of my more scientific friends are fond of proclaiming, twice is once, and once is nothing.) Marton had done as I asked, though, with diligent care, and so I had the beginnings of a pattern, which I was very keen to study.

I had decided to introduce new variables one at a time, beginning with the one I believed to be the most influential: temperature. What extreme of heat could the eggs tolerate without losing viability, and what extreme of cold? Nowadays we can control this to a very nice degree, quite literally speaking. Back then, though, the best we could do was to place the eggs in different locations, ranging from the cellars of Dar al-Tannaneen to its rooftop. At regular intervals Marton measured the temperature there, with one of the sergeants taking over the task at night. Some of the eggs were carried from the cellar to a warmer spot during the day, to simulate the fluctuation they would experience in nature; others were left in the coolness all the time, while a few lived quite cozily by a fireplace. Altogether, it made for a substantial set of data—and it was only the beginning.

An unused room in the House of Dragons became the repository of this information. I spent a day drafting a very precise graph that would show me what I knew at a glance: the horizontal axis measured days since laying, while the vertical measured temperature. On this I drew curves delineating the environment of each egg, in different colours of ink.

"It's very pretty," Andrew said when I tacked it on the wall, "but what does it mean?"

I stood, tapping my tack-hammer against my thigh, studying the graph. "It means I can see what is going on." Exchanging the hammer for a pencil, I went to the graph and began drawing hashes through some of the lines. "These are the eggs that produced unhealthy specimens. And these—" I drew more hashes, crossing them to make *X*s. "These are the ones that did not hatch at all. You can see, they are much less tolerant of cold than of heat. Which makes sense, of course, given their native environment. One wonders whether it would be the opposite with, say, rock-wyrms."

"Yes, of course one wonders that."

I ignored his flippant tone. "But it also appears that the rise and fall is important: the greater the heat, the more necessary it is that a cooling period be allowed. Without that, you are more likely to get runts and such. If the same is true for drake eggs, then it may be that our conveyance methods need revising. They bury their eggs a certain depth in the sand, you see, and the baskets used to transport them here are not nearly so large. That may mean they are subjected to too great a heat in the daytime, and too much coolness at night—or not enough, if the Aritat have been keeping the baskets by the fire. Or by their camels, even. We shall inquire. And that does not even *touch* upon humidity. Testing that will be my next step."

Andrew laughed. "What are you going to do, put them in steam baths?"

"Of course not. I need to see how humidity interacts with temperature; steam baths would require far too much heat. But closed boxes, with an atomizer to mist the air, might suffice."

He thought I was joking. He was disabused of this notion, though, when I sent him to the perfumers of Qurrat to see whether anyone sold atomizers. (They did not. That method of applying scent is more common in northern Anthiope; I ended up having to send to Chiavora for equipment. And you may be sure Pensyth gave me a *very* peculiar look when I submitted that request.)

I also had to examine the honeyseekers that had survived. These were all in one of the unused buildings at Dar al-Tannaneen, being fed on nectar extracted from the sheikh's garden, but it was already obvious that we would need a better solution. Even if I subjected the next rounds of eggs to far less hospitable conditions, we would rapidly be up to our kneecaps in juvenile honeyseekers, and the sheikh's eucalyptus trees could not sustain them all. I had inquiries out for other gardens that might suffice, and in the meantime we had even more draconic mouths to feed.

Something else happened during this time, too—but I will not tell it now, for it seemed minor at the time, and its true significance did not occur to me until much later. I note it here only so that those of my readers who care about the process of scientific discovery may accurately reconstruct the steps by which I arrived at my eventual conclusions. Laypeople often believe that understanding comes by epiphany: something important occurs, and on the instant the scientist declares, *I have it!* But the truth is that we may be blind to the import of events around us, not realizing the truth until well after the fact.

While I did all of this, Tom worked to improve the living conditions of our drakes. We began delivering charred meat to their enclosures; they will eat it in any state, from running away to very thoroughly carrion, but we hoped the scent might stimulate their appetites and encourage better health. He also began agitating for the construction of a second compound, well removed from the first. After all, if a female drake will not willingly nest within ten kilometers of a male, what effects came of having them a mere twenty meters apart?

"We aren't likely to find a suitable place here," he said over lunch one day. We had developed the habit of eating alone together in the office, where we might not offend local custom too much. (Andrew had given up on joining us, saying our conversations were impenetrable to anyone who did not have dragon blood in his veins.) "I keep wondering about that territory we went around on the way to the Aritat. I know it belongs to another tribe—but it's a sight closer to the drakes, and not too far from river transport. If the caliph gave the order, we could relocate this entire enterprise there, and I think we'd do a good deal better."

"Can he not order it?" I asked.

Tom grimaced, shredding a bit of flatbread between his fingers. "This isn't like medieval Scirland. The land doesn't all belong to the king, for him to hand out as he sees fit to barons and so forth. It's theirs, and he can't easily commandeer it. Or so I'm told."

"Can *we* approach them?" I dismissed this with a shake of my head almost before the words were out of my mouth. "Foreigners, trying to stake a claim on property in his country. Or the local sheikh's country—whichever. I can imagine how *that* would be received."

We faced a number of challenges, and our progress against them was hampered by the change of seasons. I have said before that I am a heat-loving creature, and it is true; but even the early days of an Akhian summer took their toll on me. I felt increasingly weak and light-headed, and soon found myself lying down for a little while after lunch each day, waiting out the worst of the heat, though I could not truly rest. I tried to compensate for this by working later into the night, but even then I felt exhausted, unable to focus. My digestion became poor, and even basic tasks began to feel like a burden.

Tom felt it too, but less acutely—or, I suspected, he simply shrugged it off with the stoicism expected of a man. He became concerned for my health, though, and when I attempted to shrug it off as he had, gave me a steady look. "I don't want to repeat Mouleen," he said after I rose from my couch one afternoon.

In the Green Hell I had tried to forge ahead through what turned out to be yellow fever. "I am not that ill," I promised him. "Only tired from the heat."

"Then rest," he said. "You will acclimate soon enough."

I wanted to say that I had not required any acclimation in Eriga—not like this. Another of our drake hatchlings had died, and we were going to conduct a necropsy to see if we could determine the cause. I wanted to be present for that. But Tom was better than I with matters medical, and I would not impress anyone if I tipped head-first into a bucket of viscera. "I will go visit Mahira," I suggested. "I have been meaning to do that for some time now, but I have been so busy. The gardens there are pleasant and cool, and I can inspect the honeyseekers."

Tom grinned. "Of course you can't rest without finding a way to be useful at the same time. But it's a good idea regardless. Go—and if you need to stay home tomorrow, we can manage without you."

I did not want them to manage without me. If they could do it for one day, they could do it for more than one; I did not want anyone thinking I was superfluous. But I knew what Tom would say if I expressed such thoughts to him—and he would be well justified—so I kept my self-pity behind my teeth and went.

FOURTEEN

I feel even more unwell—An unusual physician—Nour's theory—A basket for Tom—Testing the theory

You may guess that I had been avoiding the sheikh's house for more reasons than a mere crowded schedule. You would be correct in that guess.

Suhail had visited Dar al-Tannaneen twice since our return, but on both occasions he had come only briefly, and left before I knew he was there. Given my resolution in the desert, I should have been more energetic in seeking him out, if only so I could apologize for my coldness before. But it was one thing to form such a resolution; it was another thing entirely to carry it out.

I could not even be positive he was still at the house. By now the nomadic Aritat had moved to their summer quarters; Suhail might be with them, or with the men who would venture into the desert at regular intervals to collect eggs on our behalf. And even if he was present . . . what would I say? Everything I could think of seemed too forward, especially when we would certainly have an audience again. As much as I liked Mahira, I did not feel comfortable telling Suhail how much I valued his friendship with her sitting ten feet away. I could ask him how the translation was proceeding; surely that would be neutral enough? Being less than skilled at languages, I had very little sense of how long it would take him to decipher the Ngaru half of the text. Since I was fairly certain he did not know the language already, I imagined it would take a while.

That, I decided, was safe. It would show friendly warmth—an encouraging interest in a topic I knew he loved—without overstepping any boundaries. If Suhail happened upon us again in the garden, I would ask him about the Cataract Stone.

Mahira greeted me warmly when I arrived. She called for refreshments, and we spent some time chatting about my experiences in the desert. News of the kidnapping had reached her ears; she startled me with some rather fierce comments about the fate that should be visited upon those sons of dogs, the Banu Safr. "Is a prayer-leader allowed to say such things?" I asked, half scandalized.

She laughed. "In the older days, the tribes used to load an unmarried girl into a special howdah and carry her into battle as their standard. There is a long tradition in Akhia of women urging their menfolk to valour against the enemy."

It reminded me of old tales from Niddey and Uaine—though in those, of course, there is no howdah. "I hope the battles are concluded," I said. "Your brother's men did an excellent job keeping order, at least in our immediate vicinity, after that outrage."

I meant to use that comment to prepare the ground, so that asking after her other brother would not seem out of place. The words stuck in my throat, though, because I could not find a way to make them sound innocuous—not when she had almost certainly heard the poem about Suhail's own valour. Instead I gave her the gossip about Umm Azali and the rest of the Aritat, as well as I could. Mahira might live in a city, but the urge to ask for the news from elsewhere in the desert is alive and well in every part of Akhian society.

When that was done we went out to the garden, so that I might examine the honeyseekers. Amamis and Hicara were drowsing in the heat when I entered their net-draped enclosure, which meant that capturing them was the work of mere moments.

I spread Hicara's wings wide, ignoring her indignant chirps, and examined her from every angle. Then I repeated the process with Amamis. They both appeared to be in excellent health: their scales were glossy, Amamis' crest a bright sapphire blue, and neither showed the slightest lethargy in scrambling away from me once I released them. "You have done very well by them—I thank you," I said to Mahira.

"They have been an ornament to our garden," she replied. "I hope you have learned a great deal from their eggs."

The honeyseekers had fled into the trees. I peered after them, watching as they twined about the branches in search of something to nose at. "It will take time. To truly know the tolerances of their eggs, we must test all the way to the limits, and that will require more rounds than we have had so far. So long as you do not mind continuing this work, I would be delighted to leave them here—though I must find a way to repay you for your effort."

I turned toward Mahira, intending to ask whether she would like a pair of honeyseekers as a permanent installation in her garden. The offspring of my two could not mate, of course, without risk of inbreeding—but I could request another set from Lutjarro, as a gesture of gratitude. When I turned, however, the world turned with me. I swayed to one side, catching myself against a tree, and then sat down very hard on the ground.

Mahira was there in an instant, robes billowing as she sank down next to me. "Are you all right?"

"Yes, quite," I said—in that inane way one does when one is not well at all. "Only I was dizzy for a moment."

She helped me to my feet and then settled me on the bench, staying at my side lest I tip over. I could not bring myself to argue against her caution. "I have been feeling a bit indisposed for several days," I admitted. "I thought it was just the heat—I have been trying to drink plenty of water—but this is rather worse than before. I fear I may be ill, after all."

This last I said with annoyance. Disease is the near-inevitable companion of every traveller, and I had made its acquaintance far too often for my liking. Illness would take me away from my work, making me look weak in the eyes of the men I was trying to impress.

But I had also seen what happened when I attempted to work through illness. I did not want to drive myself to collapse.

Mahira said, "Would you like me to call my own physician to attend you?"

"Oh, no," I said hastily. "That won't be necessary."

"I assure you, it is no trouble. And she is very knowledgeable."

The pronoun pulled me up short. "She? Your physician is a woman?"

Mahira looked scandalized. "Do you think I would allow a man to examine my body?"

When she put it that way, I could hardly say that I took it

for granted. As some of my readers may know, the first university in Akhia was founded by a woman—the mother of one of the caliphs—and apparently she had been in favour of training women physicians, so as to uphold propriety while also caring for the patient's health. It took another two hundred years for that vision to become a reality, and even now women physicians are not so common; but the wealthy and the pious often call upon their services.

I had to admit the notion held some appeal. Over the years I have been poked and prodded in a variety of embarrassing ways by male doctors; it might be a relief to consult a woman instead. "I would be grateful for her assistance," I said.

Little did I know what I was unleashing with those words. When at last the whirlwind settled, I had somehow been transported from the honeyseeker enclosure to the women's quarters of the house, where I was laid upon a sopha and plied with cooling drinks. A serving girl fanned me, and I was not permitted to rise until the physician arrived—which she did with great alacrity, likely because of Mahira's status as the sheikh's sister.

She introduced herself as Nour bint Ahmad, and asked after my symptoms. "I have been very tired of late," I admitted, "and sometimes dizzy; I have also had frequent headaches. It may only be heat exhaustion."

But this was not enough for her exacting standards. She began to question me in detail, asking when I felt the symptoms most acutely, in what precise way they affected me, how long they lasted, and more. She took my pulse, examined my eyes and my tongue, and various other matters I will omit for the sake of propriety. (I do not mind being frank when it serves a purpose; but in this case it would not.)

As this interrogation wore on, I found myself feeling ashamed. I was startled by Nour's apparent acumen—and then, following that thought back to its source, I realized I had assumed that she, being a woman physician, would not be as knowledgeable or skilled as a man. It was, in short, *precisely* the kind of patronizing attitude I had suffered throughout my own career; and here I was, inflicting it in turn on a woman who knew more about the human body and its workings than I could ever aspire to. For heaven's sake: she had a university degree in the subject, which was far more than I could say for myself in my own field. Undoubtedly there are incompetent women physicians out there; but so, too, are there men who do not know a broken bone from a fever in the head. Despite Mahira's recommendation, I had judged Nour unfairly.

I wanted to apologize to her, but she did not know what I had been thinking; and if I had shown it in my behaviour, I could make up for it best by placing my confidence in her now. "At least it cannot be yellow fever," I said when her questioning was done. "I have had that already." Also dengue in the Melatan region and malaria after I left Phetayong, but those can be contracted more than once. Although Pensyth had supplied us with gin and tonic water as a preventative for malaria, it is far from foolproof.

Nour frowned, fingers gently clasping the front edge of her scarf in what looked like a habitual pose, assumed when she was deep in thought. "Where have you been living?" she asked.

"In the Segulist Quarter, with a Bayitist family," I said.

"And where have you been taking your meals?"

"Largely at the House of Dragons—it is an estate not far

outside the city walls. I eat a little something when I wake, but lunch is always out there, and often supper as well."

She considered this for a moment, then gave a little nod, as if an interior conversation had concluded. Turning, she called out to Mahira, who had been sitting on the far side of the room to give us some privacy. When Mahira joined us, Nour asked, "Would it be possible to keep Umm Yaqub here for a day or two?"

"What?" I exclaimed, sitting up on the sopha. "I am not *that* ill!"

Nour regarded me soberly. "I do not think you are ill," she said. "I think you have been poisoned."

I could not have been more shocked had someone thrown a bucket of ice water over me. "That—is not possible."

"How do you obtain your food?"

"From the market," I said slowly. "They send a man to fetch something in. Maazir, I think his name is."

Nour looked grim. "I would not like to accuse this man without proof. But if you stay here, and your condition improves . . ."

Despite the warm, close room, I was cold to the bone. "Tom eats the same meals I do. He has not felt unwell—or only a little so." But Tom had the constitution of an ox. He had been bitten by a wyvern in Bulskevo and shrugged it off. "God in heaven."

"He must not eat the food, either," Nour said.

If it were true—if someone was indeed poisoning our meals, with Maazir's knowledge or without—then they had gone to some lengths to be subtle about it. There were any number of things they could have put into it that would have seen us both dead within the hour, however resilient Tom might be.

Instead they preferred to weaken us, in a fashion that could be mistaken for illness. In time we would die; or perhaps it would be enough simply to disrupt our work. Either way, we had an opportunity to catch the culprit . . . but only if we did not scare him off.

"I will warn Tom," I said. "If I take food to him, secretly, he can eat that in place of what Maazir brings from the market. What time is it?"

The room's piercework shutters made it difficult for me to gauge the hour. And although the call to prayer sounded throughout Qurrat at regular intervals, I had not incorporated that into my mental clock, as the Amaneen do. "The sunset prayer will begin soon," Mahira said.

"Then I must hurry." Tom would want to finish the necropsy before the light went, which meant he would not have taken supper yet. His hardiness might allow him to go another day without serious ill effects—but I could not knowingly allow him to eat poison, not if there was any risk that Nour was correct.

The physician put her hands on my shoulders when I tried to rise. "You will go nowhere. Someone else can take the message, and the food."

"I felt well enough to come here," I said, pushing against this restraint. It did not take so very much pressure for her to keep me in my seat, though, and I knew she could tell that as well as I.

Nour said, "What if someone overhears the warning, and decides to take more direct action?"

"All the more reason for me to be there with Tom. Or do you suggest I should abandon him, when he is in peril?"

Mahira intervened before our argument could grow any

more heated. "Umm Yaqub, I will have our cook prepare a basket for him. If it is a gift from the sheikh's household, no one will think it odd that he declines supper from the market. He can be warned once he is safely away."

The mulish part of me wanted to insist on my original plan . . . but I had to admit that Mahira's suggestion was more sensible. "I should prefer to sleep in my own bed, though," I said.

Nour required me to stay on the sopha a while longer, so she could be sure my condition was not worsening. When I departed at last, shortly after sunset, I had both an escort and a basket of my own, with food enough for not only my supper but also my breakfast and lunch the next day, and strict orders to stay home from Dar al-Tannaneen.

The difficult part would be finding a reason for both Tom and myself to be absent. (Well, one of the difficult parts. I was not very good at sitting still when trouble reared its head.) Pondering this over my supper, which I was taking alone in my room, I found myself laughing wryly. "I suppose," I said to my ground chick peas, "that I might just say we are ill. Then the poisoner will think he is succeeding in his aim." Always supposing he did not take that as his cue to bring the drama to a sudden and unpleasant close.

Aviva knocked at my door before I had finished. Putting her head into the room, she said, "Your brother is downstairs."

"Oh dear," I said involuntarily, getting to my feet. "Yes, he would be. I'll come."

Andrew was pacing restlessly, and wheeled about when I entered the courtyard. "Are you all right?" he asked. Then, before I had a chance to answer: "No, of course you aren't.

I heard you collapsed at the sheikh's house. For God's sake, sit down."

"'Collapse' rather overstates the matter," I said. "I got dizzy, is all. I am perfectly capable of standing, and walking, too."

"Well, sit down for my peace of mind, won't you?" This I obliged him in, if only so we could converse about something other than my stability or lack thereof. "It isn't malaria, is it?"

He had suffered from that disease in Coyahuac, and knew its signs well. "No, it isn't. In fact—" I hesitated. Would it be better or worse to tell Andrew about Nour's suspicion? He would certainly find it even more alarming than rumours of my collapse. On the other hand, if it *was* poison, then we needed to inform Pensyth as soon as possible, so the culprit might be apprehended. Could Maazir be behind this? Or was he working for someone else? Was he a knowing accomplice, or an unwitting tool?

These thoughts had paralyzed my brain all through supper, and I was no closer to finding answers now. I wished Tom had arrived before Andrew, so I could put them to him before involving my brother. My silence, however, had alarmed Andrew. He crouched at my feet, peering up at my face. "What is it? Something worse than malaria?"

"In a manner of speaking." I scrubbed my hands over my face, which did little to clear my thoughts. "Nour—the physician—she thinks, ah. That my illness may not be . . . an accident. That someone may be arranging it deliberately."

He worked through the implications of this one blink at a time. "You mean—" He sat back on his heels, staring. "That's absurd. Who did you say suggested this? The physician who saw you is a woman?"

"Don't say it," I warned him. "She knows her business very well. I intend to test her theory, by abstaining from the food brought to the House of Dragons—the timing of my bad spells makes her think the problem is there. If she is wrong, then very well: I will seek a second opinion."

"But who would poison you?" Andrew said. "No Scirling man would do that. And we're allied with the Akhians. Why would they sabotage you?"

"Politics?" I suggested, my tone heavy with irony. "*Someone* paid the Banu Safr to kidnap us; it is hardly a stretch to think they might try other methods. Or it could be a single madman who believes we're subverting the natural order with our efforts. There's no way of knowing—not yet. But first we need to know if it *is* poison. Until then, everything else is speculation."

Perhaps my condition had dulled my wits; perhaps I was too preoccupied with the task of persuading Andrew. I had not heard the sounds behind me, and did not realize someone else had joined us until Tom said, "Poison? Are we talking about wyverns?"

"No," Andrew said, rising. "We're talking about somebody poisoning Isabella."

"And you," I said hastily—which, in retrospect, was not the best way to soften Andrew's declaration. Quite the opposite, in fact.

Tom listened, appalled, as I outlined Nour's theory. "So that's why I got a special supper," he muttered when I was done. "I *thought* that was unusually generous of the sheikh."

Andrew said, "If Maazir *is* poisoning you, the sheikh will be disgraced. I don't think he's Aritat himself—but the Aritat hired him."

"One worry at a time," I said. "I have felt no particular improvement in my condition yet—but I expect it will take more than one round of safe dining before change can occur. Can we come up with a reason not to go back there tomorrow?"

"Or just take food with you," Andrew suggested. "The two of you closet yourselves away often enough; you can hide what Maazir brought in a basket or something, then feed it to the dragons when no one is looking."

I stared at my brother in horror. "I most certainly shall not! We have no idea what such fare would do to a dragon—poisoned or not." The thought of putting Lumpy at such risk, or any of the adult drakes, was appalling. If I were to experiment with their diets, I would do so in a controlled fashion, with full knowledge of the ingredients.

Tom was pacing, hands linked behind his back. "How long will it take before we know whether the food is at fault? Will a day be enough?"

"Nour said two days, to be certain."

His mouth compressed. "By all means, let us be certain. But then what? Tell Pensyth?"

Andrew looked up, startled, from the task of retying his boot. "You're going to wait? I was going to tell Pensyth tonight."

Tom and I exchanged a swift look, confirming that we were in accord. "Don't," I said.

"Why ever not?"

Tom snorted. "Because Pensyth isn't a subtle man."

"He won't wait two days," I said. "He'll clap Maazir in irons and start a row with the sheikh. And Maazir may be innocent; perhaps the problem is with the man selling him the food. Or it might be nothing! Perhaps I am only suffering from exhaustion in the heat. I want proof, before we start Pensyth baying like a hound."

"But—" Andrew clamped his jaw in the way that said he wanted to argue, but couldn't think of any useful points he might bring to bear. It made him look nine years old, which I had good enough sense not to say.

"We will take food with us," I said. "And see what happens. I will take no further action without data."

FIFTEEN

A dirty labourer—An alley in Qurrat—Suhail's captive—Suspicious powder—Allies of the Banu Safr—Colonel Pensyth's news—What we were not told

Other people, however, were not so restrained.

When Maazir departed the next day on his usual trip to the market, I happened to be at a window overlooking the front gate. (Very well: it was not coincidence.) I do not know what I thought I might see—a pouch of poison swinging from one jaunty hand?—but I felt obliged to watch.

What I saw was one of the common labourers slipping out after him. There were any number of these around the compound on any given day; we had a great many menial jobs that needed to be done, such as tending to the livestock that fed the dragons and mucking out the enclosures, and the men who performed these tasks came and went. Some of them were city-dwellers, while others were nomads, earning a small bit of coin to purchase something before returning to their people in the desert.

The fellow I observed was of the second type, and not a particularly fine specimen of the breed, either. His clothes were patched and frayed, the scarf and veil on his head filthy with dust. He had been shuffling about as if one leg were less than hale—but as soon as Maazir was gone, his gait changed entirely. He crossed the courtyard with swift strides and was out of the compound almost before I could blink.

I stopped breathing as a suspicion formed in my heart.

It is not easy to fling oneself down stairs in a skirt; there is always the risk that you will tangle your legs and go headlong. But I made it to the courtyard and cracked the gate, peering out through the opening.

In the distance I saw Maazir. Between him and myself, the labourer, following.

Either Maazir was innocent, or he had been doing this for long enough that he no longer feared detection. (Or he was skilled enough that he knew not to look behind himself until he could make the action look casual. At the time, I did not know to consider that possibility.) As for the labourer, he was intent on his own quarry; he did not look behind, either, and so he did not see me following him.

Dar al-Tannaneen was not far from the gates of Qurrat. I nearly lost the labourer in the crowds there, and had to draw much closer than I felt comfortable with. Had he glanced over his shoulder, he would have seen me, for a Scirling woman is quite noticeable in that district, even when her dress is made of sedate khaki. I was glad to be following the labourer, rather than Maazir: the latter would not recognize the former, and I was far enough back to escape *his* eye.

And so we went, a daisy-chain of suspicion, wending our way through town. But not through the crowded market: Maazir turned off into an alley just before he reached that plaza. The labourer hurried to keep up, and I knew why. In the winding back ways of Qurrat, it would be easy to lose one's quarry entirely. Now my steps slowed, for avoiding detection there would be exceedingly difficult—even impossible. I had come out here without thinking, but continuing onward in the same manner was not advisable.

But the two men had not gone far. I peered around the corner in time to see the labourer lunge through a doorway. From within came the sound of shouts. Then Maazir hurled himself back out into the alley and came charging straight toward me.

I stepped into his path, my head empty of anything resembling a plan. I was no brawler, to tackle him to the ground. How did I propose to stop him? I was still standing there, indecisive, when he reached the mouth of the alley. He slammed into me—I do not think he even recognized me, despite my garb—and knocked me into a wall in his haste to reach the main street.

In that instant, I did the only thing I could think of. I raised my arm, pointed at the fleeing man, and shouted in the clearest Akhian I could muster, "That man just assaulted me!"

Let no one slander the gentlemen of Qurrat. Several looked up in startlement; one, understanding, took up the cry. Maazir did not make it twenty meters before someone had him by the collar and began dragging him back toward me.

I stood in the mouth of the alley, torn. Having accused Maazir, now I had to deal with him—but I suspected the true business was taking place behind me, in the building Maazir had fled.

"Bring him this way, please," I said, when captor and captive arrived. "My escort is just down here." I am not a pious woman, but I prayed with all the devotion I could muster that my suspicion would not prove incorrect.

Maazir twisted and squirmed, shouting for the other fellow to let him go, as we went down the alley. Half the market followed, it seemed; the commotion had drawn a great deal of curious attention. I stepped through the open doorway, and all the breath went out of me in relief.

Suhail was kneeling atop another man's back at the far side of the room. He had removed the dusty scarf from his head, and was using it to bind the fellow's wrists, cursing as his prisoner fought him. When I entered, it distracted him; the man got one arm free. A knife lay on the ground nearby, and the captive scrabbled for it, but it was just out of his reach. He tried to throw Suhail off, his body heaving. Suhail slammed the palm of his hand into his opponent's shoulder, flattening him to the ground, and got him tied up at last.

In that moment of struggle, I glimpsed his face. For all that the man wore the caftan and turban of a local, his features were Yelangese.

The room was rapidly filling up behind me. It did not take many people to crowd the place; the chamber was less than four meters on a side, and Maazir was still flailing about. I heard the men from the market speculating amongst themselves: this dirty labourer was my escort? Why was the other fellow tied up on the floor? Suhail got up long enough to drag the scarf from Maazir's head and use it to tie the feet of the Yelangese man, ensuring he could not escape. Then he looked at me and demanded in Scirling, "What are you doing here?"

"I could ask you the same," I said, a little breathless. "Why were you following Maazir?" Then common sense, rendered tardy by the excitement, caught up. "Mahira told you what happened."

Suhail dragged one hand through his curls, made unruly by his struggle with the Yelangese. He was out of breath himself, and a bit wild in the eyes. "You're being fed *poison*, Isabella."

That had not been proven—but it had become a good deal more likely, with the probable culprit lying at Suhail's feet. A culprit he had gone after, on his own, without warning me. "You could have been killed."

"So saith the woman who followed me here." His hands twitched at his sides, and I cannot blame the heat for the sensation that came over me then. I recognized that motion: he wanted to reach out, grip me by the arms and make certain I was unharmed. I recognized it because I wanted to do the same, and my inability to do so made me light-headed. I had lost my husband to a single thrust of a knife, not much different from the one lying at Suhail's feet. But we had an audience; I could only curl my hands until my nails cut into my palms.

Suhail collected his wits and addressed the crowd in Akhian too rapid for me to follow well. Someone bound Maazir's hands; when that was done, our erstwhile employee sagged in defeat, and dropped to a crouch in the corner as soon as he was permitted. Some of the men departed, and I caught enough of the conversation to know they had been sent to fetch a magistrate.

I occupied myself searching the room. It was a bare place, with only two small chests and some battered cushions on the floor. Wherever the Yelangese fellow was living, it was not here. The chests contained nothing of interest, just a few bundles of cloth and some cracked dishes.

I am not a legal expert in my own nation, let alone Akhia, but I knew that if we wanted to convict our two captives of anything, we would need something more than the suspicions of one (female) physician. Suhail's word might be enough, depending on how much deference was given to the brother of a sheikh—but I did not want to test it.

The Yelangese man was squirming on the floor. My first instinct was that he was trying to get away . . . but he stood no chance of squirming past Suhail and the three men still with us in the room, and he was not making any forward progress, besides. I almost bent to grab him, then remembered my manners. "Suhail," I said sharply, and he turned around.

The man thrashed as Suhail rolled him onto his back and delved into his caftan. The thrashing did him no good: Suhail's hand emerged holding a small bag of powder, which had come open and was spilling its contents over his fingers. My heart sped up. "Here," I said, holding out one of the dishes. Suhail dropped the bag into it and dusted his hands off—then stood there, eyeing his own fingers warily. "What now?"

Without knowing what the powder was, I could only guess. It had not killed me or Tom . . . but what quantity had been going into our food? I took the corner of my headscarf in my hands and stared at it as if I had never seen fabric before, then blinked and shook sense back into my head. The knife was still on the floor. I picked it up and cut a square from the scarf, and Suhail used it to wipe his hands off. "Good thing Mother broke me of the habit of biting my nails," he murmured, trying to smile.

The magistrate arrived not long after that. I delivered the dish and its contents to him, while Suhail explained that the Yelangese man had been trying to disperse the evidence. Our prisoners were bundled off to the local gaol, but dealing with them would be delayed; Suhail insisted he needed to accompany me back to Dar al-Tannaneen, after a brief detour to scrub his hands clean under a street pump.

I almost told him the escort was not necessary—that I had, after all, come here on my own, and could very well go back the same way. But I remembered my conversation with Andrew in the desert, and bit my tongue. I was glad of Suhail's company, and the gossip-mongers be damned.

We walked in silence for a few minutes. Then, abruptly, Suhail said, "Did you think you could take on those men by yourself?"

My mouth had become very dry; I wished profoundly for a glass of lemonade. "I knew I would not have to do so. Even in those clothes, Suhail, I knew you. I recognized your stride."

He looked at me, startled. Then he looked away. I swallowed, trying to wet my throat, then said, "I was foolish, yes. But so were you. What if that man had friends with him?" He was lucky Maazir had chosen to run, rather than staying to fight.

In a low voice I almost could not hear through the noise of the market, Suhail said, "I was not thinking very clearly."

The weight of everything we were not saying hung between us, as if from a rope that might snap at any moment. Suhail had seen me in peril before. He had been with me in the diving bell when the sea-serpent attacked, and had resuscitated me after I drowned. We had ridden other serpents together, stolen a caeliger, taken part in the Battle of Keonga. But at no point during that time had he been asked to sit idly by; and none of that had involved such carefully directed malice as this. He had not taken it well.

Nor had I. My hands still shook every time I envisioned what must have happened in that cramped room while I was stopping Maazir. One strike with that knife, and Suhail might not be at my side now.

I licked my lips and tried to focus on practical matters. "That man. The Yelangese. Maazir was going to meet him?"

Suhail

"So it appears," Suhail answered, straightening his shoulders. "To report in, or get more poison—I'm not sure. We'll know more once they've been questioned."

That would not stop me from speculating now. "I imagine the Yelangese want to put a halt to our work, or at least to slow it down. Anything that might hamper Scirland—and Akhia, too—in getting more caeligers. We should count ourselves lucky they haven't been out in the desert—"

I stopped dead in the street, and so did Suhail. His eyes had gone wide. "The Banu Safr," he said.

"Would they ally themselves with the Yelangese?" I asked.

"Ally? No. Not as you are thinking of it. But take payment from, yes—especially if it gave them the chance to strike at my tribe." A muscle jumped in Suhail's jaw. "The feud goes back for generations. They do not lack the will to work against us, only the resources."

The difficulties the Aritat had faced out in the desert took on a new cast in my mind. As did every problem we had faced at the House of Dragons: how many of those had been accident, and how many the result of sabotage? I blessed the discipline of the Scirling army, and the tribal loyalty that meant the most highly placed Akhians at Dar al-Tannaneen were members of the Aritat. Without those forces to bind us together, we might have had a dozen Maazirs working against us.

"Isabella," Suhail said. "I know you do not think it necessary, but—you must not go anywhere without an escort now. You *or* Tom."

It was no longer a matter of propriety. Our capture of the Yelangese agent might put a stop to their efforts . . . or it might provoke them into trying something more extreme.

"Yes," I said, feeling cold down to the bone. "I think that is wise."

I was not present for the questioning of the prisoners. Such things were considered inappropriate for ladies; Tom, who could have gone, chose not to. "If it's anything like back home, it won't be pretty," he said, grimacing.

My feelings on the matter swung wildly back and forth. One moment, I did not like to imagine the magistrate beating a confession out of either man; the next, I remembered what they had done, and I felt they had brought it upon themselves. The bag of powder the Yelangese man had tried to spill was confirmed to be arsenic, which would have been lethal in larger or more prolonged doses. Maazir's home, when searched, turned up a cache of money that could not be explained by reputable means; there were people in the market who remembered him going to that building before, several times. We had evidence even before we had the confessions.

Security became a good deal more stringent. I no longer ambled off to the House of Dragons with Andrew in the morning. Instead he came with three other soldiers, all of them armed, and met up with Tom at the Men's House before coming to collect me. It felt excessive, and I said as much—but our escort remained. There were guards at the gate of Dar al-Tannaneen, patrols of the enclosures, and daily checks of the feed for humans and beasts alike.

This state of affairs did not persist for long, however. We had scarcely settled into our new routine when the announcement came that Colonel Pensyth wanted to see us first thing that morning.

"That doesn't sound good," Tom murmured as we made our way through the streets of Qurrat, bracketed by our guards.

"Andrew," I asked, "what is this about? Have the Yelangese made some kind of threat?"

My brother shook his head. "If they have, nobody's told me. I just know Pensyth wants to talk to you."

At least he had the consideration to meet with us right away, so I did not have to fret long. Tom and I were not even asked to sit down in the waiting room before his adjutant escorted us in to see the colonel.

I wasted no time in posing him the same question I had asked Andrew. Pensyth likewise shook his head. "No, not at all. In fact, given the recent . . . unpleasantness, you may be glad to know that you will not have to worry any longer. I've just received word: we are to close down."

"Glad" was not the word I would have used to describe my reaction. I sat open-mouthed, staring at Pensyth; Tom was doing the same. "Close down?" I said, a faint and disbelieving echo.

"Yes, Dame Isabella. The dragon-breeding programme is over."

"But—" All my words seemed to have gone astray. I floundered after them with clumsy hands. "You haven't even given us a *year*! We've scarcely gathered data on their breeding habits in the wild, the incubation of the eggs—let alone tried to apply what we've learned—"

Pensyth made a gesture I think was supposed to be mollifying. "I'm sorry, Dame Isabella. This wasn't my decision: it came to me from Lord Ferdigan in Sarmizi."

"Give us a chance, at least." Tom sounded as if someone

were strangling him. "Six months, even. If we cannot show substantial progress by then . . ."

He trailed off. Pensyth sat behind his desk, impassive. Unyielding. We would not have six months; we would not have six *days*. Even in my most cynical moments, I had not imagined they would pull the rug out from under us like this. The grand opportunity, the posting that might have been the pinnacle of my career: done. Ashes. Had Pensyth been within reach, I might have slapped him.

Tom recovered before I did. His voice heavy, he said, "What are we expected to do?"

"Naturally we'll have to wrap things up here," Pensyth said, with a jovial aspect that said he was relieved we hadn't protested more. "Might as well collect the bones from the adult specimens. You can return the eggs to the wild if you like, or dissect them—it doesn't much matter. The juveniles might pose a bit of a problem, I suppose. But don't worry about tidying up the site itself; the sheikh's men will take care of that."

Bile rose in my throat at his cavalier suggestions. All our dragons, dead: not to learn anything, not because it was necessary, but simply because we no longer had a use for them. As if they were rubbish, to be disposed of by the least troublesome means, what little value possible extracted from them in the process.

I didn't hear the next few things Tom said, or Pensyth's responses. All I could think about was Lumpy. Ascelin. Saeva and Quartus and Quinta. Every dragon under our care, every living creature toward whom I had a responsibility. Soon they would be dead, and I would be on a ship back home.

The conversation ended. Tom led me from the office, one

hand on my arm, and to the devil with what people might say. He took me up onto the wall that surrounded the compound; I think he wanted to make certain I was far away from anyone else when I finally exploded.

But I could not explode. I was too devastated for that. I sagged against the hot stone of the wall and said dully, "I was right. They had already decided this was a failure, but they didn't want to blame Lord Tavenor. So they brought us in to be scapegoats." Tears threatened, burning my eyes. I tensed my jaw and forced them back. "I thought they would at least give us a year."

Gazing out over the buildings and enclosures of Dar al-Tannaneen, Tom shook his head. The wind lifted his hair, laid it down again in disarray. "This doesn't make sense."

"Oh, it makes every bit of sense," I said bitterly.

"No, I mean—" Tom stopped, hands gripping the edge of the wall. Then he turned to me, suddenly animated. "Pretend for a moment that the Akhians have gotten tired of us being here, and want us out. What do we do? Not you and I, but the Scirlings as a whole. The army."

"Apparently we go."

He chopped one hand through the air. "No. If it's the Akhians who want us out, we argue. Try to prove our worth. Even if it's just a stalling tactic—look, this enterprise, this alliance, has given Scirland a military foothold in Akhia. We're stronger than they are right now, but we need their dragons. If they decide they'd rather bow out of the whole mess, we don't just accept that; we fight it. Pensyth would be demanding we come up with something to prove our worth. But he isn't."

"So it's Scirland instead," I said. "As I thought."

"But that doesn't make any more sense. *Think,* Isabella. Perhaps this is a waste of time, and the Crown no longer believes we'll succeed. Even so—why pull out? It gains them nothing, and loses our excuse to be here in Akhia, with a Scirling military garrison. What benefit could they possibly get from this?"

None. There was no reason to close us down, except that we were no longer worth the resources spent to maintain our presence here. And however small our chance of success . . .

A small chance was better than none. They would only recall us to Scirland if they didn't *need* us anymore. If they had found a different solution to the problem.

On a breath that did not carry beyond the two of us, Tom said, "*Synthesis.*"

The artificial production of dragonbone. Not just the substance itself—we'd been able to do that for years—but its structure, the microscopic lattice that gave it its tremendous strength. We were trying to breed dragons for their bones, so we could build caeligers and other devices that would allow our nation to maintain its power in the world, to meet the Yelangese and defeat them. But if our people could make the necessary material in a laboratory, it would be a damned sight easier than what we'd been attempting at Dar al-Tannaneen.

Someone at home had figured it out. We had synthetic dragonbone, and Tom and I were no longer relevant.

Conflicting emotions warred within my heart. Synthesis would obviate the need to slaughter dragons for their bones—perhaps. Scirland would not need to kill them, at least. But we would guard the secret of the process jealously, far better than Tom and I had guarded the notes taken from Gaetano

Rossi's laboratory. Every other nation would still be reliant on natural sources to supply them. If my country launched an aerial armada, others would be forced to reply, by whatever means they could.

And even though I had hoped for that success ever since we discovered preserved dragonbone in Vystrana, I could not help resenting its effect now. Whatever the reason, it was still robbing me of my place here. I doubted the Crown would be announcing its achievement, not any time in the near future—which meant Tom and I would be going home in disgrace, the naturalists who had failed to breed dragons. I would leave behind this place, my work . . . Suhail.

Unless . . .

"What are you thinking?" Tom asked warily.

"I am thinking," I said, choosing my words with care, "that sending us home like this is very foolish."

Tom cocked his head to one side, frowning. I elaborated. "Not simply the loss of what scholarly advances we might make here—though yes, that as well. But it did not take you long at all to guess why our work was no longer needed. Who is to say another will not make the same leap?"

"The Yelangese."

"We certainly know *they've* been keeping watch on us. Other nations may guess as well. Sending us home is as good as sending up a banner that proclaims, *Scirland has found a solution.*"

Tom leaned back against the edge of the wall, crossing his arms over his chest. His energy had subsided, leaving him quiet and grim. "They won't be able to stop it—not short of serious action, at least, that would amount to a declaration of war. But it would give them time to prepare."

Our military minds would want to keep this a secret as long as they could, so as to get the advantage over our enemies. I had no particular interest in supporting that aim; wars, to me, were a thing that made my work more difficult (although honesty prompts me to admit that they have on occasion also facilitated it: viz. our presence in Akhia). In this instance, however, our goals might align. "If we were permitted to stay here and carry on our work, it might mislead them for a while longer."

He stared at me. Then he said, enunciating each word with distinct clarity, "That would make us bait."

I had not thought of it from that angle. Weighed the benefit of a smokescreen against the cost of maintaining it, yes; considered the associated risk, no. "We're already bait, Tom. Had we not met with Pensyth this morning, everything would be as it was yesterday: the two of us working to breed dragons, and the Yelangese trying to stop us."

"There's a bit of difference between swimming in shark-infested water because you're trying to retrieve something from the bottom, and staying in just because you're already there and haven't been eaten yet."

"We are still trying to retrieve something from the bottom. All that has changed is whether anybody on shore cares whether we—Oh, hang the metaphor." I pressed my fingertips to my temples. The removal of poison from my diet had improved my health, but the sun was bright, and I had left my hat behind in Pensyth's office. A headscarf alone did nothing to shade my eyes. "Look, the Yelangese have been rather less dangerous to us than some of the other things we've faced. Poison, at least, may be watched for. Diseases and storms come regardless of caution. Do you want to stay here or not?"

He pressed his lips together, still staring at me. Then he

turned and went back to his previous pose, hands braced against the edge of the wall, looking out over the compound. This time I joined him.

It was a steep mountain we had set ourselves to climb, trying to breed some of the largest and most dangerous predators in the world. I had entertained any number of doubts as to whether we would succeed—and still did. But to think only of that obscured the fact that there were splendid views to be had from partway up the slope, and satisfaction to be found in attaining the tops of various ridges, even if they were not the peak itself.

It was, apparently, my turn to wander off down the twisty byways of metaphor. In simple terms, we had done a certain amount of good work at Dar al-Tannaneen, and could still do more. Even if we failed to reach our main goal, that should not be permitted to overshadow everything else we might achieve.

And there were creatures down there in the compound whose lives depended on us. One could certainly argue that the lives of the dragons had not been improved by our interference; but having interfered, I could not simply wash my hands of them.

"Yes," Tom said quietly. "I want to stay."

I put one hand over his, pressed until he turned his hand palm-up and gripped mine in return. "Good," I said. "Now let's go talk to Pensyth."

SIXTEEN

Petitioning Lord Ferdigan—A change of habitat—A different fire in the night—Ascelin—A prisoner—In my defense—Andrew's offer

We had to choose our words carefully. It seemed quite likely that the colonel had no awareness of the laboratory side of matters; Lord Ferdigan might, but he would not thank us for opening our mouths any wider than necessary. In the end, we persuaded our military overseer to give us time, to continue the project while our suggestion was referred up the chain of command.

But we also knew better than to trust that referral to a third party. "Your title will impress him more," Tom said.

I shook my head at once. "Were I a man, yes. But he is a military fellow; women are not part of his world, except as distant kin back home that he writes letters to from time to time." (The exceptions would not be the sort of women he would listen to with any respect.) "You are also a Colloquium Fellow, as I am not. Trust in that, Tom."

"And in my sex," he said wryly. "I would accuse you of wanting to dodge politics—I suppose saying that *does* amount to an accusation—but your points are fair regardless." He sighed heavily. "Then I suppose I pack my bags for Sarmizi."

I would have gone with him, but neither of us wanted to leave the House of Dragons unattended. Even though Pensyth had promised to give us time to appeal the decision to the general, it would be all too easy for him to begin arranging the closure, on the assumption that Lord Ferdigan would tell us to follow the orders we had been given. I would stay and keep our work going.

This meant taking in deliveries of eggs, which the Aritat were bringing according to the schedule Tom and I had developed. With the aid of an interpreter, I spent some time discussing improvements to our haulage methods, based on my records of the honeyseeker eggs. I knew making alterations now would bias our data: the more mature eggs would fare better regardless, simply by dint of longer residence in their natural habitat. Unfortunately, I lacked the control data to compare this against (previous eggs having been collected so haphazardly), nor could I afford to sacrifice some of this round simply for comparison. But neither could I wait an entire year to try again with new methods. Healthy eggs, or at least the hope thereof, had to trump proper experiment design.

At least I could use the information they provided to care better for the new arrivals. Qurrat was not nearly so warm as the Jefi would be by now, so we used braziers to warm the egg sands, trying to approximate the temperatures that would prevail farther south. While I waited for those to hatch, I tried to devise an exercise regimen for our adult drakes, on the theory that aggravating them into movement would improve their health and therefore their behaviour. I also kept watch on the ongoing honeyseeker project, as well as observing the juvenile drakes in their growth (and trying a few ill-fated experiments involving proximity between them and the adults)—in short, I tried to do the work of two people, and got very little sleep as a result.

A bare week into this, I said peevishly to Andrew, "Give me one good reason I should not simply sleep here."

My brother gaped at me. "*Here?* You mean—in your office?"

"Don't be ridiculous. There's no room for a pallet; I'd have to roll it up every morning or be stepping on it all day. But there are empty rooms. Surely I could use one."

"Why would you do that, when you have a perfectly good room in the city?"

I rose from my chair and paced restlessly. Even though I was tired, the whirl of thoughts in my head made it difficult to sit still. "Because it is *in* the city. I waste too much time coming and going from there. Not to mention the concerns about sabotage. What if the Yelangese take it into their heads to attack me there? Should I endanger Shimon and Aviva, just because they were willing to have me in their house?"

That sobered Andrew. "Even so—Isabella, this is a military post. Well, sort of. My point is, you'd be sleeping down the hall from military men."

"The same military men to whom I am already entrusting my safety. I fail to see why closer residence should be a problem." My tone dared him to argue.

Andrew dragged at the front of his uniform, making an exaggerated face. "You realize what will happen if you do this, don't you? *I'll* have to start sleeping here."

I stopped in my tracks, startled. "You mean—you haven't been?"

"No. At least, not all nights." He reddened. "I, ah—made alternate arrangements."

One part of me very much wanted to ask what those were; the other part very much did not. There are things I feel it is best not to know about the private life of one's brother. "I am sure I can manage very well on my own."

"Oh, I'm sure you can. The question is whether anybody else can cope with you managing." Andrew sighed dramatically. "I'll talk to Pensyth."

Unlike my brother, Pensyth was in favour of the arrangement, as it saved him the trouble of sending an armed guard to collect me from the Segulist Quarter every morning. A bedroom was made up for me, with a local girl visiting daily to help out; I took this as a positive sign, since anything that made my circumstances here seem more permanent argued in favour of the programme continuing. In order to encourage this thinking, I slept there the very next night—and that is how I came to be present when the House of Dragons was lit on fire.

We had men keeping watch, of course, but we had not fortified the place as well as we might. In the small hours of the night someone lofted an incendiary device through one of the broken shutters, and another was set at the shed where we kept feed for the livestock. A third I think was meant for the egg sands, but it caught in one of the spindly trees that remained from the estate's long-dead gardens, leaving the branches burning like a torch.

By the time I stumbled out of bed, the soldiers were rallying to fight the various blazes. I stared at the dancing flames, a sheet clutched around me as a nod to modesty. Indecision paralyzed me: what should I rush to save? The eggs? Our records? The adult drakes could survive well enough; they were out in the open, away from anything that could easily burn, and were resilient against fire besides, on account of their extraordinary breath. But the juveniles . . . their enclosures were much closer to the flames, and smoke inhalation could be a very real danger, especially for those whose health was not good.

I hurried toward that building, hiking up the sheet so I would not trip over its edge. The air was hazed enough to sting my lungs, though I had not begun coughing yet. I reached the building where we kept the juveniles and wrenched the door open, heart full of fear at what I might find.

The air inside was surprisingly clear, on account of being closed off. It would have been better to keep it that way, but I had no lantern, and did not want to fumble around looking for one. Instead I opened one of the windows, admitting enough moonlight for me to see my charges.

Most of them were awake, roused by the noise outside. They came to the bars of their cages as I approached, poking their muzzles through the gaps, snapping at me as if to ask why I had not brought any food. I knew better than to reach out, the way I might have with dogs or horses; they did not want their heads scratched for reassurance. Trying would only lose me a finger. But I peered closely at them, looking for signs of impending asphyxia, and found none. Even the ones that had not gotten up were only sleeping, occasionally cracking an eye to glare at those who disturbed their rest.

So far, then, they were safe enough. But if the fire spread, that might change very rapidly.

What would I do if it did? Set the juveniles loose? Some of them were relatively harmless—like Lumpy, who could not move fast enough to catch anybody who saw him coming. But the eldest, feisty Ascelin, was a different matter. It was even possible he could fly away, though his wings had not seen much exercise in his life.

Would I risk that in order to avoid suffocating him with smoke? I barely even had to ask myself that question before I had my answer:

Yes, I would.

All of that, however, was putting the cart before the horse. Such measures might not even be necessary. If I opened another set of shutters, I would be able to see the fire and make a more educated decision. Before I could move, though, someone else came through the door.

The angle of the moonlight left his face in shadow. All I had to go on was his silhouette, which showed me the hunched posture of a man who does not want to be seen. He froze when he spotted me, and in one hand he clutched something I could not make out. Then he lifted it, and the blade caught the light.

It was a sword.

And not an Akhian scimitar, either. The blade was straight, its style unfamiliar to me. I did not need to know its type, though, to make the appropriate calculations. The cages were large enough that he would not be able to kill the juveniles if they hung well back . . . but some of them would not, especially if they smelled blood. Oh yes: I had no doubt that this man had come here to kill our immature drakes. He seemed too surprised to find me there for me to think I was his target.

I stood motionless, my back to the cages. I had no weapon with me; I had even dropped my bedsheet during the inspection. Armed with nothing more than my nightgown, I had no chance against that long blade.

He snapped something in a language I did not understand. The sound of it, though, told me what the shadows had hidden.

This man was Yelangese.

I retreated one step, praying Ascelin would not try to get a mouthful of my arm. Of all the juveniles for me to put at my back, he was both the best and the worst, depending on how he chose to act. "Please," I said. "I just came to make certain they were well—" This in Scirling; I could not have answered him in Yelangese if I wanted to. But the point was not to communicate so much as to delay.

He was not fooled. He came forward, far enough for me to make out his features and see him frowning at me. Another question, no more comprehensible than the first—but I suspect, based on his tone, that he demanded to know what I was doing.

A moment later, he had his answer.

I had, behind the cover of my body, worked free the hook that held the cage shut. Upon his words, I yanked the door open and stood well clear.

For Ascelin inside that cage, the man's sudden forward leap looked precisely like an attack. And so it was: one aimed at me, but my feisty charge showed no inclination to differentiate.

He got a mouthful of the man's upraised sword arm, preventing the downward stroke. The man howled and thrashed at him, ineffectually at first, then jamming his thumb into Ascelin's eye. This indeed persuaded the drake to pull back; but he took a portion of flesh with him, and the sword fell with a clatter. After that it became even more gruesome, and I retained barely enough wit to flee out the door and close it behind me. The window, I prayed, would be too small for Ascelin to climb through.

Our soldiers and labourers soon had the fires under control; the flames had not taken too firm hold before they were noticed. Only the tree was still burning brightly by then, and that only because it was judged a lesser priority. I found Andrew outside the barracks, and brushed away his exclamations over my half-clad state. "I need help with the juveniles," I said. "One of them, at least. I may have set him loose, and I cannot get him back into his cage on his own."

"Set him *loose*?" Andrew repeated, staring. "Why on earth—and in your nightgown—Isabella, what the *hell* is going on?"

"I will show you," I said. Which was, more than anything, an expression of shock: the heat of the moment having faded, I was now shaking, and trying very hard not to think about what I had done to that man. No one can witness as many dragons hunting as I have without acquiring a strong stomach; but there is a great deal of difference between watching a gazelle be crunched in a dragon's jaws and watching a man suffer the same fate. I had seen men killed in such ways before, but I hope I will never become accustomed.

What my brother said when the door to the room of cages was opened, I will not print here. Suffice it to say that it was very foul and very appalling. I waited outside while the men got the young drake under control; this was not terribly difficult, as food made him logy and slow. Once he was back in his cage, I went with Andrew to report the matter to Pensyth.

"Good *God*, woman," the colonel said when I was done

explaining. "I heard the story of what you did in Keonga, but—damn me, I didn't think it was true."

I flinched. He sounded horrified, not impressed; and well he might be. What I had done here was not admirable, however effective it might have been. The man's screams were echoing in my memory, and I had grown very cold.

Fortunately Andrew noticed this latter. "God, Isabella—here, let me fetch you a blanket." Pensyth and I sat in silence, him staring at me, me trying not to meet his gaze, until Andrew came back with one of the scratchy blankets from the soldiers' quarters. I clutched this around me gratefully, more for warmth than modesty. Desert nights could be chill, even in summer, and all the heat had long since gone out of me.

"Sir," Andrew said once I was covered, "Wardinge says we got one of them. Problem is, he doesn't speak Scirling or Akhian."

His words roused me from my half-trance. "Colonel, if you do not have anyone who speaks Yelangese . . ." Pensyth made a gesture which I interpreted as admission that he did not. "The sheikh's brother does. Suhail ibn Ramiz. And I imagine the Aritat will want to be involved in this investigation."

I also imagined Pensyth would like to keep them out of it—but he didn't stand much chance of that. His jaw tightened, and he looked over my shoulder to Andrew. My brother must have nodded or shrugged, because the colonel said, "Thank you. For that and for your . . . quick thinking in defense of this place. I'll have Captain Hendemore escort you back to your room."

Ordinarily I would have objected at being shuffled out of the way, but not this time. I took the blanket with me, and curled up tight beneath my covers until sleep finally came.

* * *

Despite my disturbed night, I woke early, out of habit. And it was a good thing I did, because no matter what had happened in the night, the business of the House of Dragons must go on.

The labourers were feeding the drakes. We tried to approximate their schedule in the wild, supplying them with meat every three days; it just so happened that this was one of their days. I tried not to look at the bloody flesh as the men dropped it in the scales, focusing all my attention on the needle and the notes I made. It was important to know how much each beast ate—even if I would have been happier not recording that Ascelin had no appetite today.

I saw when Suhail arrived, accompanied by a number of other Akhian men, but made no effort to join them. I had no wish to observe the prisoner's interrogation, and trusted that I would learn the results in due course. When the bare minimum of my duties was done, I went and sat on one of the walls, letting the hot summer breeze ruffle my scarf and the sun sink into my bones.

Andrew found me there. "Are you trying to roast yourself?"

"It is the one place in Dar al-Tannaneen I will not be interrupted," I said. "Or when I am—as now—I can see it coming, and prepare."

He settled next to me, back against the stone of the parapet. "What's on your mind?"

It was a peculiar relief not to have him ask whether I was all right. We both knew I was not, and needn't pretend. "What Pensyth said last night. About what I did in Keonga."

"The battle, you mean."

I was sitting with my knees drawn up to my chest: not a very ladylike pose. I wrapped the fingers of one hand tight around the other and looked away. "After you cut that man's throat outside the Banu Safr camp, it bothered me a great deal. Seeing you kill someone. The more I think about it, though . . . no one died when I used the sea-serpent to bring down the caeliger. But in Vystrana I provoked the rock-wyrms into attacking the boyar and his men. In Mouleen we put fangfish into the water to slow the Labane, and last night I let Ascelin out of his cage to savage that man."

Andrew—ordinarily the most voluble of my brothers—held his peace while I marshaled the words and got them out. "I have not killed anyone directly. But time and time again, I use dragons to do the work for me."

"They aren't weapons," Andrew said. "They're animals. Doing what they do. You just . . . make use of that."

"Is it any different? It might even be worse. A sword or a gun is made for killing, and does not care if its owner uses it thus. These are living creatures. They have other purposes besides murder—and they are not mine to use."

Andrew picked at his fingernails. "You keep putting yourself in dangerous situations, Isabella. You have to defend yourself *somehow*." He hesitated, chewing on his lower lip. "Do you . . . want me to teach you how to shoot a gun?"

I had not expected the offer. I had not expected anything at all; I was simply wallowing in the realization of my own deeds, without much thought for what I would do going forward. Andrew spoke with the air of a man who knew he would be banished from family holidays forevermore if word got out of what he'd done . . . but he was willing.

Was I?

I tried to envision it. Myself, with a rifle over my shoulder or a pistol at my hip. I did frequently end up in dangerous situations—and when I did, I was dependent upon those around me for defense. If not dragons, then other people: Andrew, cutting that man's throat. Dagmira, smashing a jar over Gaetano Rossi's head. The Moulish, threatening Velloin and the Yembe hunting party. Even the "pure" of Mouleen did not shy from the need for hunting or defending their land with force; they simply refrained from the act themselves, for reasons of religion. Was it any more moral to have others fight on your behalf?

I did not think it was—and yet. Had I been carrying a weapon during my various misadventures, who knew what might have gone differently? My enemies might well have treated me more harshly, because of the threat I posed. *I* might have treated *them* more harshly. There is a proverb that says, *To a man with a hammer, everything looks like a nail.* If I had a gun, it would shape my thinking; the violent response would always be there. A possibility—sometimes a tempting one. It might result in more death; and one of those deaths might be my own.

Armed or not, I might die in the field. But I would rather die failing to think my way out of a situation than failing to fight my way out.

"I should like to be able to *defend* myself," I said, choosing my verb carefully. "Not to shoot or to kill—because I do not want to become the sort of person for whom that is a standard option when trouble arises. But I know there are ways to make myself a little safer, and learning them might be valuable."

(Not long after my return from Akhia, I made an offhand mention of this conversation during a public event in

Falchester—omitting that it was my brother who made the offer. Owing to the degree of celebrity I enjoyed by then, my words were taken up by a great many people: some of them treating it as a rallying cry, others as a sign of how far our society has fallen. Of the latter I will say nothing, but of the former I will note that there are individuals who have undertaken to teach the simple basics of defense to ladies. I deplore the need for such things . . . but so long as the need exists, I cannot fault anyone for protecting herself. Especially not when I chose to do the same.)

The fruits of that conversation did not come immediately. I had the House of Dragons to take care of, and there was no privacy in which Andrew could teach me anything, unless we turned my bedroom into a training ground. But even having addressed the issue lifted a good deal of the weight from my heart; and so I was able to resume my work with a much clearer mind.

SEVENTEEN

A history of sabotage—Our chances of success—The future of Dar al-Tannaneen—Six for the desert—Wisdom and the lack thereof

Tom's news upon his return was mixed.

"We can stay," he said, putting that first because he knew nothing else he said would leave a mark on my brain until that part had been laid to rest. "Lord Ferdigan was *very* keen to send you home, on the grounds that it's all well and good for me to risk my neck, but not so acceptable for you."

"As if I have not risked my neck without his permission on many occasions," I said with a sniff. "That is excellent news—but you have the look of a man who has not said everything yet."

"Indeed." Tom dropped wearily into his office chair; his had been a strenuous journey, with no time wasted. The chair creaked in protest at this treatment. "The bad news is that we won't have any additional funding, and may even lose some."

Lose some? I dreaded to think where cuts might be made. Feed? Labour? We had our premises from the caliph; I had no idea whether we were paying rent to him or the local emir for the privilege, but surely relocating us would be even more expensive. "So much for moving the females and males a sufficient distance apart, I suppose. Why is he tightening our belts?"

Tom rubbed his eyes. "I feel like the sand has scoured my corneas right off. From Lord Ferdigan's perspective, this isn't a research programme anymore; it's a diversionary tactic. And we don't need a lot of money to be a diversion. In some ways, we're more effective if we're strapped for cash; then the Yelangese will think we don't have a prayer of making real progress."

We *wouldn't* have a prayer of it, at this rate. I went to my own chair and settled into it, much more gently than Tom had done. "Has anyone told you what the Yelangese did while you were away?"

Judging by the way Tom's hand froze in midair, they had not. It fell to me to tell him of the arson, and the man captured and questioned afterward. "It went further than we realized," I said. "The sabotage, that is. Do you recall Prima dying? He said someone crept in and gave her poisoned meat in the night, for quite a while. We thought her appetite was failing solely due to ill health; but the ill health was not accidental, and she was getting additional meals besides."

The tension in Tom's shoulders said that it was a very good thing none of the saboteurs were in front of him right now. "Then they moved on to poisoning us."

"They would have started sooner, but we went into the desert. Their leader judged that it would be better to let blame fall on the Banu Safr, rather than continue to risk revealing themselves at Dar al-Tannaneen." I sighed and sat back. The wicker bottom of my chair sagged beneath me. "What will come of this, I do not know, except that it will not be good."

Tom's voice was quiet and grim. "We thought the first act of war would be a fleet of caeligers moving into position. Instead it might be a firebomb thrown through a window."

The first act of war had been the Battle of Keonga . . . or the caeliger Suhail and I stole from Rahuahane . . . or the Marquess of Canlan sending men to break into Frederick Kemble's laboratory . . . or myself taking Gaetano Rossi's notebook from the cellar beneath Khirzoff's lodge. How far back did the chain stretch? At what point could one circle an incident and say, *This is where it began*?

For nations, it was the point at which they issued formal declarations of war. And it was indeed possible that the spark which lit that fuse would be the one that set the House of Dragons on fire.

We had come here to further the war effort, but our importance in that regard had been superceded by breakthroughs elsewhere. Our attempt to delay conflict by continuing our work had possibly done the opposite. It was enough to make me question everything we were doing here. "Tom . . . do you think we *can* succeed? At breeding dragons, I mean."

He left off rubbing his eyes and regarded me silently. His skin was as tanned as I think it could be, but still more red than tan; the whites of his eyes were slightly bloodshot. He looked tired. I did not imagine I looked a good deal better. Our lives here were not so hard as all that—they had been harder at many points in Mouleen—but there was also no end in sight. For everything we had learned, we still had no answer to the basic question we had come here to address.

"Eventually, yes," Tom said slowly. "One way or another, we'll figure it out. Or someone will. But it will take a long time."

Years, in all likelihood. Science of this sort is a matter of testing theories and methods, seeing the results, refining them and testing again. Some of that process could happen within a single breeding season, but not all. "I've been thinking about the mating flights, and the role of temperature in egg incubation. What if it plays a role in conception as well? We know the flights *must* heat the dragons tremendously—all that exertion in the middle of the day. There are species of pine whose cones do not open and deposit their seeds until a forest fire comes. What if drakes are the same? How are we to breed them without mating flights? Are we to build giant ovens for them to lounge in?" I stopped, shaking my head to keep myself from rambling on more. "We have too many questions. I could be here the rest of my life and never answer them all."

"That's scholarship. There's always more to learn." Tom sighed and leaned forward, bracing his elbows on his knees and linking his hands together. "But yes, I see your point. Are you saying you want to quit, after all?"

"*No*." My vehemence startled even me. A moment ago I had been considering that, without thinking about it directly; but the moment he asked, my indecision vanished. "I just wonder—when we will say we have done enough."

For that question, I had no answer. Tom did not have one, either, and we sat in silence for a long time before picking up our work once more.

The mood at Dar al-Tannaneen had changed. Whatever pretense we maintained, the forward momentum of the programme had faltered, and everyone felt it.

It is difficult to describe the effect this had on me. I was still working with dragons on a daily basis, in a context where I was—albeit slowly, with grudging will—being accepted as a respectable intellectual; these things did not lose their savour. And yet, I think on some subconscious level I had begun to question the worthiness of what I was accomplishing there. Despite what I had told myself about mountains and the climbing thereof, the value of views from partway up the slope even if one did not reach the summit . . . I had come here to climb the entire mountain. It was disheartening to consider that I might have to surrender that goal.

We simply had not realized how tall the peak was, and how steep its slopes. Andrew had said it, when I first arrived in Akhia: we expected that our superior scientific knowledge should vanquish this problem, even though it was sufficiently intractable as to have stumped the world for millennia. Breeding large predators in captivity is not easy, even when they are not dragons. How many years was I prepared to spend on this challenge?

I found myself staring at a piece of paper one night, contemplating what I might write to Jake. His summer holidays would begin soon; he wanted to join me in Akhia for the duration. If he came, would it be his one chance to see this country before I departed? Or would it be an acknowledgment that I lived here now, and would for the foreseeable future?

The decision might not be mine to make. Eventually the news of synthesis would become public, and at that point, the Crown would have no reason to maintain us here at all.

I had not yet dressed for bed. Although it was late, and as

usual I would need to rise early the next morning, I left my chair and went for a walk around the compound.

Guards still patrolled the site, although the Yelangese leader had apparently been the man Ascelin killed. I nodded a greeting to one, who surprised me by saying, "Is everything all right, Dame Isabella? You and Mr. Wilker are both out late."

"Tom is up?" I said. "Do you know where I might find him?"

The soldier directed me to the pits that held the adult drakes. Arriving there, I saw Tom leaning against a railing, one knee bent, his foot propped on the lowest bar. He turned as I approached, and did not appear surprised to see me.

"I've been thinking," he said.

I joined him at the rail. "As have I. But let's hear yours first."

"The *Basilisk*," Tom said. "We managed that voyage without any support from the Crown."

He and I had known one another too long for me not to guess where his thoughts might be aimed. "A voyage of limited duration and an ongoing research programme are rather different things."

"True. But that doesn't mean it's impossible." He kept his voice low; Quinta was not far away, a dimly seen shape sleeping in her little cave. We did not want to rouse her. "Between the two of us, we correspond with just about every dragon naturalist in Anthiope. We're even friends with a few. The army wouldn't look kindly on other people getting involved just yet, of course—this is still their enterprise. But when they lose interest . . ."

My mind was already racing down the path he had revealed. We would have to lay the foundations ahead of time—that was certain. If we waited until the army closed Dar al-Tannaneen down, it would be too late; our adults would be slaughtered, our juveniles and eggs disposed of by one means or another, and everything here would have to start from scratch. If we already had interested parties lined up, though . . .

Then Dar al-Tannaneen might persist beyond this moment, and beyond our involvement.

It was not the peak we had set out to scale. But it was a worthy challenge, and one I could take pride in. If I walked away from Akhia knowing I had helped create something of lasting importance, I could rest a good deal better at night.

"What thoughts were keeping you awake?" Tom asked, when the silence had grown too long.

I shook my head, smiling. "They do not matter now. You have given me a solution already."

Many people know that the International Fraternity of Draconic Research has its roots in the House of Dragons in Qurrat. I have long made a point of noting that it was Tom, not I, who first had the idea of transforming our military commission there into a collaborative research programme that would bring together naturalists from many countries. But very few people are aware that it began on a quiet night at the edge of Quinta's enclosure, when neither Tom nor I could sleep for uncertainty of what our future, and that of Dar al-Tannaneen, would hold.

I got very little sleep at all that night, my mind awhirl with notions of who to contact, already composing the letters in my head. It would not be easy, of course—but for the first time in months, I felt that my path ahead was clear.

I have never been very good at following a path.

Our second desert trip became the focus of my efforts, to the point where it bordered on obsession. I knew this might be the last bit of work Tom and I were able to conduct in Akhia, and I was determined that it would be as productive as I could possibly arrange.

The Jefi in summer, however, is not a place within human control. "You want to go back *out there*?" Andrew said, incredulous. "Isabella—you do realize it gets above forty degrees, don't you? Even as high as fifty, I've been told. And there's no water to be found anywhere."

"Now *that* is preposterous," I said. "There are oases in the Labyrinth."

My brother made a strangled noise. "Wait. You don't just want to go into the Jefi . . . you want to go into the *Labyrinth of Drakes*?"

"Of course. Why do you think it has that name? There are drakes there, Andrew, and that is what I am here to study. They nest there, they lay their eggs there—"

"—they eat people alive there—"

"It is summer. They will be dozing in the heat. And when else am I to go to the Labyrinth? In the winter it was too dangerous because of the rains, and the risk of flood. This is much safer."

"Safer" was, of course, a relative term. The Labyrinth is a treacherous place in any season. It is easy to become lost in its winding canyons; there are predators that view travellers as attractive meals, drakes not least among them. Oases exist, but finding them is more easily said than done. On paper that territory belongs to the Aritat, but at that time of year they are elsewhere, in lands that can support their herds of camels. The depths of the Jefi are abandoned to merchants and wild animals, the former tracing carefully defined routes from one water source to another, the latter often haunting the same spots.

We could not take a large group. There is often safety in numbers, but not under these conditions; more people would mean more demand for water, and we could all too easily drain a spring dry, leaving ourselves to die of dehydration. We could not stay long in any one place, no matter what intellectual temptations we found. As soon as our supplies fell to a certain threshold, we must retreat, or face the consequences.

"At least it will be dry," I said to Tom at one point, trying to make light of the dangers. "Perhaps I will finally get rid of the mold that coated me in Mouleen."

Tom and I would go; that was certain. Andrew would go as well, despite my protests. "How am I to show my face at home if I don't?" he demanded. "Mother may not approve of your work, but she would approve even less of me abandoning you to die in it. No, much better that I should die with you than show myself anywhere near her afterward."

We were not so stupid as to go alone, of course. Our guide would be al-Jelidah, the Ghalbi fellow who had assisted us during the winter. He knew the Labyrinth better than any man living: every sliver of shade, every crack where water might be found. With us would also come Haidar, who had assisted our efforts before. That made our party five, and on Haidar's advice, we should take no more than six.

I said to Tom, "I want our sixth to be Suhail."

His expression showed wariness. "Is that wise?"

"I do not care if it is wise. I do not want to see the Labyrinth of Drakes—the site of so many legendary Draconean ruins—without him at my side."

Tom was sitting on his haunches alongside Quartus' enclosure when I said this to him. He ran one hand through his hair, then wiped it on his trousers. Even this close to the river, we laboured under a constant film of dust and sand. It mixed with sweat to form a gritty paste that no amount of bathing could dispose of, for no sooner was one clean than the paste built up again. In the Jefi and the Labyrinth it would be worse, for there we would lack the water to bathe in. "You know what they will say about you."

"They are already saying it. I do not *care*." A tight sensation burned behind my sternum as I said this. My entire life I had gone back and forth between two extremes, the one disclaiming all concern for what people might think, the other carefully weighing the cost. I had spent eight months here in Akhia listening to the second voice. My patience for it was wearing thin.

Tom said, "*He* might care."

"For his own reputation? Or for mine?" I put up a hand before Tom could answer that. "He has been in the desert before—in the Labyrinth itself. I trust him to bring us out of there alive. Al-Jelidah I do not know, not truly; Suhail I do. He has saved my life before."

I gave Tom some time to consider this. It was, after all, not only *my* reputation I would be endangering, or even Suhail's.

Tom had fought to have me included at Dar al-Tannaneen, when he could have taken the opportunity for himself with far less struggle. What I did here reflected on him, too.

"Ask him," Tom said at last. "It isn't our decision to make—not alone."

"Thank you," I said in response to his unspoken agreement. "I am sure we can find a way to make this work."

EIGHTEEN

A perfectly respectable meeting—Obstacles—A solution—"Why?"—Revenge upon my brother—Cautions to the reader—Various reactions—That night

I thought about approaching Mahira for aid. She had assisted us before, arranging that meeting in the garden; she might do so again. But such an approach smacked of the clandestine, which would not serve my purposes at all. There was nothing to be ashamed of in recruiting the aid of an experienced desert traveller. If it was permissible for me to work with al-Jelidah and Haidar, why not Suhail?

Our enterprise had a small stock of official letterhead, which I appropriated for this task. That very afternoon, before I could begin to doubt myself, I wrote a message and sent it to the sheikh's household, requesting Suhail's presence at Dar al-Tannaneen at his earliest convenience.

A reply came back before sunset, saying he would come the following morning. I notified Tom of this, so that he might be in attendance for the meeting—I did not use the word "chaperon"—and failed almost entirely to sleep that night.

The next morning I rose and dressed with more care than usual, as compensation for my poor rest. I made my rounds of the site while Tom made his and, having finished before him, went to the office to await the day's next task.

It was not long at all before Lieutenant Marton tapped on

the door and opened it, saying, "Dame Isabella, Hajj Suhail ibn Ramiz is here to see you."

The distracted thought went through my mind that I ought to tell the poor lieutenant he need not be so formal with me anymore. I did not follow through on this, however, because the rest of me was occupied with a more pressing matter. "Where is Tom? He was supposed to be here."

"I'm sorry, Dame Isabella." Marton shifted uncomfortably from one foot to the other. "I think he's been caught by some business outside."

("Caught by some business," indeed. Had I known at the time what was transpiring . . . in truth, I do not know what I would have done. Perhaps it is better that I did not.)

I wavered. Should I ask Suhail to wait? It would be the proper thing to do, and yet—"Show him in," I said. As I had told myself before: there was nothing to be ashamed of here. We were conducting official business. If any prying eyes or ears spied on our interactions, they would see nothing worthy of gossip.

The formality of the entire thing had Suhail's eyebrows up as he came in. He gave me a very correct greeting, though, not even touching his heart, which might have signaled inappropriate warmth. When that was done, he said, "I understand from Haidar that you are going back out into the desert."

"Yes, in late Messis—earlier if we can manage it. And that is why I've asked you here today." I tucked my hands beneath the edge of the desk, where no one could see if I fidgeted. "You have traveled extensively in that area, have you not? The Jefi in general, and the Labyrinth of Drakes specifically. In the summertime, no less, so as to avoid the risk of flood."

Suhail nodded. "I would be glad to offer any advice I can."

"I intend that you should have every opportunity to give us that advice. I would like—" I caught myself, cursing inwardly. "That is, Tom and I have discussed it, and we would like you to accompany us."

He had guessed it before he even came there. He must have, because his head began to shake even before I finished my statement. "Umm Yaqub . . . that will not be possible."

"Why not?" I pressed my lips together, not continuing until I was certain I could do so without my tone growing too sharp. "We shall have Andrew with us. Is that not enough to make everything proper?"

"Propriety is not the problem." Suhail bent his head, looking as if he wanted to press his fingertips to his temples, banishing a headache. "Rumour is."

I gritted my teeth. "We have done nothing to encourage that."

"Nothing?" He laughed, and it carried a rueful edge. "Had I gone home immediately after you arrived in camp, that might have been true. But I did not want to flee the moment you appeared, so I stayed a few days. Then the Banu Safr stole our camels. So I went to get the camels back. While I was gone, the Banu Safr stole *you*. So I went to get you back. And now every last member of the Aritat in the desert and the city alike is reciting that damned poem, about how I crept into the enemy camp in the dead of night to rescue a lady in distress. *You* have been admirably disciplined, but I . . ." He stopped, shaking his head.

Although he no doubt intended "admirably disciplined" as a compliment, I found myself regretting what I had done to deserve it. I could not keep from sounding plaintive as I said,

"Must that get in the way? As near as I can tell, your actions against the Banu Safr have won you acclaim, not censure. I understand that your brother is concerned for your family's image—but surely it does you more good to assist in this work, upon which he has staked the Aritat reputation, than to sit idle just to avoid me."

He did not answer immediately. The silence weighed upon me, until I voiced a bitter addendum. "Or is that the precise issue? Not propriety, nor even the general weight of rumour. Me, myself. I am a scandal at home; I carry that scandal with me here. Were I another woman—one whose reputation was not in doubt—then perhaps other factors could prevail. But I am not, and so a decent man may not associate with me."

The fury and shame of it burned within me. I was so very tired of being judged in such fashion; and yet, being tired of it achieved nothing. Whatever my feelings on the matter, I must endure. The only way to escape would be to surrender, to retreat into obscurity and never show my face again . . . and that, I would not do. The path I followed had brought me to Jacob, Tom, Lord Hilford, Suhail himself. I would not surrender the hope of this man's companionship, not if there were any possible way to keep it.

"It is not you," Suhail said. He spoke with conviction—as if his conviction could convince the world. "Isa—Umm Yaqub. I have nothing but the greatest respect and admiration for you, and will defend that against any man who says otherwise. But it is on behalf of your good reputation that I must not go with you. To travel like that, with a woman who is neither my kin nor my wife . . ."

"Then what if we were married?"

I sometimes imagine there is a clerk behind a desk situated

between the brain and the mouth. It is his job to examine utterances on their way out, and stamp them with approval or send them back for reconsideration. If such a clerk exists, mine must be very harried and overworked; and on occasion he puts his head down on the desk in despair, letting things pass without so much as a second glance.

Suhail stared at me. Then he looked at the floor. Then out the window. Then, in an uneven voice, he said, "A limited-term marriage? As you did with Liluakame, in Keonga. It . . . *could* work. The Sheqari school of jurisprudence holds that such things are permitted; the Taribbi says they are not. My brother is an adherent of the Uwani school, which has not rendered an opinion either way. But it might be possible."

Until he mentioned them, I had not known that limited-term marriages existed in Amaneen legal thought. It was an elegant solution: as he said, I had done something of the kind in Keonga, when I married and then divorced Liluakame so as to satisfy the demands of my status as *ke'anaka'i*. I might do the same here, silencing the gossips by making an honest woman of myself, so to speak. Of course it would cause even greater scandal back home when the marriage ended—we *certainly* did not have such arrangements in Scirling law—but for now it might suffice.

The clerk was still derelict in his duty. I said, "It was not a limited-term arrangement that I had in mind."

Suhail went utterly still. Then, very carefully, he spoke. "Did you just ask for my hand in marriage?"

My face could not have been hotter had a drake breathed on it. But I had advanced too far to retreat; the only way out was through. "I suppose I did. Dear heaven."

We sat in silence. I could not look away from Suhail, nor

him, apparently, from me. I could have drawn his portrait with my eyes closed; I had sketched him once during our voyage, and had looked at the image more times than I should admit in the years since. I thought of trying to find him long before I knew I was coming to Akhia. I never had the courage to follow through.

As a young woman, I had naively thought that I wanted Jacob Camherst to be my friend, because I could not conceive of a man being both friend and husband. But so he had been: husband first, then friend, as we inched our way toward something like a working partnership. Ill chance, however, had taken him from me before we could progress very far. Suhail had begun as a friend, and so I had thought of him, with great and focused determination . . . but that was not the entirety of what I wanted.

He said, a little breathlessly, "Everyone says you have no intention of marrying again."

I would have asked who *everyone* was and why they thought this was any of their business—but the matter at hand took precedence. "I *had* none. Until this very moment. Intentions change."

"Why?"

It was the same question I had asked Jacob, the day he came to propose marriage to me. I felt belated empathy for him, being put on the spot in such a fashion. "Because . . . because I do not want to go into the Labyrinth of Drakes without you. Never mind the practicalities of it; that is what we have al-Jelidah and Haidar for. I do not want to see that place without you at my side. I want you to show me the ruins that inspired you, and I want you present for any discoveries I might make. Now, and always."

I paused to swallow. My mouth had gone very dry. "I—I said a thousand times that I had no interest in marrying again because marriage would almost certainly place restrictions on my life. A widow has freedoms a wife does not. But when I look at you, I do not see obstacles for my career, I see—" My face burned even more. "I see wings. A way to fly higher and farther than I can on my own."

Far, *far* too late, it occurred to me that Lieutenant Marton could almost certainly hear us, as could anyone passing by the window.

Suhail eased forward in his chair. His eyes flickered as he searched my face: for what, I could not tell you. Evidence of insincerity? Of love? Of incipient lunacy? He would not find the first; the second, most definitely; the third, quite possibly.

The clerk had woken up at his desk and was frantically sorting through his records of what had transpired during his delinquency. Stammering, I said, "But you were considering only a limited arrangement. I presume too much, suggesting—"

"You presume nothing that is not true."

I fell silent, save for the beating of my heart, which felt as loud as a drum.

"I would marry you," Suhail said, "even if it meant my brother disavowing me on the spot. Which, I should warn you, he may do."

What would my mother say? I lost one husband in Vystrana, and found another in Akhia. Suhail's was not the only family that might have pronounced opinions on this matter. "We shall simply have to support ourselves with archaeology and dragons."

Suhail laughed, and it was the light, joyous sound I had first heard during the voyage of the *Basilisk*. "I honestly cannot tell whether you are the most practical woman I have ever met, or the most deranged."

"Why can it not be both?" I said. Inside I was soaring, as I had in the caeliger, on the glider I had called *Furcula*—only this time, I would not crash. "Now, before I commit an act that truly *will* start a scandal, tell me: how does one get married in Akhia?"

When I went in search of Andrew, I found him talking to Tom, with a demeanour I instantly recognized as suspicious.

Putting my hands on my hips, I glared in mock outrage at my brother and said, "Have you been delaying Tom on purpose?"

"Oh, good God," Tom said, taking out his pocket watch. "Have I been keeping Suhail waiting?"

"Not in the slightest." I advanced on Andrew, who retreated with a sheepish and hunted look. "I do not know what you intended, dearest brother, but you shall pay the price for your interference. Have you no care for your sister's reputation?"

"I—"

"This shall be your penance. You must come with us to the judge and stand as witness to our marriage."

There are certain moments in my life that I treasure. Most of them in one way or another have to do with dragons . . . but not all. The look on my brother's face in that instant is one of the latter.

It was not *quite* so simple as that, of course. We needed a marriage contract, though it was considered sufficient under

Amaneen law for the two of us to sort it out verbally in front of the astonished judge. Suhail had to give me a bridal gift; he offered the best camels and horses and all the supplies I might need for my second excursion to the desert, and I agreed that he need not present those things to me before the marriage itself was formalized. We rushed through these matters, for after so long spent pretending we were nothing more than respectful colleagues, we were eager to have the thing done.

I feel obligated to say I do not actually recommend such behaviour to young people (or even those not so young). There were a hundred questions Suhail and I did not answer before we wed. Our heady excitement carried us over them at the time . . . but sooner or later we must come down to the ground, and crashing, to return to my previous metaphor, was a distinct risk. I was from Scirland, he from Akhia: where would we live? His people do not have family names in the same manner as Scirlings: would I become Dame Isabella ibn Ramiz, or he Mr. Camherst, or some third alternative entirely? Amaneen custom says that the children of an Amaneen man must be raised in his faith, while Segulist custom says that the children of a Segulist woman belong to *her* faith: how would we resolve this dilemma? These are but three of the issues that would have been settled in any properly thought-out marriage contract, as opposed to the hasty verbal arrangement we made that day. There are any number of men and women who have rushed into such matters, expecting their love to overcome all complications, only to find later that it is not so simple.

And yet, any warning I issue must come with the inevitable footnote: it turned out splendidly for me. I regret nothing of what I did that day (though I tease Suhail that I should have held out for more camels). Take my cautions, then, for what you will.

Tom made no objection whatsoever; I suspect he was not very surprised. Andrew seemed astonished that his interference had borne such fruit—I believe he expected *something* to blossom, but not this quickly—and kept laughing immoderately throughout the entire affair. The judge was a friend of Suhail's, educated with him in boyhood, and while he took Suhail aside for a quiet conversation when we first appeared, whatever objections he raised then were settled without fuss.

Thus was I married, scarcely two hours after I impulsively offered for my husband . . . and then Suhail and I went to share the news.

My new brother-in-law, I think, knew what had happened the moment we walked through his door. Perhaps it was only that neither of us was maintaining a pretense of aloofness any longer: we engaged in no improper displays of affection, of course, such as young people are prone to nowadays, but I could smile at my husband without fear of overstepping some bound. The sheikh's wives were there, both of them women I had met only in passing: quiet, thin-faced Yusra, and stocky Iman one step behind her. Three of their children were present as well, including the youth Jafar, who would be fostered in the desert beginning next winter. Mahira finished out the set.

I watched their reactions closely as Suhail told them of our marriage. Yusra made little effort to hide her surprise; Iman, I think, was equally startled, but did a better job of concealing it. Jafar seemed more confused than anything else, while his two younger siblings showed no sign of caring about such tedious matters. Mahira appeared troubled, which did not surprise me, but did dishearten me a little. She had encouraged our friendship; of all of Suhail's family, I had the best hope of approval and support from her. But of course she was also the most pious of them all, and I suspected—rightly, as it turned out—that her mind had immediately gone to matters religious. It is permitted for an Amaneen man to wed a Segulist woman, but that does not mean the road is an easy one.

You may imagine for yourself how Husam reacted. He did not rage; in a way it might have been better if he had. Instead he maintained a stony composure, suitable for the presence of an outsider—which is to say, myself. This composure, however, did not prevent him from making his disapproval plain.

I did what I could to mollify him. "I have greatly esteemed your brother since I first met him," I said, omitting a reminder of where and how that had occurred so as to spare Husam's sensibilities. He certainly would not want to know that my very first sight of Suhail had been when he was shirtless and diving off a cliff. "He is one of the cleverest men I know, and both brave and kind. Your tribe has given tremendous support to our work at Dar al-Tannaneen; it is fitting, I think, that the friendship of our nations be sealed in this fashion."

That last may have been laying it on with a trowel. Husam's brows drew together so swiftly I almost felt the breeze. I was happy to let Suhail take over then, telling the tale of how we reached this point and answering their concerns—for after all, he knew his kin far better than I.

The tension was made worse by my still-imperfect command of Akhian, which meant that much of the swift-moving conversation passed me by. I sat quietly, hands knotted together, trying to read expressions without being obvious about it. When Suhail suggested I should return to handle matters at Dar al-Tannaneen, I accepted with relief, even though I had a suspicion my departure was intended to give them a chance to shout at one another in privacy.

But I reassured myself as I left. What could Husam do? He had no power to mandate his brother's divorce—and even if he did, doing so would have created even more scandal than we already had.

Oh yes, there was scandal. The initial stages of it are difficult to recall now; they have been thoroughly overwritten by the romantic version that followed. Any time a man and a woman wed in haste, people's minds inevitably leap to the assumption that he has assaulted (or she surrendered) her virtue, and that the natural result of this will be arriving within the year. Such was not the case with me, of course: I assure you that while I do sometimes elide details of my activities in this tale, I have not left out *that.* But it would be months before anyone would believe I was not so burdened—months in which rumour, already quite energetic, could get the bit between its teeth and race off for the hills. One particularly nasty bit of gossip said it was not Suhail who had dishonoured me, but someone among the Banu Safr; and he was showing pity on me by taking me under his wing. Had I known who began that tale, I would have chased them down and given them a very sharp piece of my mind.

But rumour is a creature with many heads and no body, and I had no way to hunt it, any more than I could smooth over matters with my new relations. All I could do was march into Colonel Pensyth's office that afternoon and announce, "I will of course be continuing my work as before; have no fear of that. But I will have no further need of my room here, for I have wed Suhail ibn Ramiz ibn Khalis al-Aritati."

His considered, restrained reply was, "You *what*?"

"Have wed Suhail ibn Ramiz. This morning: that is why Tom, Andrew, and I left. I do apologize for the disruption. There is nothing untoward about it, I assure you—only that he is a scholar and a gentleman, one I have respected for many years. And now he is my husband."

Pensyth had grown very red about the neck. "You sat in that very chair and swore to me you didn't want a husband."

"At the time, it was true. There may not be even two men living in the world whom I would have agreed to marry, certainly not on such short notice. But I do not need two; I only need one."

My words were more than a little giddy, which I imagine did not help my case at all. Pensyth said, "Is this your idea of *avoiding* a scandal?"

My giddiness did not take me so far as to speculate out loud regarding the alternatives. (And thank goodness for that.) I merely said, "Given that I have done nothing improper, I care not a fig for what people may say. Now that I am married, I desire precisely the same thing I did before I was married: to carry on with my research. Only now I will have Suhail's assistance in full."

Brash confidence can carry one past some obstacles—but not all. Before the night was out, I had to once again eat my words to Pensyth, this time regarding my lodgings.

Suhail arrived at the House of Dragons shortly after nightfall, looking grim and resigned. "I hoped that would go better," he admitted quietly to me.

My heart beat faster. "What happened?"

"I have not been disavowed—not yet, anyway. We'll see what Husam thinks when he wakes up tomorrow morning. But neither am I welcome in the house."

I thought of my own estrangement from my family, brought about when I pursued my dreams against their wishes. The familiar ache rose up within me. In no way could I bring myself to regret what Suhail and I had done . . . but I could, and did, regret what consequences it might carry for him. "I am sorry," I said, knowing it was thoroughly inadequate.

Suhail shook his head. "Do not be. I knew this was a risk, and I accepted it gladly. But in the meanwhile—I don't suppose this place can house us both?"

"Of course," I said instantly. "I may not be able to get a larger bed until tomorrow, but for tonight—"

He stopped me with one hand on my arm. So small a contact should not have meant so much—and yet it did. "For tonight," he said, "we will find a place to stay in the city. I look forward to sharing your work with you, my love . . . but there are some parts of you I will *not* share with your work. And tonight is one of them."

PART FOUR

In which we discover
a good deal more than
anyone expected

NINETEEN

Together in the House of Dragons—Ancient words—Testing to destruction—The desert in summer—Al-Sindi—Sandstorm—Broken shells

It is a common trope of romantic tales that the heroine declares she would gladly live in a garret if it meant being with her love. I was not prone to such dramatic utterances; but looking back on my actions, I suppose it would not have been far off the mark.

We resided at Dar al-Tannaneen for the remainder of my time in Qurrat, for Suhail remained unwelcome in his brother's house. I shifted my belongings to a larger chamber (one which, coincidentally, was farther removed from the barracks in which the others slept), and we made plans for furnishing the room in a comfortable style—but it will surprise few of my readers, I think, if I say that we never followed through on those plans. Our arrangements there were haphazard, and remained so until I departed.

What need had I of furnishings? I had Suhail; I had Tom; I had dragons. Under no circumstances was I going to drag Jake with us into the desert—no matter how much he might have pleaded to go—but I wrote to him saying that he could miss the fall term at Suntley and come join us in Akhia instead. Even if my commission ended before then, I thought

Jake deserved to reunite with his new stepfather and see where Suhail came from.

Much of the clutter in our new quarters belonged to Suhail, who relocated his entire library from his brother's house to Dar al-Tannaneen. "I've had to keep half of this hidden under my bed," he admitted, prying the lid off the first crate. "It will be nice to feel like an adult again."

I borrowed his crow-bar and opened another crate. It is inevitable, I suppose, that one cannot unpack a box of books efficiently, at least not when the books belong to someone else; I was immediately diverted by looking through them. Of course I could not read three-quarters of their titles, as they were in Akhian or some other language I did not know—but that did not stop me from looking. And when I lifted a heavy green volume from the bottom, I found something I *did* recognize.

"Is this Ngaru?" I asked, pointing at the symbol on the front cover.

You may think it strange, but I had quite forgotten about the rubbing of the Cataract Stone I gave to Suhail. He and I had rarely been in the same place since then—and when we were, our minds were fully occupied with other troubles (such as Maazir and the Yelangese poisoner), or else we were busily pretending to be near-strangers to one another. It was not that the Cataract Stone had never crossed my thoughts again; rather that it never did so at a point when I could ask Suhail how he was getting on with it.

As it turned out, he had not gotten very far at all. He said, "That was one of the books I had to hide under my bed. Which is a very great pity, since I had to sell my soul to Abdul Aleem ibn Nahwan to get my hands on it—that's a glossary and grammar of Ngaru." A mischievous grin spread over his face, and he took the volume from me. "But I suppose, now that I am the idle husband of a prominent naturalist, I must occupy myself with *something*. And I have no idea how to do needle-work."

Even with his aptitude for languages, it was slow going. Suhail had never studied Ngaru before obtaining that book from his fellow scholar, and had devoted the months between then and now to the necessary first step of familiarizing himself with it. Translating the inscription was a painstaking process, and he warned me at every turn that he would need an expert to verify his text before he would be at all confident in the result. Indeed, he would not even share what he had with me until he worked his way through the entire piece. It is a very good thing that the House of Dragons kept me busy, or I would have hovered over his shoulder until he went out of his mind with distraction. Even though ancient civilizations and dead languages have never been my greatest love, I was champing at the bit to know what the stone said.

He unveiled the fruits of his labour one night over a private dinner. "The beginning of it is not the kind of thing to make anyone's heart beat faster, except perhaps a scholar of early Erigan history. It is a list of names—a lineage, I think, for some early king. Then it goes on for some time about how that individual caused the stone to be set up in the ninth year of his reign—"

"Yes, yes," I said impatiently. "Get to the interesting part."

"Are you sure?" This time his grin was more diabolical than mischievous. "I could read that part to you, if you like, complete with footnotes about my uncertainty regarding case endings—"

"We are alone, Suhail. There is no one to see if I throw food at you."

He laughed. Then, composing himself, he recited:

We are the patient, the faithful, those who continue when all others have abandoned the path. Obedient to the true masters, we make this stone in their name, in their hand as we remember it. Here the gods will be born anew: the jewels of the precious rain, the sacred utterances of our hearts, the transcendent ones, the messengers between earth and heaven. On their wings we will ascend once more to the heights. May the blood of the traitors be spilt on barren stones of their sin. Hear us, gods of our foremothers. We keep the faith, until the sun rises in the east and the Anevrai return.

Rapt though I was, that did not preclude my mind from seizing upon his words and picking them apart for meaning. "The sun rises in the east *every* morning. Either that is an error in your translation—which I doubt—or an error in their carving, or else some kind of ancient idiom. In which case we will likely never understand what they meant. 'Gods of our foremothers' . . . I suppose they were matrilineal, as many Erigan peoples are today. But what does 'Anevrai' mean?" My breath caught. "Ngaru post-dates the fall of Draconean civilization, does it not? Is—is that what the Draconeans were called?"

"It might be." Suhail was grinning from ear to ear. "Or it is the name of their gods. I cannot tell, from one text alone."

And a brief text at that, if one discounted all the folderol about lineages and such. But there were hundreds, perhaps even thousands of texts out there. "Now that you can read the language, though—"

Cataract Stone

He held up a cautioning hand, stopping my excitement before it flew away with me. "I cannot read Draconean. Not yet."

I stared at him, confused. "But you know what it says."

"Yes. My next challenge is to figure out *how* it says that. Which symbols say 'gods' in the Draconean tongue? Which ones say 'faithful'? Are those single words in their tongue, or several? How do their verbs conjugate? What order do they phrase their sentences in? I gave it to you in Scirling, but in the Ngaru order you would say 'stones barren' instead of 'barren stones.' I cannot even be positive that the Draconean text reads the same—though 'in their hand as we remember it' suggests that it does."

His explanation deflated me. I had believed this single key would unlock everything at once. In reality, it was not nearly that simple. "Even so . . . is it helpful?"

Suhail's eyes went wide. "Is it *helpful*? It is a gift from God himself, the Preserver who kept this stone safe through the years, the Bountiful who gave us this treasure that may not have any equal in the world. Without your discovery, we might have laboured another ten generations without ever knowing as much as we know today."

His praise warmed me right down to my toes. "Are you confident enough in your translation to have that friend of yours look it over?"

My husband bit his lip, looking at the paper. "I—yes. Perhaps. I'd like to refine it a bit more, first—Ngaru verb tenses are quite different from Akhian or Scirling—"

I laid a gentle hand over his. "Then here is what I suggest. Give it to him when we depart for the desert; that way you will not fuss about like a mother hen while he works on it.

When we come back, you can make preparations to publish the result."

"*We* can make preparations." He turned his palm upward and gripped my hand firmly. "Both of our names will be on this. You have my word."

He did not spend every waking minute between then and our departure on perfecting his mastery of Ngaru. As Suhail admitted, sometimes the best thing for one's work was to step away for a time, to freshen the brain with other exercise.

Tom and I gladly ceded the preparations for our second expedition to him, as he knew far better than we what might be necessary. My own attentions were much occupied by the honeyseekers, for I had several more months of data now, and had to decide what should be done with the experiment while I was in the desert.

My purpose, you must remember, was not to find how best to encourage the healthy propagation of the breed. It was to test the limits of their hardiness—or rather, the hardiness of their eggs—and determine which factors were the most influential. There is a phrase engineers use: "testing to destruction." It is not enough to know that a beam is strong; they must find out how much weight it can bear before snapping. The only way to do this, of course, is to pile on weight until it *does* snap.

This was the point I had reached with the honeyseeker programme. The plan I drew up involved extremes of both temperature and humidity, with multiple eggs in each scenario to ensure that any one failure was a pattern, not a coincidence. I could not subject them to any great influx of cold, as our budget did not stretch to cover large quantities of ice, but heat was easy to arrange. Lieutenant Marton had instructions to increase this one step at a time until he was certain no eggs could survive.

You may think it is cruel to subject unborn beasts to such stresses, in the knowledge that some will be harmed by it, and some even killed. You are correct. It is also, however, the only way to learn certain vital facts. I would not do such a thing lightly, and having learned what I can from it, I would not do it again. But I cannot regret my decision to test the honey-seeker eggs so rigorously, for it wound up bearing unforeseen fruit upon my return from the desert.

We departed for the Jefi once more in the second week of Messis: myself, Suhail, Tom, Andrew, Haidar, and al-Jelidah, with the best camels Suhail could provide. In hindsight it was an absurdly small group, and sorely under-equipped for our eventual needs. But of course we did not know that at the time, and Suhail's preparations were entirely reasonable for the circumstances. For my own part, based on my previous excursion, I believed that I was prepared for this journey.

I was *entirely* wrong.

In past volumes I have claimed that I am a heat-loving creature, and it is true. But there is heat, and then there is the Jefi in summer. Perhaps the simplest way I can convey the difference is to say this: had Tom and I been kidnapped by the Banu Safr in that season, we both might have died.

The air was dry even in winter; in summer it became positively desiccating. I thought at first that I perspired surprisingly little. Then I realized the moisture was evaporating nearly as quickly as it formed, and in fact I was losing water at a shocking rate. There was no point between our departure from Qurrat and our eventual return when I was not thirsty, not even after I drank—for we could never indulge ourselves as fully as we wished. We had to conserve not only the water we carried but also what we found, for some of the springs we relied upon took hours to refill even a few liters, and the well-being of our camels necessarily took precedence over our own comfort. What water we obtained was bitter and unpleasant to drink, and it reeked of the hide skins in which we kept it.

Grit worked its way into every crevice. It was under my fingernails, in the folds of my ears. I half expected a grinding noise every time I blinked. The sun was more than punishing, it was torturous; its light beat down from above, then reflected off the sand and struck a second time from below. On Suhail's advice, we added eye veils to our headscarves, restricting our vision but also protecting our eyes against the constant glare. We painted our lips with grease to reduce chapping, but our exposed hands did not fare so well. The paste that supposedly protected against the sun helped a little, but even with its aid, we were still miserably charred.

I cannot fault Andrew for snarling at one point, "Why the *hell* did I let you talk me into this?" I even forbore to remind him that he had wanted to come along, which under the circumstances I think was quite noble of me.

And it was only Messis: not yet the height of summer. We departed so early—well before hatching might begin—because Tom and I wished to see estivating dragons, drowsing in their rock shelters. But it meant we would be out here a dreadfully long time. Two of the camels we rode were in milk, and what they provided was a welcome alternative to and supplement for water; camels can extract moisture from plants that are inedible for humans, so by allowing them to graze and then drinking their milk, we could extend our supplies somewhat. When our food supplies were sufficiently reduced, we would slaughter and eat one of the pack camels; if necessary we would do this more than once. Such measures are necessary, when undertaking a journey of this sort.

Luck smiled upon us at first. We crossed tracks in the desert that al-Jelidah identified as belonging to fellow Ghalb, because they were from donkeys instead of camels. We followed these for a day and found the Ghalb camped at a Banu Zalit well. They were a small group, a family of eight, which is common for their tribe. Our Akhian companions exchanged news with them, as is obligatory among the nomads (enemies excepted), and learned that there was a drake not far away. I believe they thought us mad when they realized we wanted to go *toward* the beast, rather than away from it, but we parted from them in amity, and wasted no time in hurrying toward our mark.

I have been close to dragons on many an occasion, including riding upon the back of one. There is something especially hair-raising, however, about sneaking into the lair of one while it sleeps.

"Like al-Sindi the thief," Suhail said with a wide grin. This turned to mock outrage when he learned that none of the Scirlings in the party knew that tale; he told it that night after we ate our meager supper.

This was not as comforting as it might have been, for al-Sindi, as my more literary readers may know, is the thief who crept into the lair of an estivating drake in search of its golden treasure. But there was no gold, and the drake woke while he was there; al-Sindi was forced to flee deeper into its lair. This being a fairy tale, the lair was an improbable complex of twisting passages and bottomless pits. There are many variant episodes in the tale of al-Sindi, recounting what strange wonders he found in the byways of the drake's lair, but many of them end badly for the thief.

"Moral of the story," Andrew said when this was done. "If the dragon wakes up, run *out* instead of *in*."

"Or else trust the clever slave-girl you meet along the way," Tom said. "The bits where al-Sindi listens to her are the ones where he ends up alive and rich at the end."

We did not find golden treasure in the drake's cave, nor did we have to flee in any direction. So long as one moves quietly and does not tread upon the dragon's tail, it is possible to get quite close to an estivating drake without disturbing it—even close enough to measure its rate of breathing. This, like all of the creature's bodily functions, slows down tremendously during estivation, which is part of how they survive the summer months when food becomes more scarce.

My own breathing slowed down while I was inside, even though I knew that mere air was unlikely to wake the beast. Every sound seemed excessively loud: the scratch of my pencil, the shift of my feet on the stone, the quick beating of my heart. That latter even made me contemplate whether an ear trumpet would improve one's hearing enough to measure heart rate as well: I was not *quite* foolhardy enough to try taking a sleeping dragon's pulse directly.

Our party did not linger long, however, because we had another goal: a particular egg cache we had marked during the winter, which had been left untouched by the Aritat for this very purpose. It lay just outside the canyons and gullies of the Labyrinth of Drakes, and if the eggs hatched early enough, we might hope to find a second clutch in the area—I was personally hoping for one within the Labyrinth itself—and record that one, too.

Nature, however, was not inclined to oblige us.

It was a gusty day, which I found quite agreeable. The wind kicked up a good deal of grit, but it cooled me a little as well. So long as I kept my face turned away from the wind, the weather seemed a pleasant change of pace.

Our Akhian companions knew better. Al-Jelidah saw the warning signs first: a haze on the horizon, which grew with alarming speed. He spoke sharply to Suhail in the nomad dialect, and my husband's face lost all its good humour on the spot. He began twisting in his saddle, looking in all directions—for what, I did not know.

"Is there a problem?" I asked.

"Sandstorm," he said. "We have to find shelter."

I knew of sandstorms, of course—but I knew of them in much the same way that I had known the Jefi was hot in summer. Intellectual understanding fell *far* short of the reality. I was bemused at the rapidity with which our party moved: following a hasty consultation, which revolved around whether we had time to reach a good place to make our stand, or must settle for a closer but less adequate option, we chivvied our camels into a gallop.

As fast as our beasts ran, the storm moved faster. By the time we reached a small hillock that dropped off in a rock face on the other side, the distant haze had become a distinct cloud. When I say "small," I mean it very strictly: the bluff was scarcely a meter and a half high, and not long enough for all six of us. Suhail directed me to crouch at the base of the rock, with Tom and Andrew on either side of me and our camels so close that, were they prone to rolling, they might have crushed us. He and the other two Akhians reversed this ordering, crouching on the leeward side of their camels, for lack of any other shelter.

"Dab this inside your noses," Suhail said, handing us the little jar of the grease we had been using to protect our lips. Mystified, we obeyed. "Now stuff your ears with these rags. Tie your scarves over your faces, as tightly as you can. Use extra scarves on your foreheads, low over your eyes—leave only the smallest slit. Tie them *over* your eyes, if you can endure a blindfold."

When each of us finished this task, he tilted our heads backward enough for him to pour a few drops of water over our noses and mouths, wetting the fabric. Through the slit between my two scarves, I could see al-Jelidah and Haidar doing the same to themselves. "Keep your hands tucked inside your clothing," Suhail added. "The wind may scour you bloody, otherwise."

No more did he have time for. By then I could hear the strange, hissing roar of the wind—like other storms I have encountered, but with the alien touch of sand particles sliding over and past one another at tremendous speed. The light was beginning to turn red as the leading edges of the cloud eclipsed the sun. Suhail covered his own face with quick, practiced hands, and took shelter in the lee of his own camel.

Over the growing clamour, I shouted, "How long will we stay here?"

"Until the storm is gone!" Suhail shouted back.

I wanted to tell him that this was a singularly unhelpful answer. Of course we would remain there until the storm was gone; what I wanted to know was how long that would be. In my naivete, I did not realize that was the only answer he could give me . . . for a sandstorm may last anywhere from minutes to hours.

I cannot tell you how long we endured that one. What hour it had been when al-Jelidah saw the cloud, I do not recall; all I know is that much of the day was gone by the time we emerged. In between, there was misery.

A sandstorm *assaults* you, as even the most driving downpour does not. Rain sliding down the inside of your clothes is unpleasant, but it does not threaten to trap you, weighting your body while more piles up around you, pinning your legs. I saw at one point that my camel was periodically shifting, rising slightly from her couch to step free of the sand building around her; on the assumption that she knew better how to survive this weather than I did, I mimicked her.

Would that I had a camel's ability to pinch my nostrils shut against the dust. Grit caked my scarf, and slipped through where I had not tucked the edges well enough; despite that protection, I found myself coughing out bitter masses, constantly feeling as if I could not get enough air. I learned soon enough why Suhail had directed us to grease our nostrils; without that, my skin would have cracked and bled.

I wished desperately that my husband were at my side. I knew why he was not: he was more accustomed to enduring such challenges than my Scirling companions, and so had given us what shelter the little bluff could provide. Much of the time I had my eyes closed anyway, to protect them against the scouring wind; when I opened them, I could scarcely make out Tom and Andrew through the red cloud. Suhail, on the far side of Tom, might as well have been in Vidwatha. But I would have derived comfort from seeing even his silhouette, as a reminder that such things *could* be endured.

The sound was ultimately the part I hated the most. It reminded me of the time in Bayembe when an insect had gotten inside my tent, and its buzzing threatened to drive me mad. This was worse, because it was deafening, and it went on for what seemed like an eternity. One of the scraps of rag stuffed into my ear fell out; attempting to replace it, I opened an unwise gap in the defense of my scarf, and nearly choked on dust. For the sake of my breathing, I left that ear unblocked, and the hissing roar of the wind was loud enough that I felt partially deaf on one side for some time after. Half deaf, half mad, I crouched between my camel and the stone, and prayed with unwonted fervor for this trial to end.

By the time it did, I had so lost all sense of reality that I did not trust it. Not until Suhail came and chivvied my camel to her feet did I believe we were safe, that the blue sky clearing above was not some hallucination.

When I stood, sand cascaded from every fold of my clothes, inside and out. The skin of my face stung as I unwrapped the two scarves; peeling them away, I saw that their edges were daubed with blood. The gap between them, narrow as it was, had allowed the wind to score my skin, flaying the top layers. Suhail bore similar marks. He wet a rag and offered it to me; my breath hissed between my teeth as I cleaned the area of grit.

I lifted my head from this task to find him offering me a tired, dusty grin. "We have made it through water and sand," he said: this, and the gale that had blown us to Keonga. "Give us snow next, and we will have collected the full set of storms."

"Do not tempt fate," I said, but I could not help smiling in return.

We never would have found the cache of eggs without al-Jelidah's aid. I consider myself an observant woman, particularly where visual matters are concerned, but the desert I returned to was not the one I had left four months before. Expanses of greenery were gone, consumed by animals or simply dried up and blown away. In areas of sand dunes, the very dunes themselves had migrated. And even a short time away from the terrain had eroded my memory, so that every gully or outcropping of rock looked like every other.

But when al-Jelidah brought us to the spot, there was no question of finding the egg cache itself. Bits of it were strewn across the ground for meters in every direction.

In a voice made thin with dryness, Tom said, "God *damn* it."

I stared at the wreckage, feeling as hollow as the remnants of the shells. We had missed it. All our haste, and we were still too late.

The Akhians dismounted and began to quarter the ground. Suhail picked up fragments of shell and conferred with al-Jelidah in the nomad dialect. Then he raised his voice and called out to us in Scirling. "It was animals. Hyenas, perhaps.

There are still signs of their digging, and tooth-marks where they broke into the shells."

I sagged atop my camel. Too late, yes—but not because we had failed to estimate the hatching season correctly. Predators had beaten us here.

When I persuaded my camel to kneel and went to examine the wreckage, I saw what Suhail meant. The eggs had not been cracked from within, as if by a hatchling struggling to get out. An outside force had broken them, in some cases all but crushing the egg completely. "Does this happen often?" Tom asked, gesturing with a shard of shell.

Al-Jelidah shrugged and said something, which Suhail had to translate for us. "It depends. He says that sometimes the drakes fail to dig their nests deep enough, or the wind uncovers the eggs."

I went to one of the pack camels and pulled out the notebook where I had written my original observations. "This one was no shallower than the rest. Do you think the recent sandstorm exposed them?"

Suhail shook his head immediately. "No, the storm didn't reach this far. And this happened longer ago than that."

So even had we hurried more, we would still not have found the cache in time. It was cold comfort.

We camped a little distance away that night, and had the type of scant meal that was all too common during that journey: tough, tasteless flatbread baked in the ashes of our fire, with a tiny bit of coffee to wash it down. It was the month of fasting in the Amaneen calendar, but travellers are exempt from that requirement; Suhail had promised Mahira that he would make up for it when he returned to Qurrat.

Tom and I pored over our maps, but to little avail. All the

other caches we had marked had been harvested by the Aritat and sent to Qurrat. If we wanted to observe a hatching in the wild, we would have to find another clutch . . . and quickly.

Al-Jelidah shrugged when we said this to the group. He was Ghalbi: he knew the desert like no other. He had not needed Scirling naturalists to find eggs before, and he did not need them now.

But searching would not be easy. "The Labyrinth of Drakes," I said, touching that spot on the map. "We did not mark clutches there, so they will not have been harvested. And drakes are known to lair in that area."

We had been planning to go there regardless—but it had been a later stage in our plans, not our sole hope for seeing a hatching. "Finding buried eggs, without being eaten by predators along the way . . ." Suhail mused. "Not an easy task. And travellers often get lost."

Andrew roused enough to say, "*You've* been there."

Suhail grinned. "In my foolish youth. And a few times in my equally foolish maturity. I'm not saying it can't be done—only warning you. The depths of the Labyrinth are not for the faint of heart."

"The faint of heart would not be out here in the first place," I said. "Let us enter this Labyrinth, and see what we may find."

TWENTY

In the Labyrinth of Drakes—Searching for eggs—The Watchers of Time—Hatchlings—Dragonsong—Smooth stone

I have tried many times in my life to sketch the Labyrinth of Drakes, and failed every time.

Mere pencil or ink cannot capture the place. Even photographs cannot do it, for such an image can only show you a limited slice of the whole, and the true experience of the Labyrinth is to be surrounded by it. The terrain there is spiderwebbed with canyons, until one cannot truly say whether the high ground is broken by these depressions, or the low ground is interrupted by hills and plateaus. In many places the canyons become so narrow, one might be in a corridor rather than out in the wild. Over the ages, wind and rushing water have carved the stone into fantastical shapes, fluid and twisting, exposing the striations of the rock.

This is where the Draconeans of southern Anthiope chose to settle, the location that many have long believed to be the heart of that ancient civilization. It was a more habitable place back then: they built dams to protect the canyons against the sudden floods that make it so lethal in winter, and dug wells to supply themselves from artesian sources, which have since become clogged and unusable. For shelter they reached into the stone, carving out chambers that are among the wonders of the archaeological world. Elsewhere they built their temples and walls out of enormous blocks, but here they had no need; they merely hollowed out what nature had provided.

We passed the first of these ruins not long after entering the Labyrinth. "The Gates of Flame," Suhail called these sculptures, and I could see why. The draconic shapes melded beautifully with the rich red and gold of the stone, wings reaching skyward. (These are sadly marred by bullet holes: too many passing travellers, both nomads and foreigners, have found them enticing targets.) I scrutinized them as we approached, trying to guess whether they were meant to depict desert drakes, or some ancient kind now lost. Perhaps the dragons they had bred? Presuming they had bred only one variety; I had no reason to assume the Draconeans of Rahuahane had cultivated the same type of beast on a tropical island as their cousins in a maze of canyons on the far side of the world.

I soon realized, though, that if I looked only for monumental works like the Gates of Flame, I would miss half of what there was to see. There were doorways set into the rock all over the place, and jagged piles where the hollowed cliff faces had given way at last. "One of these days," Suhail murmured, eyeing a particular spot as we rode past. When I raised my eyebrows at him, he grinned and said, "Cranes and sufficient labour to haul the rubble clear. What might we find inside?"

Though I was no archaeologist, I could see the appeal. Draconean sites had been thoroughly looted during the millennia since that civilization's fall. Even the cavern he and I had found on Rahuahane had been in a ruinous state. In all likelihood many of those collapsed chambers were empty—looters had tunneled into some of them centuries ago, hunting remnants they could sell—but the possibility was tantalizing.

We were not going to answer such questions on this trip, though. Indeed, the only reason I had as much time to explore the ruins as I did was that I could not be of much use in looking for eggs. The drakes did not lay them on the canyon floors; their clutches would have been washed away by the winter floods. They had to seek out higher elevations, the plateaus above and the terraces partway down, where the canyon walls were not so steep. We knew well the sort of location they favoured, sandy enough to allow for digging, and exposed to the sun. But what a dragon can reach by flight and what a human can reach by climbing are not always the same thing.

Al-Jelidah was accustomed to this work, and scrambled about with phenomenal ease, clinging to minute protrusions of rock with fingers like steel bars. He went farther and faster than anyone else in the party. Suhail was not far behind him, though, using ropes where he could to assist his climb. "There are statues and inscriptions in some rather unlikely places," he explained with a laugh, when I expressed my surprise. Tom, Andrew, and Haidar tramped about on the easier paths, searching every nook and cranny of the Labyrinth for possible clutches.

Which left me with the camels. Oh, I searched when I could—but my clothing hampered me, and even when I donned trousers, I lacked the strength and physical conditioning of my male companions, and could not get nearly so far. (Remembering this, I took the precaution of training before my next expedition, which came *very* much in handy.) I consoled myself by working on a map of the area, which Suhail said might be the first accurate attempt anyone had made since Mithonashri a hundred and fifty years before.

Our search took us deeper and deeper into the Labyrinth. One clutch we found had been raided by predators, like our original target; another had already hatched, which made me fret with impatience. Tom and I conferred and agreed that we should move onward, rather than studying the signs left behind at that one. What little we might learn was not worth the risk of missing the event itself elsewhere. If all else failed, we could always come back.

Suhail steered us a little, at the end. Not so far as to potentially miss a good spot—he would never have put our work at risk for a mere side trip—but when the choice came of going either left or right, he chose left, because he knew where it would lead. And so, on a morning in early Caloris, when the light was at its most dramatic angle, we emerged from a canyon barely wide enough for our camels to find ourselves facing the Watchers of Time.

If you have seen any images from the Labyrinth of Drakes, you have seen this site. The Watchers are five seated figures, fully twenty meters in height, carved into the sloping face of a canyon wall. They have the draconic heads and wings so typical of Draconean statuary, and seem to be gazing to the ends of eternity itself. Between them are four doorways, and above is an intricate frieze, depicting small flying dragons and human figures in chains.

The space that lies beyond those doorways has long been a mystery. All four open onto the same shallow antechamber, from which only a single archway gives access to the larger

The Watchers of Time

space within. This must have once contained furniture, paneling, or something else similarly flammable, for the walls of that chamber are covered with soot, which has almost completely obscured the murals that once decorated every square inch. Only bits and pieces can be made out, and efforts to clean away the soot have in many cases removed the murals as well. There is hope nowadays that our methods have improved, and the ancient artwork of that place might be seen at last . . . but so far, it has come to naught.

It was not what I had come to the Labyrinth to see, but even a woman as obsessed with living dragons as myself could not help marveling at the place. Had I grown up with such relics nearby, who is to say that I, too, would not have formed a fascination like Suhail's? The Draconean ruins in Scirland are few and disappointing. The Watchers of Time took my breath away.

We camped nearby that night. Suhail admitted he had once laid his pallet within the antechamber itself—"But never again," he said with feeling. "I hardly slept a wink that night. I was convinced the Watchers knew I was there, and did not approve." I knew what he meant. Though I am not a superstitious woman, I did not want to sleep with their stony eyes on me; we went around a corner to a spot out of their sight.

We stood watches during the night while we were in the Labyrinth, for the groundwater allows vegetation to persist through the summer—which attracts various herbivores—which, in turn, attracts carnivores. Our tiny fires, built from camel dung, were not enough to keep them away. I alone was not expected to stand sentry, less on account of my sex, and more on account of having refused Andrew's offer to teach me to shoot . . . but that night I slept very little regardless, thinking of the Draconeans and the world they had known.

The next morning my companions searched the area, while I stayed below and sketched the Watchers. (It was hardly necessary, as they have been a popular subject for every traveller who passes through the area and even some who have never even seen them—but I could not look upon those ancient guardians and not wish to render them with my own pencil.) We would not be able to stay long, and knew it. There had once been a well nearby, whose site Suhail pointed out, but it was so thoroughly collapsed that it would be less effort to dig a new one entirely. For water we would have to go some distance. One of our milk camels had foundered after the sandstorm, and the other was not giving as much as we had hoped.

From high above, I heard a triumphant shout.

I twisted on my seat to find Tom standing at the edge of the plateau across from the Watchers. He was a dusty blot against a sun-bleached sky, but he waved his hat to attract my gaze, and put his other hand to his mouth to direct his voice. "Up here!"

He had scraped his hands bloody getting up there—a fact I discovered after Suhail led me by an easier route. (I say "easier"; it is not the same thing as "easy.") But his suffering paid off, for he had located a clutch of eggs, nestled in the cup of sand above.

From a dragon's perspective, the site was ideal. The plateau was high enough that it received almost no shade, except in the very late morning and afternoon. It had a little dip in its center, though, which caught sand that would otherwise have blown away; and in this sand, the dragon had laid her eggs.

(I had the utterly fanciful thought that *she* had laid them: the first drake whose mating flight we observed, the one I lost track of when al-Jelidah prevented me from riding onward into the Labyrinth. The odds of it were small . . . but my mind does not always weigh odds rationally.)

From a naturalist's perspective, the site left something to be desired. It was not close to water; furthermore, if Tom and I wished to observe the hatching, we would either have to sit *in* that cup with the newborn drakes—not a very wise idea—or else climb an even steeper hill a little way off and watch through field glasses.

This last, as you may imagine, is what we chose to do, while Andrew and al-Jelidah took our camels and went to acquire water.

There is nothing like an intellectual victory to distract one from miserable heat and thirst. We had found the clutch just in time: the very next day, when Tom and I were still trying to tent our cloaks over ourselves as shelter from the sun, the eggs began to hatch. I lay full-length on the burning stone for hours, field glasses glued to my face, putting them down only when necessary to sketch what I had seen. Suhail stepped around and over us with fabric and sticks, trying to make sure we would not die of heat exhaustion while we were too busy to notice. By the end of the day I had an excruciating headache, but I hardly cared—for I had, at last, seen desert drakes hatch.

Tom and I had both read Lord Tavenor's accounts of the hatchings at Dar al-Tannaneen, of course. Many of those eggs produced unhealthy results, though, and we could not be certain how the change in their circumstances had altered the process. Watching that day, we treated the entire affair as a new observation, discarding all of our assumptions and noting every detail, no matter how small.

The eggs were nearly spherical, which is common among birds that lay their eggs in holes (where there is no risk of them rolling away). Their colour was pale and sandy, but speckled here and there with darker spots, like the eggs of sand grouse—in both cases, we surmised, as camouflage against predators that sought to find and raid the nests. The shell had become hard since the laying, which is not universal among dragons: some lay leathery eggs, like those of reptiles, but others are more like those of birds. The hatching drakes used an "egg tooth" to break through the shell; this is actually a specialized scale, and is shed soon after birth.

Where our observations diverged most from those of Lord Tavenor was in the matter of the shell membrane. This was a good deal thicker than he had reported, and it became apparent that before the drakes broke free of their shells, they had to shred that membrane. "Why so thick, do you think?" Tom asked me without ungluing himself from his field glasses.

"Perhaps it is a holdover from the more leathery type of egg," I said, propping myself up on one elbow so I could sketch with the other hand. "The harder shell could have developed in response to environmental factors, but the more flexible interior remained."

It was a nice theory, and I held to it for many years. Tom eventually conducted experiments, however, that gave us a more accurate explanation: the inner membrane of a desert drake egg is a highly specialized material that responds to heat. This connects to the yolk by means of the chalaza, the thready component one sees upon pouring an egg into a glass, and actually supplies the drake with energy supplementing that of the yolk itself. At the time we did not know this, though. All we knew was that the drakes showed a surprising amount of vigor upon emerging from their shells, and were soon stumbling about without having been fed a single thing.

There are few things more hideous and adorable than the newly born of any species. The drakes had the benefit of scales, which kept them from looking like raw flesh the way so many avian hatchlings do; but they were gawky and pale, and much prone to plowing their faces into the sand when their weight got ahead of their feet. Far from cannibalizing one another, they showed a startling degree of sociability: as night fell, they gathered together among the remnants of their shells, forming a pile to keep themselves warm.

Tom and I had to retreat from the plateau before the light was entirely gone. We were not much more graceful than the drakes as we made our way down to our camp on the canyon floor, and without my observations to distract me, I felt in full the consequences of a day spent under the sun's merciless eye. Though I did not say it to anyone at the time, I was more physically wretched than I had been when the Banu Safr kidnapped us—albeit less sunburnt. I drank every drop of water Suhail gave me and passed out on my bedroll, too tired even for the whirl of my thoughts to keep me awake.

Even so, I found myself rousing again about two hours later. A sound had disturbed my sleep, quiet and low, but persistent. When I rolled over, I found Suhail was sitting up, arms loosely linked across his knees. "What is that?" I whispered.

"I think it is the drakes," he said.

It was a steady, soothing hum, in shifting chords as voices

dropped out and came back in. The result was not precisely musical—even I, not blessed with much sense of pitch, could tell the various notes conflicted at times—but it was beautifully eerie in its way, like the howling of wolves, but gentler. "They are . . . singing to one another?"

Even in the darkness, I could make out his smile. "Purring, perhaps. Like cats. There are stories of this, but I've never heard it myself."

After a moment he lay down again, and I pillowed my head on his shoulder. I cannot tell you how long I listened to their aimless song; it followed me into sleep and shaped my dreams. But those moments, however many there may have been, have remained in my memory as among the most priceless of my life: enduring a rough camp in the Labyrinth of Drakes, with a man I loved warm at my side, listening to the dragons sing.

Three days passed before we could investigate the nest directly, which is the length of time it took for the drakes to abandon it for good. I will not trouble my readers with too many details of this period, as it is all but prelude to what came next; I will say only that the time was physically unpleasant, for we were down to our last mouthfuls of water, barely enough to keep body and soul together, and I no longer had the joy of new discovery to distract me.

Fortunately Andrew and al-Jelidah returned on the third afternoon, bearing as much water as they could harvest from the spring without draining it or keeping us waiting for too long. Even then I could not drink my fill—but that water, bitter and goat-flavoured though it was, tasted more glorious than the finest wine.

"Do we want to look for another nest?" I asked Tom.

He thought about it, biting his lip, then finally shook his head. "By the time we find one, it may well have hatched. And we've pressed our luck rather far already." Jackals had gone after the camels on the trip to the spring, and my brother had been forced to hide in a crevice to avoid a drake that had woken briefly from its slumber. Suhail had found another lair not far from our current location; we all had our fingers crossed that the dragon there would remain in estivation until we departed. No doubt Tom was thinking of all of these things when he said, "I'd rather finish this one properly, then head back."

We had missed the hatchings at Dar al-Tannaneen (in favour of seeing the natural version out here), but we could do some good with the new drakes. "As much as I hate to say it, I agree. Let us see if the drakes are gone yet: if they are, we might leave as early as today."

The last of the drakes had indeed departed. They were sufficiently harmless at this stage that Tom had followed two of them when they wandered off the previous day, watching their first, inept efforts at hunting, but in that terrain we could not afford to pursue them far. A corner of my mind was already considering what sort of preparation would be necessary to observe juveniles out here—but whatever the answer might be, it certainly amounted to more preparation than *we* had made. I therefore turned my attention to the remnants of their nest, which at least had the courtesy to stay in one place.

Bits of shell were scattered all over. Initially we left these where they lay, scrutinizing the cup of sand from all edges before stepping into it and disturbing the tracks of the drakes.

Then we began to gather up the shards. Among them we found a few shreds of membrane, which had escaped the notice of the hatchlings; most of that material had been eaten. We had brought a small quantity of formaldehyde with us, sufficient to preserve the soft tissues of one hatchling (if occasion arose); we used it instead for the membrane, so we could study it at leisure back in Qurrat.

Because this was the sole hatching we had been able to observe, we wanted to be thorough. We gathered up every last scrap of shell we could find—uncovering evidence that the site had been used more than once—and when that was done, I sat for a time in the cup, running my hands through the sand to make certain we had not missed any.

My fingers brushed stone.

This should not have been unusual. I sat atop a great pile of stone, after all; it stood to reason there would be some at the bottom of this cup. But that should have been rough, and what I touched was flat and smooth.

Curious, I dug away some of the sand to see. This was easier said than done, as sand of course tends to slide right back to the bottom of any hole; but I was able to find what I had touched. It was indeed quite flat—not a figment of my tactile imagination, brought on by too much sun. And as I ran my hand across it, my fingertips found an edge.

I can only imagine what I would have looked like, had anybody been watching me. I knelt on the sand, flinging handfuls of it to the side like a drake preparing to lay, trying to clear enough ground to see. The stone was perhaps twenty centimeters wide, and featureless—but so regular in its shape that it could not be a natural accident. It was a separate piece, on one side set into the rock, and on the other . . .

Some part of me, I think, knew what I had found before the rest of me put it together. For when I raised my voice, it was not my fellow naturalist to whom I called out.

"Suhail!"

Whatever note he heard in my voice, it brought him from the floor of the canyon to my side in an astonishingly short time. He knelt in the hole I had made, laying one hand on the shaped stone. "Here," I said, and guided his fingers downward.

He felt what I had: a second stone, set below and in front of the first.

In a voice no louder than a few grains of sand slipping past their kin, he whispered, "Stairs."

My heart was pounding in a way that had nothing to do with exertion. I said, "It is only two blocks. It might be nothing more." Or it might be a *great deal* more.

Suhail said, "We have to see."

Andrew and Tom had followed him, but more slowly. By the time they reached us, he and I had revealed a bit of the second step, and thrust our hands deeply enough to find a third one below. "We have found something," I said breathlessly, "only I do not know what—"

"Water," Suhail said. "We need water. This will collapse in on us if we do not wet it down at least a little. No, it will only evaporate—" He stopped, hands clenching in frustration. There was no timber we could use to brace the sides of our pit. Then he looked all around the cup, five meters or so across. "Baskets," he said. "Whatever we can load sand into, and then throw it over the edge."

Despite our excitement, we were not so reckless as that makes it sound. I credit this to Suhail, who clung to the rock of his professionalism even as a storm threatened to sweep him away. We did indeed pour out the sand—but carefully, in a single spot, where we could examine it for any bits and pieces that might be mixed in. It fell to the other four, poor souls, to carry these down from the cup and bring the empty saddlebags back up, while Suhail and I dug out the stairs.

Because of this caution, our progress was slower than it might otherwise have been. We dug our pit wide, clearing an area around the top of the staircase down to the bare rock; this revealed a shaft cutting downward through the stone, which alleviated our fears of collapse. Then we dug out the staircase itself, from one wall to the other. We only made it through the first step that day, and a bit of the second, and when nightfall came we were exhausted.

Sitting around our camel-dung fire after it became too dark to dig, we looked at one another in silence. At last I broke it. "I do not know what may be at the bottom of those stairs," I said. "But I do know that I cannot walk away without at least *trying* to find out."

"They must be Draconean." This came from Suhail, who was staring fixedly into the distance. "There is nothing about their appearance to say, not yet—but the location. Directly across from where the Watchers sit. As if that is what they are watching. It cannot be accident."

"Are there any legends or historical records of other civilizations here?" I asked. He shook his head. "Then it is very likely theirs, for that reason if no other."

An unrecorded Draconean ruin. It might be nothing: a passage to an unremarkable chamber, used in past ages to store supplies. It might have been—likely had been—looted centuries before, by someone who never noted its location for posterity. But it was not on the lists of remnants in the Labyrinth. No modern person, apart from the six of us, knew it was there.

Andrew laughed, spreading his hands. "Is there a question here? *I'm* staying. Good God, what kind of man could walk away?"

By the expression on his face, al-Jelidah could. He was no scholar; his interest was in what he got paid to do, nothing more. But so long as we paid him to carry bags of sand down from the plateau, he was perfectly willing to do that. And Haidar, of course, was Aritat. He would not abandon his fellow tribesman.

When I looked at Tom, a tired grin crept upon him. "I'm game," he said. "As they say: when you find the dragon's lair, you must look inside."

TWENTY-ONE

The staircase—A door—Bones in the corridor—Rebellion—Something missing—Too many fairy tales—The murals—Two backward feet—A narrow gap—More broken shells—A chip of stone

It was absurd, of course. Six people, subsisting on camel's milk and the water that could be hauled from a spring a full day's journey away, digging out a staircase with tiny hand shovels. The shaft was narrow enough that only one person could dig as the hole grew deeper; we took it in shifts. Had it been much longer, we would have been forced to abandon the effort. Our rations were growing perilously thin, even with Haidar hunting to supplement them, and while we would not have starved there in the Labyrinth we might have starved on the way out. But the farther we got, the less any of us could bring ourselves to walk away, even when common sense said we should.

Fifteen steps, from the top of the plateau to the base of the staircase. We had uncovered six when Andrew called out, bringing us all hurrying to the shaft: the vertical wall of the far side had ended in a lintel. At that point there was no possibility of leaving, for we all wanted to know—*had* to know—what lay at the bottom.

Suhail took over digging for a time, relinquishing his position only when it was time to pray. Mere words cannot do justice to my husband's patience: the desire to tear through the ground must have burned like an inferno in his heart, but rather than hastening his work, he slowed down. And his care was rewarded, for he soon uncovered a mass embedded in one wall below the lintel, which turned out to be the twisted, broken remnants of a bronze hinge.

Where there had been a hinge, there had once been a door. The lack of a door told us something had happened—something that almost certainly crushed our unspoken hopes of an untouched site. But we dug on.

And the sand came to an end. Suhail, digging out the doorway, broke through into air. I was sitting at the top of the stairs when he did, awaiting the next bag of sand to carry away, and had to restrain the urge to climb over him and put my eye to the hole. "Can you see anything?" I asked.

"I need a light," he said, and I scrambled to call down to the camp.

A match was brought. Suhail put the flame through with a cautious hand. It continued to burn, telling us the air inside was good. I was not the only one holding my breath.

Suhail peered through the gap for a long moment, then pulled back. "A corridor," he said. "The walls are carved, but I cannot make out details. We'll have to clear the doorway."

He would not let us hurry, no matter how any of us chafed—Andrew in particular. We worked downward to the last of the stairs, continuing to dig long after there was enough space to climb through. Our efforts revealed the other hinges, and then, at the bottom, the reason Suhail had insisted on caution: the broken remnants of the door.

It was not in very good condition. Lighter rainstorms would only penetrate the top few feet of sand, but there must have been the occasional deluge, which sent water all the way to the bottom of the staircase. Only portions remained, and those sadly decayed. I had a few brushes with me, on the chance that we would have enough water for me to try a bit of painting; these were put to use instead in brushing sand off the fragile wood. Laid bare, the door told a story.

"Looks like it was bashed in," Andrew said.

The four of us were crouched on the steps above, leaning over one another to study the scene. Suhail traced one hand through the air, not touching the wood. "Struck here, I think—and it broke the panel near the top, tearing away a portion still attached to the hinge. That must have rotted away entirely."

Tom broke the silence that followed. "What was in here, that it merited breaking down the door?"

Was. Whatever had been here was undoubtedly long gone. But I knew Suhail's views on archaeology: even if the great treasures had been looted, we might still learn any number of things from the shreds that remained.

Suhail eased the cover of a notebook beneath one of the pieces of wood and tried to lift it. The fragment crumbled as he did so. "Damn," he said. "We can't possibly carry this back. It won't even survive going up the staircase." He turned, putting one hand on my knee. "My artistic, keen-eyed love, my angel of the pencil. Can you record it?"

Imagine, if you will, that you are sitting at the entrance to a previously unidentified Draconean ruin. Any number of wonders may lie down the dark stone corridor that stretches before you . . . but you are not exploring them, because you have undertaken to draw a picture of a broken, half-rotted door. Not just the door, either: also its hinges, and the green, corroded mass that was once the latch, and the shape of the frame and staircase that accompany it.

It is a mark of how much I love Suhail and esteem his archaeological acumen that I did as he asked, rather than trampling across the decaying wood of the door to see what lay beyond.

When that was complete, we removed what we could of the door, which in the long run was only its metal fittings. These we wrapped in scraps of cloth, and then—at last—we proceeded.

Four of us went: Haidar and al-Jelidah remained outside with the camels. Suhail took the lead, but I followed with my hand in his, one step behind only because we could not comfortably walk side by side. He and Andrew carried lamps, and their light showed us that the tunnel, hewn out of solid stone, was carved all along its length: the striding figures of Draconean gods, winged and dragon-headed, with humans bearing offerings to them. "If you ask me to stop and draw all of these before we explore to the corridor's end, I shall *kick* you," I whispered to Suhail. He laughed.

(Why did I whisper? It was not as if there were anything down there I might disturb by speaking too loudly. But I could not have raised my voice for all the iron in Eriga.)

Then Suhail stopped, so abruptly that I ran into his back.

He was not looking at the walls any longer. I followed the line of his gaze, and saw something on the floor up ahead.

Andrew, peering around me, said, "Is that . . . are those *bones*?"

It will not surprise you, I expect, that I thought immediately of dragonbone. There is no evidence the Draconeans had the art of preserving them, and good reason to believe they did not, apart from what nature may have occasionally provided; the chemical knowledge necessary for that is rather more advanced than they likely had. But the last time I discovered a pile of bones in an underground space, they had come from dragons.

These, however, were human. We advanced slowly, as if the skeleton might rise up and attack us; Suhail held his lamp out like a shield. The four of us clustered together instinctively, courtesy of too many lurid tales of haunted Draconean temples.

Up close, however, the bones were merely sad. They lay as their owner had fallen, slumped against the wall—and to my great surprise, they were not entirely bare. Water had not penetrated this far, and so the body had naturally mummified in the cool, dry air. The preservation was imperfect, and his clothes hung in nearly absent tatters . . . but one could look at his cadaverous face and see an ancient person there.

"He's got a knife," Andrew murmured.

We arrayed ourselves around the body, touching nothing. Andrew was right: there was a dusty bronze blade under the corpse's hand, as if he had dropped it when he died. Tom lowered his face nearly to the floor, peering at the body, and said, "There's something caught between his ribs. It might be the point of a spear."

"A broken door, and now a dead man," I said. "What *happened* here?"

His voice trembling faintly, Suhail said, "Isabella, I *will* ask you to draw him. And, yes, the carvings on the walls. But not yet." Even his scholarly discipline knew limits.

We went onward. Now that we knew to look for them, we spotted dark marks on the floor, on the carvings along the walls, that might have been bloodstains. Then the corridor came to an end at another door, and this one was not broken down; it stood a little ajar.

My heart felt as if it might leap right out of my mouth. Suhail looked back at us. I do not know what Tom and Andrew did, but I nodded emphatically. He removed his headscarf, wrapping his hand in the fabric—he later explained this was to keep the oil and sweat of his hand from touching the wood, made delicate by the ages—and eased the door open far enough for us to slip through.

The room beyond was as you have seen it in pictures: a rectangular space, its corners dominated by four statues standing with wings and arms outspread. The spaces in between were carved and painted, their colours undimmed by time, for they had not seen light since the downfall of Draconean civilization. Those murals alone would have made the site a worldwide treasure, for they are better preserved than any we have found elsewhere, and from them we have gleaned a hundred details of the ancient Draconean religion.

The remaining contents were few, with signs that the place had been looted long before we set foot inside. A bronze tripod had once stood in the center of the room. Now it lay on its side a little distance away, the bowl fallen from its top, dented and forlorn. By the left-hand wall there was a splintered pile of wood, with shards of clay beneath; these proved to be tablets, each carved with Draconean text, which we have since pieced back together. Chains hanging from the ceiling still held primitive lamps: shallow bronze dishes that would have been filled with oil, judging by the soot that marked the ceiling above.

One of those lamps had been torn from its moorings. Below

its empty chains lay two more bodies, as well preserved as their companion out in the corridor. It took no careful observation to see how one had died: his head was crushed from the side. The other we could not judge, for he lay under the first, and no one wanted to move him.

Andrew muttered a profane oath, looking at the two of them. "So the myths are true. The Draconeans didn't just fall—they were overthrown."

Common sense argued that a few dead men did not a rebellion make. My instinct, however, agreed with Andrew. Those men had not died of natural causes; they were killed in a fight. Given the state of preservation here, that must have happened in ancient times, with sand sealing the place for millennia afterward. Their weapons, from what we could see of them without touching the bodies, were crude bronze: assuredly not the best Draconean civilization could produce, and not what defenders of this temple would have been armed with. They must be invaders, rebels, the ones who had kicked in the door and come down here to despoil this place. No other site in all the world preserved a moment like this one did, and the moment thus presented to us, out of the distant past, was one of war.

Suhail's eyes were wide in the lamplight, drinking in every detail. The wonder I felt upon seeing a dragon in flight was written in the soft parting of his lips, the stillness of his body, as if the slightest movement would cause this all to collapse into dust and dreams. He and I had found a Draconean site before, on Rahuahane, but that one had been wrecked like all the others. This one was almost pristine, and I could only begin to imagine the effect it had on him.

I was not the only one thinking of Rahuahane. His voice

almost as dry as the air, Tom said, "This beats that other ruin you found all hollow."

And then Suhail said, "This is wrong."

It brought us all around to stare at him. "What?" Andrew said.

Suhail's free hand curled in the empty air, as if to grasp a mirage. "Rahuahane. Can you not *see*?"

I cannot fault the other two for failing to grasp his point. They had not been on that cursed island; they did not know the conversation we had there. But I looked once more at the statues in the corner, and I understood. "These are the figures you told me about—the fertility gods, or guardians of the young. Whichever they are. The ones we found at that hatching ground."

Now Andrew was staring at me instead of at Suhail. "Hatching ground? Rahooa-what? When did you find a ruin?"

I had shared many things with my brother, but not that. He was too likely to tell someone, or go haring off to the Broken Sea to find it for himself—and that was *without* me telling him about the firestone. But I could not spare the attention to explain it to him right then. "This has all the marks of a hatching ground, for the dragons the Draconeans bred. But where is the hatching ground itself?"

With that question in mind, the site's purpose became obvious. Even if one were not a specialist like Suhail, familiar with theories about the particular variety of statue looming over us from the four corners, the murals told the tale. The processions of people were not merely bearing offerings; they bore them to gods who stood over radiant spheres—eggs. I could not understand all the symbolism, but I did not need to. There ought to be eggs here, and there were not.

The room was not so terribly large that a pit for eggs could have somehow escaped our notice. Tom even went to the bodies fallen in the corner and peered under them, on the small chance that they concealed anything of interest. The bowl that had stood atop the tripod was not nearly sufficient to hold such a burden. "Unless there was only one egg at a time?" Suhail suggested doubtfully.

But the inside of the bowl was charred, indicating they had lit fires inside it. "Even desert drake eggs do not incubate in flame," I said. "Likely they burnt offerings or incense here."

A muscle jumped in Suhail's jaw. "I should not be frustrated," he said, with a disbelieving laugh. "On Rahuahane we made the discovery of a lifetime; here we have made the discovery of the century. To be so lucky twice is a gift from God himself. But—it feels incomplete. I am *certain* there should be more."

Andrew spun in a circle, arms flung outward. He was grinning like a fool. "Al-Sindi! In the stories, there's always a secret door."

"You," I said severely, "have been reading too many fairy tales."

Then we all fell silent, looking at one another. Tom offered, with a cautious air, "The walls—they're scarred in places."

So they were. Chips of stone had broken off the carvings, and not in the places one might expect from a fight. I looked around the room again, this time thinking less about the walls, more about what had taken place within them. "These men break in. Are the defenders here when they come, or do they surprise the invaders in their work?"

"They're here," Andrew said immediately. "The way the

fellow out there fell—he was facing someone farther down the corridor, not fighting against someone coming in." He paced a circuit, shining his light on stains and scattered piles of decayed cloth. "There's more blood here than just those two could account for. Maybe some of the defenders died, too. If so, their bodies were taken away later."

Tom took Suhail's lamp and examined a section of scarred mural. "After the invaders left, I'm guessing. *Somebody* hacked at the walls for a while. Not in any systematic way, I don't think—it looks more like frustration at work. If we pretend for a moment that there *is* a door here somewhere . . . they might have lost their tempers when they failed to find it."

"Is it even *possible*?" I said.

"A secret door?" The grin spreading across Suhail's face would not have looked out of place on an eight-year-old boy. "Yes. It would have to be—" He whirled, gazing upward, orienting himself relative to the plateau above. "This direction." He pointed at the wall that held the entrance to the corridor. "Unless it is underneath us entirely. There is no space for it in the other direction, and if it were to the left or right, it would have to be *very* small."

We had tramped up and down from that plateau often enough to all have a very good sense of its dimensions. "Or else another corridor," I said. "It would almost *have* to be a corridor, or else an exceedingly small room; otherwise it would overlap with the path we came in by. But how on earth would it open?"

Andrew actually bounced in place, so great was his excitement. "Some kind of hidden lever or knob! But we should be careful; we might trigger a trap instead. Then poison darts will come shooting out of the walls, or the ceiling will drop on us—"

Suhail laughed. "I think we can rest safe on that count. There has never been any proof that the Draconeans built traps into their sites."

"There's never been anything like this, either," Andrew said—which was true, albeit not a very compelling argument for improbable traps.

Given the room's intricately carved decoration, though, finding the trigger for a secret door (always supposing one existed in the first place) would be easier said than done. The invaders seemed to have tried without success; what were the odds that we would do any better? In our favour, we did have more time to search than they likely had, if there had been a rebellion under way at the time. But we could not press and pull on every square centimeter of the walls.

When the first hour of random prodding failed to produce any results, however, that was precisely what Suhail proposed. "We have to be systematic," he said. "Otherwise we will waste our effort, revisiting points we have already tried, and perhaps miss the bit we need by a mere finger's breadth."

Just then we heard a startled Akhian oath from the corridor. It was Haidar, come to make certain we had not all perished; instead he had found the first body. The hour was getting late, though it hardly made any difference in the depths of the temple. "We'll come back to this tomorrow," Tom said. "It's waited for millennia; if there's anything else for us to find, it can wait a few hours more."

Andrew and Suhail both made faces like their mothers were telling them to leave off playing and come have a bath. I believe I controlled my expression better, though not my heart. But with my concentration broken, I found myself ravenous, and Tom had a point.

"First thing tomorrow," I agreed. "And I shall not sleep a wink tonight."

Upon our return the next morning, I did not take part in the Great Secret Door Search. Instead I brought my sketchbook with me, along with every lamp we had, and set to work documenting the interior of the temple.

Nowadays this sort of thing is done with photography, and had we known we were going to stumble upon a priceless Draconean ruin, we would have brought a camera with us. (A camera, and someone to work it: none of us knew how to operate such a thing.) But the photographic methods of the time, being quite new, had one great flaw, which was that they required very long exposures—hardly ideal for capturing living subjects like dragons, who have no interest in sitting for their portraits. We might have gotten some value out of photographing them asleep, or recording their habitat; but I could do the same with pencils and paper, and those are much less finicky about temperature and the interference of grit. A camera was far more trouble than it truly would have been worth . . . or so we had assumed.

Standing once more in the temple chamber, Suhail shook his head at his own folly. "If I had the self-restraint the Merciful and Compassionate gave a rabbit, I would seal this up and ride back to Qurrat, then come back here with proper supplies and assistance. This site deserves better than we have given it."

"We have not damaged anything," I said, to reassure him.

His expression appended the word "*yet.*" "At the very least, you should let me sketch things as they are now. I would be here for weeks copying everything in full—to begin with, I would need watercolours—but I can record the important points, at least. When that is done, if we have not found anything else, we can go back to Qurrat as you said."

"*You* can go back to Qurrat," Andrew muttered. "I'm not leaving until I find treasure."

While the others began a systematic exploration of the wall, then, I set to work drawing. I began with the three bodies, and then the door to the chamber, but those were very quick sketches. My true interest was in the murals, of which there were five: one on each side of the entrance, two on the side walls, and an enormous one covering the back wall.

The large one was the procession of offerings. This was laid out in the customary manner of Draconean art, with the human figures a fraction the size of the dragon-headed ones, and all standing in the peculiar combination of profile and facing posture that looks so odd when one is used to modern techniques of perspective. The procession stretched out in horizontal rows, each one separated from the rest by a decorative band filled with writing. "Prayers?" I murmured to myself, laying down lines with a quick hand. The inscriptions I made no attempt to replicate; those would be better done as rubbings. "Or some kind of proclamation, perhaps?"

There was a good deal more writing on the left-hand wall, this time arranged in vertical columns, with each character painted in red. It was exceedingly strange, seeing the bright colours in this chamber, not only in the murals but on the statues. Close examination of other relics had shown that at least some Draconean statues used to be painted; but we are accustomed to seeing them as plain stone, and this has given their civilization an austere quality in our imaginations. Now, however, we had proof that they had loved colour as much as modern man.

I resorted to quick scribbles to represent the writing on that mural, putting my main effort into the egg that sat at the bottom, underneath the red columns and atop an elaborate altar-like shape. Again, rubbings would be more helpful in the short term than me drawing every character by hand. The murals to either side of the door I bypassed for the time being; Suhail, Andrew, and Tom were too much in the way.

That left me with the right-hand wall, which is the one I had the most interest in to begin with. This one showed actual dragons, which are much less common in Draconean art; most of their decorations depict humans or dragon-headed figures. But two winged reptiles dominated the upper part of the wall, flanking yet another inscription, and I was very keen to study them more closely.

My first thought, when I saw them the previous day, was that they might depict the kind of dragon this civilization had bred—a variety that seemed to have since gone extinct. If that were the case, however, then the breed in question had not been much different from our modern desert drakes. The creatures on the wall looked a good deal like the ones I had been chasing and feeding all year, allowing for a certain amount of artistic license: their scales were painted in gold leaf, making them far brighter and more splendid than any real beast, and the odd perspective of the Draconean style made them look rather like flowers squashed flat between the pages of a book.

But they had the broad, delicate ruffs I knew so well, and

the fan-like vanes on their tails. I was forced to conclude they were indeed the familiar breed, or at least their very close cousins. If *those* had been hatched here, then it meant two things: first, that the Draconeans had raised more than one variety of dragon (for I was certain the kind we had found on Rahuahane were not desert drakes); and second, that an ancient civilization had succeeded where Tom and I had failed.

It was a disheartening thought, and no amount of telling myself that it was silly to feel disheartened in the middle of such a tremendous discovery changed my mood. I devoted myself to documenting this wall with assiduous care . . . and that is when I noticed something peculiar.

Even with all our lamps, the light was less than ideal. I picked one up and carried it to the wall, so I might get a closer look.

"Oy!" Andrew said. "I need that, or I'm going to lose my place!"

"Put your finger on it for now," I said, distracted. "This dragon's foot is wrong."

The silence from behind me was disbelieving. Then Tom said, "Wrong how?"

"It's on backward. As if the seamstress wasn't paying attention, and sewed it on upside down."

Andrew snorted. "It's Draconean art. It always looks strange."

By then I had gone to the other dragon. "This one, too. Their feet ought to be facing toward the edges of the wall, even if the claws dangle. Instead they're cocked inward, as if—"

"As if pointing at something." Suhail had gone outside again to pray. The month of fasting was supposed to be a time of piety; even if he was not observing the fast itself, he felt obliged to attend to his devotions—all the more so because he was spending the intervening time in a heathen temple. He had returned while I was distracted, and came now to stand just behind my left shoulder.

"And their scales are wrong, too," I said. "That is—the entire depiction of their scales is very stylized, but we are used to that. I mean that even for the style, they are on upside down. But only on these hind legs."

We had brought measuring tape with us. Tom fetched it and, with Suhail's assistance, stretched it out to form a line from the left-hand dragon's foot. He said, "I don't know exactly what angle we should follow, here. The top of the foot? The medial line of the metatarsals? It makes a difference."

The two dragons were not perfectly symmetrical; their feet were not cocked to the same degree, meaning that any lines we drew from them would not intersect in the middle of the wall. The left was cocked higher than the right, skewing the intersection to the right as well. I said, "All we need is for it to direct us to the correct area. Once we have that—"

I had only just begun to run my hands over the wall. But the tip of my index finger brushed something—not anything noteworthy; only the irregular shape left between the carved marks of a character—and when it did so, the stone shifted slightly. On instinct, I pressed, and the bit of stone slid into the wall.

Something clicked.

I had crouched to search, and now shied back with such alacrity that I landed on my rump. Above me, with a clatter of chain and a ponderous, grinding sound, a portion of the wall swung inward.

Less than ten centimeters. It shuddered to a halt after that, its mechanism corroded and clogged with the slow accumulation of grit. But it was a secret door, and it had *opened*.

With slow care, Suhail knelt at my side. I think his intention was to help me to my feet; but having knelt, he stayed there, his hands on my shoulders, staring at the door. As if his knees, like mine, had gone too weak to bear weight.

Andrew whispered, "I *knew* it."

His faith had been stronger than mine. We had searched for this thing; we had assembled arguments for the possibility of its existence. But theories are one thing, and proof quite another. And if the invaders had not found this door—as it seemed they had not—

Then whatever lay beyond it would be pristine. A Draconean site, wholly untouched since ancient times.

I got to my feet, then helped Suhail up. He was still staring at the wall, hardly blinking. I licked my lips, swallowed, then inhaled deeply and said, "I for one am *very* eager to know what is beyond that door."

Tom looked to Suhail, but my husband seemed to have lost the power of speech. "Well?" Tom asked. "Will it damage anything if we force the door open?"

The question brought Suhail to rationality once more. "It might," he said, in a shallow, cautious voice. "From the sound, I think the mechanism is stone and bronze, which is why it survived; wood or rope would have snapped at the first pressure. But it is not working smoothly any longer. We may not be able to close the door again."

Then he blinked and drew what I think was his first real breath since he returned from his prayers. "Whatever we find in there," he said, fixing each of us with his gaze, "we must *not* touch it. No matter what it may be. We may look only. Then we will close the door if we can, and go back to Qurrat, before this treasure lures us into stupidity or starvation."

"Or both." I reminded myself to keep breathing. It was

remarkably easy to forget. "All of this, of course, presupposes we can get the door open."

Tom and Andrew put their shoulders to it, both of them being stronger than Suhail. The panel made very unpleasant noises as it moved, but move it did. The wall proved to be approximately twenty centimeters thick, and beyond it was darkness. When the gap was large enough for my hand, I put a match through, as Suhail had done at the staircase, to test the air.

His voice trembling, he asked, "Can you see anything?"

"No," I said. "Not from only a match's flame. But the air is good."

The men redoubled their efforts. Soon, however, the door ground to a halt . . . and the gap it left was not very large.

Andrew made an anguished noise. "We *can't* just leave it like this! To hell with the mural—do we have a hammer? We could smash the edges off—"

"No!" Suhail yelped.

I stepped up to the crack and measured myself against it. "I think I can fit through. It will be tight, but possible."

I should not have looked at my husband when I said that. His expression was that of a man who has glimpsed Paradise, and been told he may not enter. Contrition gripped my heart: as tremendous as this moment was for me, of the two of us, I was not the archaeologist. How would I feel if he went on to see some new kind of dragon, while I stayed behind? "Never mind," I said. "It has waited this long; it can wait a while longer."

"No," Suhail said again, this time in a softer voice. "We cannot leave without knowing, and I will not destroy this door just to see. If you can fit through, then go."

Tom sighed when I turned to him. "I would say, *Do you think that's safe?*—but I know what your answer would be. If this turns out to lead into the back end of a drake's lair, though, please do think twice before settling down to sketch it."

Andrew said only, "You are both my most favourite and least favourite sister in the world right now."

I was, of course, his only sister. Squaring my shoulders, I addressed the task of sliding through that narrow gap.

I had to exhale completely to fit through, and lost a button even so. It was a tight enough squeeze that I suffered a moment of worry as to what would happen if I got stuck. But then I was through, and Suhail passed along my notebook and pencil and one of the lamps. Before handing me the latter, he took my hand and kissed it, his body blocking this from the sight of the others. In a voice meant only for me, he murmured, "Come back and tell me of wonders."

"I will," I said, and turned to face the next step.

I was in a narrow corridor, running parallel to the wall. Suhail had been right; the hidden chamber lay back in the direction of the entrance. Not far ahead, the passage descended in another staircase, to a level below that of the previous room. By my calculation, the lower level must be at least halfway down the plateau.

For the sake of my companions, I called these details out to them. "There are murals here, too," I said. "Painted, like the ones in the room, not the plain ones in the first corridor. All of gods—there are no human or dragon figures here that I can see." A mischievous impulse seized me, and I added, "Shall I stay and draw them, before continuing on?"

The chorus of "*No!*" from behind me bid fair to shake dust from the ceiling, but it also made me smile and fortified me for the mystery ahead. When I raised my lamp, my hand no longer shook.

At the base of the steps, the corridor turned right again. Here, however, there was no door. The moment I rounded the corner, my lamp threw its light forward, and the chamber returned it in glory.

Even in its heyday, the hatching pit on Rahuahane must have been a rough, provincial thing. What I saw here was the exemplar: a square chamber carved and painted in the finest detail, with steps in the center leading up to a low, round platform. Unlike the room above, this one was still furnished. There were tables, stands, vases and bowls; gold and alabaster, coloured enamel and precious wood . . . an immeasurable treasure of unbroken Draconean artifacts.

Almost unbroken. One of the low tables had been upset, its dishes knocked to the floor. When I advanced into the room, I understood why.

Empty fragments of eggshell lay in the sand-lined center of the pit. There were no skeletons: of course there would not be. Those would have fallen to dust after the hatchlings died. Stains and a few bones from what looked like birds remained in or around some of the dishes; undoubtedly the ravenous newborns had devoured every scrap they could while they waited for their caretakers to return. Left alone, hunting for more sustenance, one of them must have knocked over the table. But the bottle atop it had held some kind of oil, not food, and its contents had spilled out to soak the bare earthen floor.

My lamplight fell upon marks pressed into the earth.

They were tracks. Footprints, left behind by the newly hatched dragons, as they wandered back and forth in search of food that would never come.

The Hatching Chamber

Later on, I was objective. I drew the tracks, measured them, took casts and tried to work out how many different individuals had trodden in that patch of oil-soaked ground. They were a priceless scientific discovery, and I valued them as such.

In that moment, however, I was not objective in the least. I envisioned the history that had transpired here—little hatchlings abandoned on the day of rebellion, starving to death in this beautiful and lifeless chamber—and I wept, tears rolling silently down my face. The Draconeans had never truly been people to me, only an ancient civilization who worshipped and bred dragons and therefore posed some intriguing puzzles. But the bodies up above had been people, individual men who lived and died; and the tracks here told the story of lives that had vanished without any other trace. Whatever had happened in the Labyrinth of Drakes, so many ages ago, it had carried a dreadful cost.

I do not know how long I stood there, my tears drying on my face. After a while the thought came to me that I was wasting precious water, crying like that; and so I came back to my senses. I hurried to the foot of the stairs and called up, "Are you still there?"

Suhail's answer was impatient, disbelieving, and full of love. "Where do you *think* we would have gone?"

"There is a hatching chamber," I said as I came up the stairs, my voice catching a little. My knees trembled, but I refrained from putting my hand on the wall, lest I mar something. "It is untouched. Very much so. It looks as if there were eggs abandoned here, which eventually hatched, but the dragons themselves never made it out. I will want to search for teeth and talons—anything that may have survived."

"Those should tell us whether it was in fact desert drakes

they were breeding," Tom said, full of excitement. He had undoubtedly been looking at the murals and drawing the same conclusions I had.

"Indeed," I said, reaching the top corridor. Suhail held his hand out through the gap, and I went to grasp it—but then I stopped short. "Hullo there," I said, diverted. "What's this?"

I had not taken a very good look at the back of the door when I first came through. Now that I did, I saw a piece of rock wedged under the bottom edge. Its faces were fresh enough that I thought we had broken it free in pushing open the door; it had then fallen into a spot where it prevented the door from opening any farther.

"What do you see?" Suhail demanded, in the tone of one who is about to perish of curiosity.

I pulled the stone free and said, "Try the door again."

Andrew threw himself against the panel almost before I was done speaking, and the door grated open a little more. It still did not go far . . . but it went far enough. Through the newly widened gap, I could see Andrew standing with his hands on his hips, glaring at me. "You couldn't have looked behind the door *before* you wandered off to make discoveries without us?"

I would never have told him this at the time (and have debated admitting it now)—but a part of me was glad he had not been there when I found the chamber, for then he would have seen me weep for ancient hatchlings. I was not even certain I wanted to share so private a moment with Tom. But Suhail brushed the marks of tears from my cheeks with a gentle hand, and I smiled up at him. "Come. Let me show you wonders."

TWENTY-TWO

Return to the Watchers' Heart—My reputation changes—Lieutenant Marton's report—Quite a lot of spit—My theory—Changes at home—Four times as much

Much of what happened after that is *extremely* public knowledge. We sealed the site—even going so far as to carry that pile of sand back up to the top and pour it into the staircase—and returned to Qurrat. Through a heroic effort of will, neither Tom, nor Andrew, nor I breathed a word about what we had found in the Labyrinth. This was to give Suhail time to secure the place properly—a task which ultimately took him to the court of the caliph in Sarmizi. I went there myself much later, but was glad not to face the ruler of Akhia during this delicate phase; as my faithful readers know well, I do not like dealing with politicians.

The Labyrinth is not incapable of supporting human habitation, even in summer. Rather, maintaining a presence there requires a tremendous outlay of resources. This the caliph was happy to provide, once he understood the value of what we had discovered. Before the winter rains came, an expedition returned to the Watchers' Heart (as the site has become known) to record it properly and begin clearing the hatching room of its treasures.

Suhail led this expedition, of course, and I went with him,

to collect any remnants of the ancient hatchlings. (Tom remained in Qurrat to oversee the House of Dragons and its transition to a less military purpose.) Jake accompanied us as well, having arrived in Akhia shortly before the excavation team departed. I did not tell him our destination until we were safely away from civilization, and found my caution abundantly justified: he whooped and danced about so much, he fell off his camel and broke his left arm. This put only the most negligible damper on his spirits, for he had Suhail as his new stepfather, he was out of school, and we were taking him to see a treasure out of legend. It lacked only the sea to make his happiness complete.

Of the archaeological treasures taken from the Watchers' Heart you can read elsewhere, in abundance. Where my own work is concerned, I found less than I expected, and more. Less in the sense that there were no teeth, no claws, and only a scattering of delicate scales. But that very lack told me that what had hatched there were almost certainly *not* desert drakes.

The general response when I published this information was an assumption that I had simply overlooked the missing remains. This, however, is a slander against both my own professionalism and Suhail's. He oversaw all efforts at the site, and took precautions that were extraordinary for the time (though quite standard now). Nothing could be removed until its original position had first been recorded with a photograph; then it was photographed again, from all angles, once clear of the site. Only when this was done would he allow another item to be removed.

Nor did his caution end there. We sifted every bit of sand that had been removed from the staircase, making certain there was nothing more than ordinary pebbles mixed in, and took equal care with the interior of the site. Every bit of sand and dust from the hatching chamber was screened to a minute degree: that is the only reason I found the scales. Had there been teeth or other materials there, we *would* have found them.

When I was not peering at a tiny speck of rock to see whether it might be relevant, I made rubbings of every inscription in the place, then put myself to work recording the murals properly. I was not able to finish this task before the winter rains came, but I made good progress. As for the inscriptions . . . Abdul Aleem ibn Nahwas had finished refining Suhail's Ngaru translation, and gave a copy to him before we left Qurrat. Whenever he could snatch a spare moment, Suhail was chipping away at the Draconean text of the Cataract Stone, seeking the correspondences that would enable him to puzzle out the phonetic content, and from there begin to identify vocabulary, grammar, and so forth. We had new inscriptions to read, and could not wait to discover what they said.

We did not speak of that aspect where anyone could hear, not until the text was ready for publication. There was already more than enough publicity surrounding the Watchers' Heart: journalists from half of Anthiope had flocked to the site, some of them ill-prepared enough for the hazards of the desert that Suhail had to negotiate with the Ghalb to find and rescue those who might otherwise have perished. But this did not deter them from wandering by our camp in the hopes of seeing the hidden chambers, interviewing Suhail or myself, or both.

This is the point at which my public reputation underwent

a revision of truly awe-inspiring proportions and speed. Scant months before, I had been the notorious woman who wed the man reputed to be her long-time lover on shockingly brief notice. With our discovery, however, we became the romantic tale of the century: two brilliant eccentrics, destined to be together, marrying in a whirlwind of passion for soft-hearted men and women to sigh over in envy. While I cannot dispute the "eccentric" part, and have a healthy respect for both my own intelligence and Suhail's, I could not help but laugh at the image of us that journalists and gossips presented to the world.

I am glad I was in the desert for the worst of it, safely insulated from the stories spreading through Qurrat and beyond. Natalie compiled a scrap-book of articles published in Falchester, which she presented to me upon my return to Scirland; I can scarcely read some of them without expiring of laughter or embarrassment. But on the whole, my sudden transition from notoriety to genuine fame was a boon to my career, and so I cannot complain overmuch.

One other thing amuses me, looking back on that time. So much attention was focused on the discovery in the Labyrinth of Drakes—and rightly so, for the Watchers' Heart has never been truly equaled by any archaeological site since (though the city of Jinkai, buried in volcanic mud, comes close). Virtually no one apart from myself and Tom, however, paid the slightest bit of attention to my work with the honey-seekers.

The turning point there came when the winter rains drove us out of the desert at last. Lieutenant Marton had faithfully carried out my orders regarding the egg incubation programme, and came to report to me almost as soon as I returned to Dar al-Tannaneen.

I knew something was amiss as soon as I saw him, for he was wringing his hands fit to dislocate a finger. "What is wrong, Lieutenant?"

"The data," he said. "That is—one bit of it. A honeyseeker, I mean. One of the honeyseekers. It's wrong. Not like the others."

"Has it fallen ill? Which one?" I reached for the files in which I kept all my notes on the hatchlings.

The reference number he gave me, however, was not yet in my files, as it belonged to one of the eggs that had been incubating during my absence. I closed the ledger in front of me and said, "Lieutenant Marton. Take a deep breath, and tell me precisely what is amiss."

He obeyed, straightening his shoulders. "I did as you asked, Dame Isabella, increasing the temperature. Well past the point where I expected all of them to die. But one of the eggs hatched anyway. And the thing that came out of it is—different."

My chair nearly toppled over as I stood. "Show me."

I saw immediately what Lieutenant Marton meant. Had I encountered this hatchling in the wild, I would have thought it very similar to a honeyseeker, but not quite the same. A related species, perhaps. Female honeyseekers are a dull green, and their mates black-and-yellow, with a bright blue crest; this one was female and had a similar shape to her body, but her scales were solid orange. Her body was even more attenuated than usual for her kind, and sported a much finer crest. All in all, she was not nearly so mutated as Lumpy—in fact, she seemed quite healthy—but she was, as Lieutenant Marton had said, *wrong*. This was not what a honeyseeker should look like.

Earlier in this volume I said I was eliding a certain incident whose significance was not apparent to me at the time. My mind returned to it now, in light of this new data.

Some months before, one of the hatchlings had become vexed at me for manipulating his body to obtain measurements of his growth. To express his annoyance, he had spat on me—the defense mechanism of honeyseekers, which acquires its toxicity from the eucalyptus nectar they consume.

Their saliva is not *very* toxic. It is neither as choking as a swamp-wyrm's breath, nor as corrosive as the spray of a savannah snake. But it can irritate the skin, causing an unpleasant rash, and so I had hurried to wash the affected skin (leaving the honeyseeker to enjoy a brief freedom, before I returned and finished my measurements). Afterward, though, I noted that my skin was not even a little red.

"Lieutenant Marton," I said. "How many times have the honeyseekers spat on you?"

He looked puzzled. "I don't know, Dame Isabella. A dozen times, at least. Probably more."

"How much has it irritated your skin?"

"It doesn't bother me, Dame Isabella," he said stoutly. "So long as I wash it off within a few minutes, I don't have any problems."

A few minutes was long enough for the full rash to set in, and even prompt washing leaves one with redness and tender skin. But I needed more evidence than that.

Marton categorically refused to let me use myself as a test

subject—even going so far as to roll up his sleeves and take one of the juvenile honeyseekers directly out of my hands. My attempt to reclaim it produced the first test, as it provoked the creature into spitting on Marton's bare arm. "Might as well do the rest," he said with a hint of triumph, and reached for the next one.

I gave in. Soon a full dozen honeyseekers had spat on him, and I had written on him with my pen, marking each place where the saliva struck with the appropriate reference number. Half an hour later, there was no effect from any of them.

"Maybe it's because we're keeping them in cages?" he speculated.

"That should not matter," I said. "We are still feeding them eucalyptus nectar. It should show up in their saliva." (Had I been in less of a rush to test my theory, I might have been wiser and asked Tom to chemically analyze samples, rather than using Marton as my canvas.) "And that does not explain your orange honeyseeker, either." The creature had hatched despite being subjected to temperatures that ought to have been lethal.

Nor were those the only anomalies. I went back through my records, examined each juvenile closely; I thought about the swamp-wyrm eggs that had been transplanted to the rivers of Bayembe. Some had failed to hatch, and others had hatched unhealthy specimens, just as we experienced here at Dar al-Tannaneen. But the ones that had been healthy, the ones that had grown . . .

They had been different, too.

I showed the orange honeyseeker to Tom and Suhail, laid out all the data I had. It was not nearly enough for a strong theory, and I had learned my lesson about publishing ideas before I thought them through sufficiently—but I trusted those two men above anyone in the world. They would not mock me for getting something wrong. I took a deep breath and said, "I think dragon eggs are not merely sensitive to handling. I think the environment in which they incubate actively changes the organism that results."

Tom was examining the orange honeyseeker from every angle, ignoring her furious spitting. "You think they aren't toxic because they didn't incubate in nests of eucalyptus leaves."

"I didn't want to strip the sheikh's trees bare. We've been using tamarisk leaves—I didn't think it would make a difference."

I was not the only person in this enterprise who lacked caution. Tom wiped some of the spittle from his arm and tasted it. He made a face. "Salty."

Suhail's eyes went very wide. "Tamarisk trees can take up salt from groundwater."

"Swamp-wyrm eggs in clear, running water," I said. "Rather than the silty morass of Mouleen. We already know the Moulish change the egg's environment to influence the sex of the creature that results; Mr. Shelby says that works with some reptile eggs, as well. He says it is based on temperature. What if, with dragons, it can affect more than sex?"

"That," Tom said, "would be a *hell* of a thing to study."

It would require an absurd number of eggs. If the honeyseekers were anything to go by, not all mutations worked out well; many were lethal. One would lose a great quantity before one had anything like a stable breed of orange, salty honeyseekers.

But on a long enough timeline, it might be possible. And

who knew how many centuries the Draconeans had spent on dragon-breeding, gradually shepherding wild stock toward something of their own making?

"When you think about it," Suhail said after I expressed this thought, "it isn't *that* much different from what we have done in breeding livestock. A great deal of the selection happens earlier in the life cycle, is all. And the rate of change is, shall we say, more *dramatic*."

I could not help smiling at him. "I see our discussions in Coyahuac about animal domestication left a mark on you. Let me officially recant what I said then: I am now firmly of the opinion that they *did* domesticate dragons. A breed they created through altering the environment of the eggs; a breed that has since gone extinct, or else mutated beyond easy recognition—for it is likely that whatever they made was unfit to survive on its own. Oh, if *only* we had a proper skeleton to study!"

"We have found a hidden temple, footprints, petrified eggs, and a stone we can translate," Suhail said, ticking the items off on his fingers. "Who is to say that a skeleton is not out there somewhere?"

The odds were small . . . but I would not give up hope. "If there is, then we will find it."

Suhail and I parted for a time that winter: the obligations of dealing with the Watchers' Heart kept him in Akhia, while Tom and I had to report to Lord Rossmere concerning our own commission. (Also Jake had to return to school, though he protested mightily.)

"I would call this a successful failure," Lord Rossmere said once we were settled in his office. "You did not manage to breed dragons, but we kept Yelangese attention diverted for a good long while. And that discovery of your husband's, Dame Isabella, has turned into a diplomatic coup for us with the Akhian government."

I smiled sweetly at him. "I am glad that *our* discovery has brought so many benefits."

His frown said he had not missed the stress I laid on that word. "Yes, well. Under the circumstances, the Crown has decided it would be best to let the research in Qurrat continue in a more generalized way. Who knows? Maybe you'll even find a way to harness dragons for a more active combat role, the way the Keongans do."

Tom cleared his throat. "My lord, neither Dame Isabella nor I are interested in carrying out more military research. We would be happy to go on studying drakes, to further our store of knowledge—but not to use them in war."

Lord Rossmere brushed this off with the air of a man who thinks he can talk his opponent around, but Tom and I were utterly firm on that point, both then and in the weeks to come. We did not like the clear implication that the breeding programme had been a smokescreen for the synthesis efforts from the start; we did not like being treated as the Royal Army's lackeys. Suhail had enough influence now in Akhia that Dar al-Tannaneen would survive, with or without Scirling involvement: if Lord Rossmere tried to force the point, the emir of Qurrat would reclaim the property and re-establish it as a research site under his own authority. Which would hardly free us from the noose of politics, of course—that cannot be escaped, wherever one goes—but it made a useful stick to bludgeon people with in an argument.

And I soon had quite a strong arm with which to bludgeon. Not long after our return, Tom and I received the news that we were both to be rewarded for our recent deeds: he with an elevation to knighthood, becoming Sir Thomas Wilker, and I with a peerage.

I burst into laughter when I heard the news. "Me, a lady? You can't be serious."

But they were quite serious. I was to be granted the barony of Trent, in the county of Linshire. There were various complications on account of my foreign marriage, but the peerage solved one problem in the course of creating others: Suhail and I took the opportunity to adopt Trent as a shared surname, dodging the linguistic and social contradictions we had ignored up to that point. Miss Isabella Hendemore had become Mrs. Isabella Camherst, then Dame Isabella Camherst; now, at the age of thirty-four, I acquired the name by which the world knows me: Isabella, Lady Trent.

Only a few of my readers, I think, will understand why my elevation felt almost like an insult.

Tom understood. "It's a slap to the face," he said, pacing an angry circuit across the carpet of my study. "Not that you don't deserve it—you do."

"And you deserve more than a knighthood," I said.

"They'll never make me a lord, and we both know it. But why haven't they made you a Colloquium Fellow?"

I could feel my mouth settling into an ironic line. "Because I have not yet published anything of sufficient scientific import."

"Bollocks," he said bluntly. "You've published as much as I have. More than a great many of my *fellows*." He scarred the word with heavy sarcasm.

We both knew the real answer to his question, of course. I was not a member of the Philosophers' Colloquium because I was a woman. "If I am right about the effect of the environment on incubation, and I publish *that*—"

Tom's leg jerked as if he almost kicked one of my chairs. Instead he sat in it, scowling like a thunderhead. "We have to achieve twice as much, in order to get half as much reward."

There was no answer I could make to that. It was true . . . but neither of us could do a thing about it. Except, of course, to achieve four times as much. To be so exceptional, they could no longer shut us out; and having done that, to hope that those who came after might be judged on equal terms with those who should be their peers.

It is not a dream easily attained. We have not truly attained it in my lifetime. But I was more determined than ever to do my part.

I therefore went to the wall and pulled down the map hanging on a roll there. It was decorated with little tags, marking the homes of different draconic breeds around the world. Once Suhail came to Falchester, he and I would update it with major Draconean sites. Somewhere in the world, our two passions must intersect and form the picture I sought.

Turning to face Tom, I smiled and said, "The answers are out there somewhere. And together, we will find them."